Secrets, Lies and Fireflies

ANGIE FOX

Also by Angie Fox

THE SOUTHERN GHOST HUNTER SERIES
Southern Spirits
A Ghostly Gift (short story)
The Skeleton in the Closet
Ghost of a Chance (short story)
The Haunted Heist
Deader Homes & Gardens
Dog Gone Ghost (short story)
Sweet Tea and Spirits
Murder on the Sugarland Express
Pecan Pies and Dead Guys
The Mint Julep Murders
The Ghost of Christmas Past
Southern Bred and Dead
The Haunted Homecoming
Give Up the Ghost
Dread and Buried
Death at the Drive-In
Secrets, Lies and Fireflies
Garters, Ghosts and Wedding Toasts

THE MONSTER MASH TRILOGY
The Monster MASH
The Transylvania Twist
Werewolves of London

THE ACCIDENTAL DEMON SLAYER SERIES

The Accidental Demon Slayer

The Dangerous Book for Demon Slayers

A Tale of Two Demon Slayers

The Last of the Demon Slayers

My Big Fat Demon Slayer Wedding

Beverly Hills Demon Slayer

Night of the Living Demon Slayer

What To Expect When Your Demon Slayer is Expecting

THE WANDERLUST MYSTERIES

Death at the Ice Hotel

Death on the Queen Mary

SHORT STORY COLLECTIONS

Haunted for Christmas: The complete collection of Southern Ghost
Hunter short stories

A Little Night Magic: A collection of Southern Ghost Hunter and
Accidental Demon Slayer short stories

Secrets, Lies and Fireflies

NEW YORK TIMES BESTSELLING AUTHOR

ANGIE FOX

MIB
Moose Island Books

Chapter One

The salty-sweet smell of dill and batter filled the air as I crouched behind the fried-pickle stand, my stomach tight. "This is our moment," I whispered, gently stroking Lucy's silky fur. My little skunk and I had spent months training for this day, and now it was time to show Sugarland what we could do.

Lucy's nose twitched as I ruffled the little tuft on her head and gave her a quick peck.

"You missed," a familiar voice teased. I looked up to see Ellis Wydell, my handsome boyfriend, tapping his cheek.

He deserved a little love too, I supposed. After all, he was pulling double duty that afternoon as skunk handler and beauty consultant.

Could I pick 'em or what?

I straightened and kissed his cheek, feeling his weekend stubble. "You're both spoiled."

"Happily," he replied, his dimples deepening as a pair of my grandmother's church friends winked at us and tittered as they strolled past, rose perfume wafting in their wake.

The smell always reminded me of her.

It seemed half of Sugarland, Tennessee, had gathered in the town square for the annual Pet Parade and Festival. Wagging tails and excited barks mingled with the sizzle from food trucks and chatter from vendor booths. Bright striped tents housed the town's biggest adoption event of the year, lining up all the way from Main Street to the stately old city hall.

Best of all, the entire shindig benefited the Sugarland Animal Sanctuary. I couldn't have been prouder of my town or the turnout.

"I don't think I've ever been this popular," Ellis said, nodding to Nancy Tarkington from the mayor's office, who was making balloon animals for the kids in the circle drive behind us.

"I should have known you'd make an unfairly handsome prince," I said, tugging on a gold button on his Disney ensemble. His royal blue coat accentuated his broad shoulders, while the fitted white pants showed off his athletic build. A gold sash across his chest completed the look. "This is what happens when you let Lucy pick your costume."

He grinned, and I couldn't help but admire his chiseled jawline. "Anything for my girls."

We'd snagged a private moment near the historic library with its imposing front columns and weathered brick walls. On the left side, under an arched window, a Civil War cannonball was still lodged in the foundation.

It was the perfect backdrop for Lucy's agility contest debut.

We'd already marched in the parade, Lucy bouncing along in her fairy princess costume, wings bobbing with every step.

But she already had a reputation as a town beauty.

Now it was time to showcase her talent.

"Let's go," Ellis said, leading the way around the grandstands to the grassy center of the square. Jumps, tunnels, and weave poles dotted the lawn under the watchful eye of our town founder, Colonel Ramsey Larimore, as he sat atop his horse, immortalized in Tennessee limestone.

I gave Lucy a final once-over, making sure her tiara was secure. "You're going to do great." She'd nailed every run on our backyard practice course. I leaned in close, lowering my voice. "And don't forget our surprise trick at the end."

That was sure to wow the judges.

"You're sure she needs the wings?" Ellis pondered in the tone he usually reserved for more official matters.

It was his analytical nature that made him Sugarland's finest police officer.

"She's been training with them." Plus, they looked great on the jumps. I'd selected my sparkly green tank top to match. But I'd kept the rest of my outfit simple—white capris and sneakers. Lucy was the star.

I smoothed the cowlick behind her ear. "She's ready."

"Almost." Ellis reached into his pocket and then tied a big pink bow onto Lucy's tail, his large hands surprisingly deft. "For luck," he said, stroking her head.

Gorgeous.

She swished her tail happily.

I scooped her up and linked an arm through Ellis's as we headed for the starting line. "My grandma always said, 'When in doubt, put a bow on it.'"

A burly fellow with tattooed arms strolled past, his eyes widening at Ellis's princely attire. "Who knew Sugarland's toughest lawman had a soft side?"

I did.

And I loved every bit of it.

The festival's happy buzz carried us along. I waved to Mr. Hartley, the library director. He'd taken over when Sheila Ward retired. I grinned when I saw Judy Donovan from church. She made the best cheesy chicken and Ritz cracker casserole on this earth—then I spotted Mrs. Hummerman at the check-in table. The head judge clutched her clipboard, her wire-rimmed glasses perched on the end of her nose like they were afraid to get too close to her beady eyes.

I shot her my brightest smile. "It's a beautiful day to race."

She glanced at Lucy's number 13, her mouth twisting. "I still say nobody wants to see a skunk in this competition." She smirked when she saw my mood falter. "Skunks are smelly vermin. Even ones who dress in lace and bows."

Ellis shot her a long look. "I think you've confused judging with being *judgmental*."

Lucy tensed, probably because she felt me do it.

I pasted on a smile, determined not to let Mrs. Hummerman get to me. "I appreciate all the work you put into this competition."

And I did.

"Kill them with kindness," I told Lucy once we were out of earshot. It was my mom's favorite saying. Though at this rate, one more sugary smile from me and Mrs. Hummerman might keel right over.

The contest forms never specified dogs only. They didn't even require contestants to be mammals. I'd half expected to see Annie Libardi's cockatoo weaving through the poles. That bird was wicked smart. Almost as smart as my skunk.

And in a few seconds, we'd show Mrs. Hummerman and everyone else exactly what skunks could do.

The scoreboard was done in multicolored chalk on a slate board framed with silk daisies. Bree from the animal rescue stood proudly next to her creation. I gave her a wave.

She wore her trademark cat-eye glasses and a vibrant yellow tank top she'd knitted herself. Everything Bree did, she did with her whole heart.

The top three scores stood out, each marked with a gold star:

> Biscuit (Corgi) 9.92
> Princess Pawsome (Lab mix) 9.95
> Sir Barksalot (Poodle) 9.99

The announcer's microphone crackled.

"Next up, Verity Long with Lucy!" Pete from Rural Radio boomed. He paused. "Lucy is a... Is this right? Skunk."

Ellis squeezed my arm. "Show them what two princesses can do," he said, planting a quick kiss on my head.

The crowd in the fold-out grandstand erupted in cheers as Lucy and I took our places at the starting line. Up close, the course loomed larger—the jumps higher, the tunnels longer—far more challenging than anything I could have rigged in my backyard.

I suddenly wished we'd trained harder.

But no. We had this.

I clutched Lucy close as her little paws started pumping. She wanted me to put her down.

"Soon," I promised.

"Verity!" my friend Maisie called from the back row, her wild gray hair barely contained in a long braid. She held up a poster board that read *Skunks Rule, Poodles Drool!* in stark black-on-white.

I waved at her, then spotted a real-life gangster in the crowd. Well, a dead one. He appeared in semitransparent gray, wearing the same 1920s pin-striped suit he'd died in. Frankie lived on my property with me, ever since I'd accidentally trapped him there. When he lent me his power, I could see the ghostly side of Sugarland. These days, he kept that connection open all the time. After our last adventure, he was living his best life and his ghostly energy had grown so strong he barely noticed sharing it. And I was enjoying it.

Mostly.

I supposed I was always grateful to know exactly what was happening in Sugarland, with the living and the dead. Over the years, Frankie and I had used his power to solve murders and uncover long-buried crimes. We'd even unearthed a trove of lost pirate loot.

"Let me know if you need any help!" he hollered. "I got a way with the judges," he added, patting the holstered revolver under his jacket.

Naturally.

Frankie had lived—and died—thinking gangland shakedowns solved all life's problems.

"I'm good," I mouthed, sparing a grin for his sweet Victorian ghost of a girlfriend, Molly, who cuddled next to him.

I held Lucy still while the referee attached a timing chip to her collar.

Right in front of Molly sat Mrs. Gremmelter, my old high school lunch lady. Like Frankie, she appeared as she'd died, which had probably been at or after work since Mrs. G sported a hair net and a crisp white smock and pants in the afterlife. She chatted animatedly with Miss Felicia, my late Sunday school teacher, whose *Hang in There* cat T-shirt and ankle-length skirt were a familiar sight.

The living instinctively gave the ghosts a wide berth, creating pockets of emptiness in the stands. Still, there were more vacant seats than I'd expected, the gaps making the crowd feel oddly sparse.

The race official approached with his scanner. Lucy's new tracker gave a sharp *beep,* and I glanced at my watch with a pang. The race had run ten minutes over. My sister, Melody, would have been forced to leave by now. The Kids' Craft Fair at the library had been due to start as soon as the race had been scheduled to end.

My hand drifted to my pocket, closing around the small object Melody had pressed into my palm after the parade. It was her lucky charm, a tiny brass thimble passed down to her from our grandmother. The metal was worn smooth from years of nervous fiddling. My sister was with me in spirit.

The referee raised his hand and pointed to the starting line.

This was our moment.

"Ready, Lucy?" I gave her a gentle scratch behind the ears. "Let's show them what skunks can do."

Lucy's tiny black nose twitched, and she pawed the ground, her eyes locked on the course ahead. She coiled like a spring, ready to prove skunks belonged in any race in Sugarland.

The official raised his flag. "Ready?" He whipped it down. "Go!"

Lucy shot off like a furry bullet, with me hot on her heels. "Weave poles," I called, pointing ahead. She zipped between them with a grace that would make a border collie swoon.

"A-frame," I called as she shot out from the last pole, her little legs pumping furiously. Lucy scrambled up and over without missing a beat. The judges scribbled on their clipboards, eyeing both her speed and form.

Mrs. H was the only one frowning.

Lucy would win her over.

As long as I kept up.

I dug deep, lungs on fire as I put on a burst of speed. Lucy pulled ahead as we approached the tunnel. "Through," I panted. I could've sworn she'd never run this fast.

A whiff of something acrid hit me as she vanished into the blue tube. Smoke? I glanced around but saw nothing amiss. The tube shook as she powered her way through and emerged in a blur of black and white.

Time was crucial, but so was accuracy. "Jump," I gasped, legs burning as she raced for a bar that loomed much higher for a ten-pound skunk than a ten-pound dog.

Lucy cleared it with a swish of her tail.

And the next one.

And the next one!

My heart hammered as we flew through the rest of the course —over the tire jump, across the seesaw. We'd show Sugarland who was the number one pet!

With each obstacle, the cheering from the stands intensified. Even Mrs. Hummerman's pinched expression had melted into something resembling begrudging tolerance.

We'd take it.

Lucy blazed across the finish line to the click of the official's stopwatch. I stumbled after her. But she wasn't finished yet.

With a final burst of energy, Lucy reared up on her hind legs and twirled for the crowd, her beribboned tail fanning out like a feather boa.

The grandstand erupted. Maisie's *Skunks Rule!* poster bounced wildly. The ghosts leapt to their feet. Or at least they floated higher than usual.

"Up!" I called, bending down, like we'd practiced. Lucy dashed straight up my back and onto my shoulder. I stood, my heart pounding in time with the applause.

"You were amazing," I gushed, still catching my breath.

Lucy gave my cheek a nuzzle.

Ellis wrapped us both in a bear hug. "That was incredible! You two just made Sugarland history!"

The judges huddled together with their heads bowed in intense discussion. All except for Mrs. H, who stared us down.

"She looks like she swallowed a bug," I said under my breath.

"More like her pride." Ellis stroked Lucy under her chin.

"The lowest score is dropped," I assured him, wiping sweat from my brow. "We have a chance. Especially if we ran the fastest."

Lucy took advantage of my distraction to wriggle out of my arms and leap into Ellis's surprised but steady embrace.

"She's got good taste," I said as Lucy nuzzled against his broad chest, her paws kneading his jacket.

My breath caught as Bree posted Lucy's score. The crowd's chatter swelled as I stared, hardly daring to believe it.

"Lucy wins!" Maisie shouted, her wild gray hair flying. Lucy sprang from Ellis's arms to dance in victory circles, and the grandstand erupted in cheers. Ellis swept me into a kiss.

The official ushered us out onto the field, where Miss Sugarland tottered over in her tiara, sash, and impossibly high heels. She presented us with a gleaming trophy and an oversized hundred-dollar check.

"Stand close together now." Reporter Ovis Dupre arranged us, camera ready. "Big smiles for the Lifestyle section."

"Wait." I pulled out the small ribbon Mom had sent. *First Place Skunk* gleamed in gold on blue.

Miss Sugarland helped me drape it over Lucy.

"I had it handy just in case," I said, my cheeks warming.

Oh, who was I kidding? My skunk would've worn that ribbon either way.

I held Lucy high, her fairy wings glittering. The crowd's cheers swelled, a tidal wave of love for our little skunk. I caught Ellis's eye, and his proud smile said it all. My girl had won more than a race.

Then a shout sliced through the celebration. "Fire!"

I whirled. Black smoke trailed from a second-story window of the Sugarland Library.

Melody.

My sister was inside.

The festive crowd shattered into screams. My feet moved before my brain caught up, Lucy squirming in my arms as I raced toward the blaze.

"Verity!" Ellis's hand clamped my arm. "Stay back," he ordered, already in police mode. He tore past me toward Detective Marshall and Chief Royce.

I'd stay back when my sister was safe.

I dug out my phone, dialing Melody as I ran.

She didn't pick up.

I tried again.

No answer.

Sirens wailed, but panicked crowds had flooded the fire lanes behind the tents. Ellis worked to drive people back, clearing a path for the trucks.

Heat slammed into me at the library steps. Thick, black smoke bled from the upstairs windows, staining the sky black. Coughing patrons streamed from the main entrance.

"Have you seen Melody?" I asked Skip Lebowitz and Millie Dryer. I received only shakes of their heads in response.

A chain of children emerged, tiny hands linked, led by wild-eyed librarians counting heads. Parents darted in, snatching kids, adding to the chaos.

I caught Lucas, Melody's second-in-command, at the end of the line. "Where's Melody?"

"She should be right behind me." His terrified eyes swept the crowd. "I don't see her."

"Is she still in there?"

"I don't know," he said, scooping up a crying kindergartener.

A sickening crack split the air. Fire burst through the roof of the turret that had graced the library's corner for a century and a half, flames twisting high into the sky.

More sirens wailed in the distance, but still no trucks. My stomach lurched as precious seconds ticked away. An upstairs window exploded in a shower of glass and smoke. Then the first truck whipped a sharp right into the square by the pet-adoption tents. My stomach lurched as its side caught a tent support cable. Metal shrieked, canvas ripped, and the whole mess crashed onto the truck. Firefighters spilled out, yanking at the tangled wreckage. Dogs barked, and cats yowled, fleeing in all directions. Ellis bolted toward the chaos, his princely cape flapping behind him.

I looked to the library as precious seconds ticked by. Smoke billowed down the main stairs.

My heart plummeted with it.

There was no sign of my sister.

Chapter Two

My stomach churned as I scanned the panicked crowd. Melody wasn't with the other librarians gathered near the fried-pickle tent. She wasn't anywhere near her fiancé, Alec Duranja, who was helping Ellis free up the fire truck. My little sister, who'd always counted on me, was still in the building.

This was bad.

It would be just like Melody to hole up in the burning library, getting people out instead of taking care of herself.

Lucy squirmed in my arms, her tiny claws catching on my faux pearl bracelet. I'd forgotten I was holding her. What kind of person brings a skunk to a fire? I spun around, spotting Maisie frozen in horror as she watched our town's history burn.

"Hold my skunk," I ordered, thrusting Lucy into her arms.

"Verity, don't you dare—" she began, clutching Lucy while I bolted up the library steps.

Heat seared my face as I reached out to steady the soot-smeared blonde in pigtails stumbling down the stairs. The caustic smoke burned my throat, making my eyes water.

"Bethany! Your boys okay?" I shouted, grabbing her arm. At her frantic nod, I added, "Have you seen Melody?"

Bethany shook her head, clutching a toddler to each hip, tears streaming down their faces. "No, I'm sorry," she choked out before rushing away.

"Emma!" I called to the teenager guiding her younger brother through the haze.

"I'm fine," she warbled, pointing toward the crowd. "I see my mom." Good. I spotted Mrs. Lawson waving frantically as she darted away. She was safe.

But still no Melody.

Then a familiar face emerged from the smoke—Mr. Watkins, who'd volunteered at the library longer than I'd been alive. His silver hair was slick against his head, his glasses askew.

"Mr. Watkins!" I seized his arm. "Where's my sister?"

He coughed, eyes wild. "Still inside. Making sure everyone's out."

My heart sank.

"Melody!" I inched closer to the entrance, the heat making my forehead break out in sweat. The doorway gaped like a smoke-belching beast daring me to enter. Every instinct screamed at me to run the other way, but Melody was in there.

I spun around, searching. "Ellis?" But he wasn't by the fire truck anymore. Neither was Duranja.

The lawn teemed with onlookers, their faces a mix of horror and morbid fascination. Officer Jameson and Detective Marshall corralled the crowd, their voices hoarse from shouting directions. Officer Roberts, off-duty but all business in jeans and a Sugarland PD T-shirt, cleared a path for the incoming fire trucks. Sirens wailed in the distance.

Hurry up!

Me rushing into a burning building would only add to Melody's troubles, but somebody had to make sure she was safe.

"Frankie!" Relief flooded me as he materialized on the step next to me.

He squinted at me through the smoke. "You need to be in back with Molly and the girls."

"Not hardly." He should know me better by now.

We both jumped as a thunderous crash from inside the library sent a fresh wave of heat billowing out. I stumbled back, choking on the smoke.

My chest tightened. "I need you to go inside," I wheezed.

He looked at me like I'd asked him to dance naked. "You're nuts. That's an inferno."

Not yet, but it would be.

"You'll be fine," I choked out. "You can't feel the heat." His hair didn't even flutter in the breeze.

His eyes narrowed. "You don't get to tell me how I feel."

"Melody is in there." And I didn't have time to strike a deal.

"Melody can take care of herself." He gritted his jaw. "She knows what she's doing."

As if that made sense. As if I hadn't helped him a million times before.

"You want to bet her life on that?"

Frankie's face darkened. "You don't get it. Heat is energy, and that's all I am. It's Afterlife 101, sweetheart. You can haunt a place before it burns. You can haunt what's left. But you never haunt an active fire." He flung both hands toward the side lawn. "See?"

A cluster of Confederate ghosts huddled near the old oak tree, lost and confused. I'd never seen them like this. The library had been their home since the Civil War, when it had served as a military hospital. Usually, they were a rowdy bunch, playing cards and bragging about their battle scars. Now they stood frozen, staring at the flames.

"I play cards with those guys." Frankie jammed a finger in their direction. "They died in there, and they stayed in there. None of them have set foot outside since 1863, and you want me to go *in*?"

"It's not about what I want," I snapped. It wasn't *for* me.

Then I spotted a lone Union soldier. He stood apart from the rest, his back ramrod straight, his untamed hair and trimmed beard unmistakable.

Matthew.

"If you won't help, he will."

I started down the steps, eyes locked on Matthew, refusing to waste another second arguing with Frankie.

The gangster materialized right in front of me, blocking my path. "I am *not* letting you do that."

"You don't have a choice." I ducked to the right.

Frankie cut me off. "He's the type to let you follow him in."

So what if he was? "It's getting done." I walked straight through him.

"Eee-yah!" he bellowed as I felt the icy, stomach-curdling, bone-crackling, wet awfulness of the dead.

"You asked for it," I said, my knees going weak as I plowed forward.

"You're insane," he screeched, nearly face-planting as he blocked me again. He cursed under his breath. "Fine." He furiously wiped away my touch like I'd dropped Sea-Monkeys down his shirt. "You win. You happy?"

"No." I was shaky, light-headed, and scared out of my mind.

"I can't believe I'm doing this," he groused before shrinking into an orb and zipping into the library.

I turned, trying to shake the wet ick, so tempted to follow him I had one foot on the bottom stair before I caught myself. Going in blind would be foolish.

There was a slim chance Melody had slipped out the back. But, no, I would have seen her in the yard.

I spotted Bree nearby, her sunny yellow knitted top streaked with soot, her dark skin ashen with shock.

"My friend Tina just got out." Bree swallowed hard. "She was in the map room. A few of them went out the back."

Hope surged. "Did she see Melody?"

Bree shook her head. "Only three people went that way. Most everybody else was upstairs with the kids' crafts."

They would have gone out the front. And they should all be out by now.

Except Melody.

Fire tore across the roof, devouring the aged shingles. Sirens wailed in the distance, still too faint.

Too slow.

Smoke leaked from around the window frames. I followed it up, up, then froze.

Shock rippled down my spine. I couldn't believe what I was seeing. Because there, in the second-floor window nearest the stairs, my grandma Delia watched me.

She'd been my rock. My confidante. The one who'd taught me to love Sugarland as much as she had.

She'd also been dead for six years.

I lived in her home now, the one she'd entrusted to me. And there she stood, clear as day in the window, looking the same as always. Well, maybe a little changed. She appeared as translucent and gray as any other ghost, but it was unmistakably her. Those high cheekbones, her chin dipped down.

Her arm lifted, twisted. Almost as if she were beckoning me.

"Didi?" I'd seen a hundred ghosts, in all kinds of ways, but I still couldn't wrap my head around this one.

Then she began to fade.

"Wait!" I ran to get a better look.

Grandma Delia's silver hair was coiled in its usual crown braid. She wore the patchwork dress she'd died in, lovingly pieced from the leftover scraps families had donated for Sugarland's centennial Quilt of Unity. None of us had expected to lose her that day. The tradition had gained new meaning when Grandma transformed the remnants into a dress, saying, "Every scrap represents a piece of us. And I couldn't let one piece go to waste." In a way, it had been the perfect send-off. She'd died that night in her rocking chair on the back porch.

Not a day had passed I hadn't thought of her. I'd always hoped she'd appear to me, but not like this.

If she was here now, Melody must be in real danger.

Her energy surged once more. Before I could think, Grandma thrust her entire body through the window. "Upstairs. Now."

It was her. She was here. And her tone brooked no argument.

"What are you doing?" Bree called after me, but I was already sprinting up the steps. "You can't go in there!"

Could and would. Grandma knew something, and I wasn't about to waste time debating.

The world narrowed to a haze of smoke and flickering shadows as I plunged into the library. Darkness consumed me before I'd made it five feet into the marble lobby, broken only by the angry glow of flames along the back wall of the reference room.

Fear clawed at my throat, threatening to paralyze me. I forced it down. I was a Sugarland girl, and I knew this library by heart. I shoved my shirt up over my nose and mouth against the bitter stench of burning paper and wood.

"I knew you'd come." Grandma's voice echoed urgently in my ear. Her image was weak but steady. She beckoned from the top of the staircase to my right. "Quickly."

"I'm here." I crouched low and ascended the wide wooden steps toward the kids' area.

"This way," she said as I reached the top.

She swept down the short landing into the activities area. Tiny chairs littered the floor around a cluttered crafts table. Light from the front windows cut eerie shapes through the thickening smoke.

"Keep going," she urged as my eyes watered in earnest. She led me past the abandoned crafts, through rows of chest-high shelves stuffed with children's books. An ornate fireplace loomed, a relic from the original build. Next to it stood a fort of cushions under a canopy. I stumbled over one as we rounded the corner—

And nearly collided with my sister.

"Melody!"

She appeared dazed, her blond hair a tangled mess, her sleeveless silk tank torn and stained with blood.

I gripped her shoulders. "The fire's bad. We need to get you out. Now."

My sister shook her head frantically. "I can't. Olivia's missing."

My stomach iced over. "Missing?"

I knew about Olivia. Her mom couldn't afford childcare, so she walked to the library after school each day. Olivia loved to read, and Melody loved that little girl.

Melody looked past me, searching as if she could will Olivia to appear. "She didn't want to make crafts. She wanted to read. I left her in the fort by the fireplace, but she's not there."

I hadn't seen her go outside, either.

"It's okay," I promised, fighting down panic. Of course Melody wouldn't leave without the little girl. Neither would I. "We'll find her. Together."

I went to take my sister's hand but froze as Grandma Delia materialized directly behind her.

Melody grabbed my hand. "It'll be like hide-and-seek when we were kids."

Except I could never find her.

I stiffened. "Didi's behind you."

"Grandma?" Melody gaped. "That's good, right?"

Not if we ran out of time.

"This way," Grandma said, whirling around and zipping deeper into the library.

I squeezed Melody's hand. "Stick with me."

She moved fast, but we stayed close. Shelves loomed through the thickening smoke. We ducked under a sagging *Baby Your Baby* quilt-making banner and passed a Lego castle to reach a book cart behind the Reading Request counter. There, wedged between a box of Sugarland's Pet Parade coloring books and a stash of water cups, was an alcove just large enough for the book cart. And inside, eyes round with terror, was Olivia.

Melody rushed forward, her gentle voice at odds with the creaking floorboards. "Hey, sweetpea. We've been looking for you." She scooped the girl into her arms. "Ready for an adventure?"

Olivia clung to Melody like a baby koala, her tear-streaked face buried in my sister's neck.

"Let's be brave like Captain Whiskers from *Calico Cat Superhero Squad*."

Olivia nodded.

"Here's your power cape," I snatched a quilt off the wall and draped it over Olivia's face and arms.

"There's not much time," Grandma warned.

I nodded. "Let's go."

We hurried toward the stairwell, the flames crackling louder with each step.

Grandma stood sentinel on the landing in front of a glass display case labeled *Sugarland Suffragettes: Sweeting the Path to Progress*.

"Thank you," I murmured, rushing past her.

"Wait," she commanded as Melody hurried ahead with Olivia. "There's something else you can't leave without."

Chapter Three

Grandma Delia's ghostly form shimmered. Her finger thrust toward the glass-front display case. "Get this. You need it."

"Of course, Didi." I didn't think twice. I reached for the ornate brass closure, yanking my hand back with a hiss as searing heat bit into my fingers. Mercy. The building was on fire. Of course the metal was hot.

"Hurry," Grandma urged.

Gritting my teeth, I hooked my sleeve over my fingers and wrenched the case open. Inside, sepia photographs of stern-faced women stood amid a collection of pins and yellowed pamphlets proclaiming *Votes for Women*. A delicate teacup sat in the center.

Grandma swiped her hand through all of it and pointed to a weathered white sash at the back.

I grabbed it, having no idea why I'd need such a thing when a fresh wave of smoke hit me, searing my lungs. I doubled over, coughing violently, my eyes watering. Now I got it.

Grandma was trying to save my life.

I pressed the sash over my nose and mouth, the musty fabric filtering the smoke. My breath came in ragged gasps, each inhale like breathing cement.

It was thick. It was everywhere. I wasn't even sure which way I was facing anymore.

Flames crackled in front, behind—I couldn't tell anymore. Sweat poured down my back as waves of heat pressed in from all sides. My heart pounded in my ears, and for a terrifying moment, I froze.

A shimmer rippled through the air directly in front of me, like heat waves on asphalt. A silver orb appeared, its surface swirling with light.

I nearly sobbed with relief. "Frankie?"

"For the love of Pete! I told you I'd handle this!"

I opened my mouth to respond but succumbed to a coughing fit instead.

"Get down. I'll get you out," he huffed. "As usual," he couldn't help but add.

Yes, down. I dropped to my hands and knees, clutching the sash over my nose and mouth.

Frankie zipped down to eye level. "This way," he urged. "And make it snappy."

I crawled after Frankie's glowing form, the pungent smell of burning wood filled my nose, and I pressed the sash tighter. I touched the curve of a stair.

"Now down."

My palms stung against the hot floorboards, and my world shrank to a hazy gray.

"Do. Not. Pass. Out!" Frankie shouted in my ear, jarring me back to myself.

I crawled down the first stair.

"You just had to run into a burning building, didn't you?" Frankie griped. "Even Frisky Pete knows better than you."

Now he was comparing me to his broken-down racehorse? "Not. The. Time," I wheezed through gritted teeth.

I crawled down the second stair.

"Oh, you're going to hear all about this after I get you out of here."

No doubt I would. *If* he got me out of there.

I inched down into the darkness, the wood groaning beneath me. I had to speed up. *Go faster.* I felt it in my gut like a countdown. But each stair was a gamble. Would it hold? Or would it break and send me plummeting?

A crash echoed from below, and I froze.

"Double time, sweetheart," Frankie pressed, losing his swagger. "I'm serious."

My heart hammered as I picked up the pace. The smoke had grown thicker. I could barely see Frankie.

"Hey, you're gonna be fine, kid," Frankie said. "This is nothing."

He was usually a better liar.

"We've been through worse," he added, with false cheeriness.

Now I knew we were in trouble.

His orb was moving faster now, and I struggled to keep up.

Slow down! I tried to say it, but my voice came out as a squeak.

"This reminds me of the time we tried to torch Jimmy Big Head's speakeasy and ended up setting fire to our own getaway car."

My mind swam. It would feel so good to sit for a second.

Frankie zipped straight at my face, making me jolt.

"Of course, that was nothing compared to the time we smuggled illegal fireworks inside a shipment of coal. Whole train car went up like a Roman candle. Luckily, it was the boss's birthday, so we said it was for him."

"Can it, Frankie," I gasped.

"Not my style, doll. You knew what you were getting into when you hosed my ashes into your dirt."

Never in a million years could I have imagined this.

I doubled down, forced myself to keep moving. When I thought I couldn't crawl another inch, my hand met level ground. The bottom of the stairs!

"Safe! Just like when we fixed the World Series in '32!"

"You didn't," I wheezed.

He probably did.

Frankie zipped to the left.

I struggled after him, arms trembling.

"Almost there, kid. Just a little farther," Frankie coaxed. "Hey, that's what I said to Johnny Numbers right before I introduced him to Suds's pet python, Squeezy. They really hit it off. Till death did they part and all."

This was going to be the death of me, one way or the other.

The heat was unbearable now, pressing in from all sides. Sweat stung my eyes. I lost my bearings again as a loud crack echoed above us, followed by an ominous groan.

"Move it! Move it! Move it!" Frankie shouted.

I scrambled forward with everything I had. The world lurched, my vision narrowing to a pinprick. Boots thundered around me.

"It's her!" Hands gripped me under the armpits, lifting me off the floor. "Get her out!"

A sudden gust of cool air hit my face.

A pair of firefighters hauled me down the front steps of the library, my feet barely touching the ground. The crisp afternoon air rushed into my lungs, a shock after the suffocating smoke. I doubled over, heaving as I coughed and retched. I gasped, desperate for air between each painful hack. Each short breath scraped my raw throat, but I gulped it down greedily.

The sash slipped from my grasp, catching on my arm. One of the firemen tossed it over my shoulder without breaking stride. I recognized him as he yanked off his breathing apparatus. Wally Roan. His dad ran the hardware store. His uncle married my mom. I tried to say hi, but it came out as a wheeze.

Through watering eyes, I caught glimpses of the crowd. Blurred faces gaped, and hands covered mouths. A figure in blue and white pushed through the throng. Ellis. Still in his Disney prince costume, now smudged with dirt and oil.

"Verity!" He rushed to my side, matching the firemen's pace.

His jaw dropped, his gaze darting over me. "What were you doing in there? Are you okay?"

"She's okay," Wally promised, his voice gruff.

I managed a raspy cough.

Ellis escorted us to the fire truck parked on the circle drive out front, his hand hovering over my back like he wanted to snatch me up and carry me the entire way. Wally and the other fireman eased me onto the bumper, and an oxygen mask was pressed to my face.

"Deep breaths," a paramedic instructed, adjusting the straps around my head, the plastic slick against my skin.

I inhaled, the cool oxygen soothing my burning lungs. Ellis paced nearby, running his hands through his hair. He turned to a passing EMT, gesturing urgently toward me.

"She needs to be checked out," he said, voice tight. "I have no idea why or how long she was in there." His jaw worked. "Too long. Her hand is burned. Her arm is cut."

No kidding? I looked down at my arm and saw blood.

The EMT nodded, already moving in my direction.

I didn't recognize her. Evidently, they'd called in units from out of town. After what felt like hours of oxygen and prodding, along with the bandaging of a throbbing burn on my hand and a shallow bleeder at my elbow, I felt okay. Lucky, really.

That was when I looked up to see Olivia standing a few feet away with her mother behind her. Soot streaked her face, but she was otherwise unharmed. "Thank you," she said shyly before flinging her arms around my neck.

I returned the tender hug and could see how Melody had fallen in love.

"Me too, sis," said Melody, eyes red-rimmed as she wrapped an arm around my back. "You did good."

So did she.

Her fiancé, Alec Duranja, hovered near, like she'd break if she got out of his sight. I supposed I didn't blame him, as Ellis was doing a fair job of looming, too. The paramedic had already asked him to stand back twice.

The only person I didn't see was my grandmother.

Then a familiar grunt pierced the air. "Lucy?" I breathed into my mask, creating more fog than sound.

Maisie edged past the worried boys, with Lucy in her arms. She shook her head slightly, obviously glad to see me. "You gave us quite a scare, kiddo."

My skunk squirmed, paws outstretched. She leapt, landing heavily on my lap. I buried my face in her fur as she circled once, twice, then curled up against me. She always knew exactly what I needed.

"Fire's out," Duranja said to Ellis, his voice low and steady.

A small army of firefighters emerged from the library, peeling off their breathing masks, coiling hoses, talking on their two-way radios. They must have called in at least two other towns.

Smoke seeped from the historic brick building and into the clear blue sky. The library—my library—would never be the same. Scorch marks marred the once-pristine facade, and shattered glass littered the ground. Water cascaded down the steps, carrying ash and debris. The air was thick with the smell of burnt wood and paper. How many irreplaceable books had been burned, drenched, and ruined?

Melody's young assistant, Lucas, hovered behind her, his blond hair slicked with sweat and ash. "I'm sorry. I'm so sorry." His voice cracked. "I should never have left you."

My sister placed a hand on his shoulder. "I told you to get the kids out, and you did."

His blue eyes were wide, haunted. "A real man would have—"

"What?" she prodded. "Left the children? You did your job." She gave his shoulder a squeeze. "Go help Tina make sure all the parents have found their kids."

"I think he's just in shock," I said. We all were.

Melody took my hand and Olivia's as well. Her grip was tight, as if she were still a little afraid she'd lose us both. "At least we're all okay."

"Thanks to Didi," I said. And despite losing him somewhere, I had to add, "You too, Frankie." Hopefully, he was lurking nearby. "Thanks for being there for me."

It was a big step for the gangster. Doing the right thing. Risking himself for me. Helping me without me having to bribe, blackmail, or otherwise coerce him.

Frankie had grown a lot since I'd first met him, and when push came to shove, he was my friend.

Even if he didn't always like to admit it.

A little while later, the screen door on my back porch creaked as I pushed it open. "We're home, girl," I said to Lucy, who nestled in her sash against my chest.

The familiar scent of lemon kitchen cleaner and old wood mixed with the tang of smoke clinging to my clothes.

I paused in the doorway, scanning my empty kitchen. I'd half expected to see Didi. If not on the lawn after the fire, then here.

"Grandma?" The word came out raspy.

No answer.

I'd looked for her on the long driveway leading to the house. I'd searched for any sign of her on the back porch. She'd want to check on me, right?

I wavered across the worn linoleum, one hand trailing along the kitchen island. The library's sash hung heavy around my neck, a reminder of how close I'd come to...well, joining Grandma.

I glanced behind me. Just in case.

But I was alone.

Out the kitchen window, I could see the white-painted porch gleaming in the late afternoon sun. It stood empty save for the gently swaying porch swing and my collection of potted geraniums near the stairs. It had been Grandma's favorite place, and it was mine, too.

The screen door stuck a little as I eased my way back out into the fresh air.

Lucy hopped down out of my arms, her claws clicking against the wood boards as she explored, her sash trailing behind her. I eased my way over to the porch swing and leaned back, grateful to be whole and unharmed. Grateful for my sister and my skunk as I closed my eyes and listened to the birds in the yard, the familiar creaks and groans of the old house settling.

"I'm here, Grandma," I whispered. "Where are you?"

Chapter Four

I cleared my throat and tried again. "Grandma?"

The only response was the distant chattering of squirrels and the whisper of the breeze.

My phone buzzed with another text from Ellis.

Everything okay? Need anything?

He'd questioned why I'd charged into a burning library alone. He'd tried to make me swear on Grandma's grave to find him next time—as if Grandma hadn't been the one who'd beckoned me into the fire in the first place. He'd dropped me off and had practically wanted to carry me up the back steps. But he'd been on borrowed time. The festival had closed early, and all units had been ordered to the site to help manage cleanup and crowd control.

I typed back a quick reassurance. *I'm safe and happy on the porch*, adding an extra heart emoji and a cute cartoon skunk for good measure.

Lucy hopped up into my lap and nuzzled against me. I stroked her silky fur, my mind drifting back to the library. Grandma had been there, helping me, guiding me. I'd always wanted that from her, ever since I'd seen my first spirit. But now? Nothing.

I sighed and looked toward Grandma's prized rose garden. What was the point of being a ghost hunter if I couldn't spend time with the one spirit who mattered most?

I sat for no telling how long, hoping to catch a glimpse of her familiar silhouette or hear the echo of her laugh. I'd even have settled for a whiff of her rose perfume.

The sun dipped lower, casting shadows over the apple tree and the pond across the yard.

My phone buzzed. Ellis again.

I'm not going to keep saying this, I promise, but next time you run into a fire, tell me, and I'll run into the fire for you.

Ah, but he couldn't see my grandma.

"I'm going in now," I said to her in case she was listening.

The porch swing creaked as I stood with Lucy cradled in my arms. Maybe a bath and some clean clothes would help. As I reached for the door handle, a cool breeze brushed past, carrying the faintest hint of rose.

I spun around, but the porch remained empty.

It could just be from the garden. Still, a small smile tugged at my lips.

Maybe she wasn't completely gone after all.

After bathing Lucy and myself, I rebandaged my hand. The cut on my arm had been nothing much, and it felt good to be in clean pajamas and fuzzy socks. Lucy seemed to agree with her fur all fluffed and blow-dried.

We made our way downstairs, my damp hair leaving a trail of droplets on the worn, wooden steps.

"Ready for a little dinner?" I asked, surprised when she dashed for her princess bed. "Truly?" I asked, following her through the dining room into the parlor.

She blinked up from underneath the plastic turret.

"I'll make you something anyway." Lucy brought out the Italian grandmother in me.

I didn't want her to go hungry.

But as soon as I stepped into the kitchen, I realized why my skunk had taken to her bed.

Frankie stood in the middle of the oak-topped island, smoking. And I don't mean he'd lit up a cigarette in my house, which would have been bad enough.

No, the gangster stood ramrod straight, glowering at me while he kind of, sort of looked like he was still on fire. "Oh, Frankie." I touched a hand to my chest.

Wisps of smoke curled from the sleeves of his pin-striped suit. Glowing embers spiked from his white Panama hat, and if I wasn't mistaken, from the jagged bullet hole in the center of his forehead—the one that had killed him.

He shot me a look that could cut glass. "You did this to me."

"Not exactly," I hedged. Although he did have a point. Frankie wouldn't have gone anywhere near the library if I hadn't insisted.

Oh my.

He looked like he'd gone ten rounds with the devil's own flamethrower. And heaven help me, it really was my fault. I cringed as a lick of fire darted from his bullet hole, burning a matching hole in the brim of his hat.

Lucy bolted straight for the back door. I let her out, wishing I could follow.

Frankie stalked through the kitchen island, heading straight for me. "I told you." His voice boomed, growing louder and hollower with each word. "Ghosts and flames don't mix."

"I can see that." He'd been telling the truth and then some. Not that I'd doubted him. But we hadn't had a choice. "Melody would have died." I'd barely made it out myself, and I'd had help. "You know what that's like. We risked everything to save your brother's family when their afterlives were at stake."

He flexed his jaw. "That's beside the point. You always say we're a team."

"We are." We made a great team.

Well, most of the time.

When Frankie felt like it.

"You said you'd stay outside." He jabbed a finger at me, realized it was on fire, and shoved it into his pocket.

"I did." But he had to realize. "I didn't change the plan on purpose. Grandma beckoned me inside. Melody needed my help on the second floor." When I'd run into him, he'd been coming from the lobby. "Did you even go to the second floor?"

"Of course not." He tossed his hands up. "It was too dangerous."

I opened my hands. He'd proved my point.

"Argh!" He spun in place, which only whipped up flames on his shoulders. Before I could react, he rushed me, looming over me with only inches to spare.

I shuddered when I felt the heat coming off him. He was usually so cold.

"I went in. For you," he grated out. "I knew my limits. I played it smart." He brought a hand to his forehead, then dropped it. "I would have come up aces if you hadn't made me stay to save your butt. Now look at me!"

I retreated a step. "You don't look bad," I said quickly, trying to focus on the positive. His lower half wasn't on fire at all.

He ground his jaw. "Well, I hope you enjoyed Frankie's Fire and Rescue, because I'm done helping. Forever."

Oh, please. "You don't mean that."

He notched a chin up. "That's what Sammy Three Fingers said right before I stuffed pork chops in his pockets and locked him in the lion cage at the circus. He figured out real fast I don't fool around."

"Pork chops?"

"I've always had a flair for showmanship."

Sometimes I forgot how ruthless Frankie could be. "But you don't want to go back to being the lone wolf, only out for yourself." He'd been miserable then, and his plans hardly ever worked. That was how he'd ended up with a bullet in his forehead.

"Life's a lot simpler on my own," he huffed. "When I want to shoot somebody, I pull the trigger."

"You do that anyway."

But Frankie was on a roll. "No committees. No feelings. No group vote. Just me, my favorite gun, and a whole lot of peace and quiet."

A rather large ember fell away from his shirtsleeve and sizzled onto his shoe. I followed it down and noticed the historic sash I'd taken from the fire had slipped off the kitchen island. I hurried to retrieve it.

Smoky tendrils followed Frankie as he paced. "I tried to play the hero, and see where it got me? I look ridiculous."

"You look like you care about me."

He sneered. "That's even worse."

"Okay," I said, placing the sash on the counter, racking my brain to find a way to cheer him up. I was a little scared to think it might be permanent. "Think of your friend who died in his underwear."

Frankie's eyes narrowed. "Handsome Henry," he gritted out. "He'd shoot you between the eyes for noticing."

"How could I not?" The ruthless hit man was doomed to wander eternity in boxer shorts with a dad bod. Didn't change the fact he knew a hundred ways to kill a man. "He still scares me half to death."

"Stop trying to make me feel good," Frankie griped, stopping directly under my fire detector.

That could be a problem.

He closed his eyes. "I might never be a stand-up guy, but I'm trying to be a better guy. I even tried to be your friend." Never mind he'd said the word *friend* like he'd been asked to hug a cactus. Then he was back to the glare. "Stunts like this don't help."

"I'm sorry you got hurt." Honestly, I was. "What you did today was really brave. You didn't think twice. You just went for it."

Frankie's impulsive streak had backfired plenty of times, but today, it had saved me.

The corner of his mouth ticked up. "I was pretty terrific."

"You're my hero," I said simply.

His ears tinged a deeper gray. "That's what Molly said." He removed his hat and fiddled with the brim. "Sounded better coming from her."

"I have no doubt."

He slicked back his hair. It was usually a futile gesture, since it rarely changed from how it looked when he died. Now it scraggled like somebody had attacked it with a cake beater, the parts that weren't singed off entirely.

Poor ghost. "You're going to be okay, right?"

He shoved the hat back onto his head. "I've had worse."

"Truly?"

"I could tell you stories." He pulled a silver cigarette case out of his suit coat pocket and flicked it open, frowning when he saw his Pall Malls were already smoking.

"No smoking in the house," I reminded him.

His forehead crinkled. "Too late."

The sash on the kitchen island twitched. I blinked hard, but before I could question my eyes, it slid forward as if pushed by an invisible hand.

"Frankie, look," I gasped as it dropped to the floor with a gentle thud. "Did you see that?" I rushed to pick it up.

He stashed the cigarette case in his pocket. "Yeah, I see. An old sash is more important than me still being on fire."

"Someone's trying to tell me something." I traced the fabric. "Grandma?"

"Oh, perfect. The lady who told you to go into the fire. By all means, let's take her advice," Frankie bit out, smoke literally curling from his ears.

The sash was a relic, its once-pristine white faded to a mottled ivory. *Votes for Women* was hand-sewn across its length in neat, precise stitches. A purple stripe adorned the top, a green one at the bottom. And as I turned it over in my hands, an odd weight caught my attention.

"Come see. This feels like metal," I said, pinching the bottom edge.

Grandma used to sew round weights into formal dresses to help them hang right. But this weight was long, with a rough edge that had no business touching silk.

Frankie glided closer, curiosity temporarily overriding his annoyance. "Why is this more interesting than me?"

"I'm not sure yet." I found the seam and worked it, coaxing the object through a hole where the stitches had frayed. A metallic glint caught the light as it slipped free.

Frankie swore under his breath. "It's a key."

"An old one." With a long stem and a filigree handle at the top. Swirling vines surrounded a flower bud under a star.

His face lit up. "You think that's what your grandma was going for all along?"

"It can't be." She wouldn't have risked my life like that. And she'd directed me to Melody first.

But she had wanted me to grab the sash.

"You think she's got cash stashed somewhere?" He rubbed his hands together, thankfully without sparking new flames. "Maybe a pile of jewelry?"

I very much doubted it. Grandma had never been the cash-and jewelry-stashing type. "This isn't her sash, so whatever this key unlocks, it's not hers."

"It'll be ours if we find it," Frankie said, warming up to the hunt.

Who was I to discourage him? I had a feeling I'd need his help. "I don't know what this key unlocks, but I'll bet it's important."

Why else would someone hide the key?

I gripped it tight, feeling its weight. Grandma had wanted me to have this.

The gangster nodded, suddenly all business. "All right. I know what we need to do next."

"Oh, goodie." Another Frankie scheme.

What could possibly go wrong?

Chapter Five

Frankie paced the kitchen, his smoky form leaving wispy trails behind him. He stopped abruptly, spinning on his heel to face me. "All right, here's the plan." He smacked at an ember hovering near his ear like a mosquito. "First, we gotta cut your grandma out of the picture. I don't trust her."

"You don't trust anybody." That was his problem. And frankly, if I had to pick one of them to team with, it would be my grandma. "You do realize I'd give anything to see her again."

Frankie spread his hands. "She's unreliable," he said as if he knew anything about it.

I squared my shoulders. "Didi is my rock." My North Star. I'd patterned my life after the lessons she'd taught me. "What happened today shows me she's still watching over me." As far as I was concerned, that was a good thing. A wonderful thing. "I wouldn't have been able to save Melody without her."

"And then she poofed out and left you in the middle of a fire." Frankie threw his hands up, sparks flying.

"I'm sure she couldn't help it," I said, stiffening. It had been terrifying and awful, but I refused to let it affect our relationship.

If we could still have one.

His eyes narrowed. "That's not what you'd say if *I* left you alone in an inferno."

"But you didn't. You were my hero." He'd been able to help, and he did. I'd gotten out, and I was thankful.

"Remember that." He rested his hands on his hips. "I was there. She wasn't. I'm here now. She's not—"

He didn't have to rub it in. "What's your point?"

The corner of his mouth curled up. "I'm in charge."

Bless his heart. "We'll agree to disagree."

"I hate to break it to you, kid, but your grandma's gone." Frankie patted out a flame on his third knuckle. "She lives in the light. Her type will shoot right up after they die. They don't have to worry about getting in. Or going the other way."

"Wait," I said, closing the distance between us, feeling the heat. "Is that why you stayed? You're worried about where you might go?" He hadn't exactly been a Boy Scout. Still... "You've changed a lot since I first met you."

The gangster's expression darkened. "I don't want to talk about it."

"All right," I said, keeping an eye on him even as the ghostly smoke stung my eyes.

"We're not talking about me," he snapped, a flame erupting from his hat. "We're talking about the goody-two-shoes souls. The ones who just assume they're worthy of the light. It's all candy and unicorns for them." He yanked off his hat and swatted it against his leg.

"Frankie—"

"Sometimes, they come back from fancy town when someone they love is in trouble. If they can," he added grudgingly. "But they never stay long."

Well, he hadn't met my grandma. "Didi will be the exception." I felt it. I knew it. Or maybe I just hoped really bad. There had to be an explanation for why she'd disappeared earlier. "She didn't appear as powerful as you."

"Who is?" Frankie wondered aloud.

Lots of ghosts. But Grandma's image had flickered even before the fire had gotten worse. Considering the heat still had Frankie burning, there was no telling what it had done to Grandma's weaker energy.

Still, I knew one thing for sure. She might have lost her strength, but she loved me with all her heart. Death couldn't change that.

I notched my chin up. "Didi knows we saved Melody, and she'll be back to make sure I'm safe, too."

Frankie shot me a curious look. "We'll agree to disagree."

"Don't steal my line," I warned him.

But he'd already moved on. "The question is—" a wisp of smoke curled from his furrowed brow—"why did your grandma direct you to the key?"

"Maybe she didn't. Maybe she wanted me to have the sash to help me breathe during the fire."

Frankie tilted his head. "She could have told you to use your shirt."

True.

The gangster drew up straighter. "I think your grandma had you grab that key because the keyhole is somewhere on your property. Some place you've never seen."

I'd like to believe that, to think we had some sort of family legacy stashed in a basement safe or behind a cupboard. "The trouble is, I don't have any mysterious keyholes." I knew every inch of this place. "Besides, how would Didi know about a key hidden in a suffragette's sash? She was born in 1936."

"Ghosts talk."

Maybe. I studied the sash for any sign of who might have owned it.

"In any case," Frankie said, opening his hands magnanimously, "we'll find out what this key opens, clean it out, and split the take ninety-ten."

"Seriously?" This was what he was worried about?

"Okay, eighty-twenty," he ground out.

"The eighty being yours," I said dryly.

"It's my plan."

"To use a key to open a lock." A key I found. That only I could use.

He ignored my very well-made point. "We can start the search in the attic. Then maybe hunt down all the old stuff you had to sell. Then I can have Suds do a deep dive in the basement. He's good with tunnels."

"Are you done?"

"I'm only getting started."

That was what I was afraid of.

I left the sash and key on the counter and turned to face Frankie. "This isn't a treasure hunt. I simply want to see my grandma."

"Fine, but then you'll have to offer her a cut from your twenty percent," he warned.

If he weren't already suffering, I'd set him on fire myself. "This isn't about money, Frank!"

Smoke billowed from his collar. "Don't call me Frank."

"Grandma led me into the library to save Melody, not find some key."

"Yet she had you grab that sash instead of running." He strolled through the kitchen island toward me. "And how did the fire start? I say something is going down. On the ghostly side and in the world of the living, and we need to get out in front of it for once."

Dread settled in my stomach. "What could possibly be going down?" We had no reason to assume anything nefarious was happening. "You're too used to sneaking around."

Frankie's eyes bugged out. "You're too used to trusting everybody."

Wasn't that a good thing?

I shook my head, glancing out the window above the sink to the warm light of the setting sun. "I suppose it wouldn't hurt to try to learn what the key is for."

"And your solution will be to ask everybody in town while waving around the key and telling them where you found it."

"That's not my plan at all," I balked, although it sounded like a good idea to me. "With any luck, Grandma will come back and tell us herself."

After all, she'd been the one to help me find it.

"Well, that's just terrific," he shot back. "So, tell me. How many years do you want to wait around this time for her to show up?"

A scratch at the door interrupted our debate. I opened it to find Lucy twitching her tail expectantly.

It was dinnertime. "Are you hungry, sweetie?" No doubt she was also thirsty after her race today.

But as soon as she spotted Frankie, she scampered away, her tiny feet pattering on the porch.

"I'll bring it out to you," I called after her, closing the door. She could dine alfresco.

"What did I ever do to that skunk?" Frankie asked, popping his head through the back wall to watch her go.

"Nothing at all," I assured him. The gangster loved animals. It was one of his few redeeming qualities.

This one just didn't love him back.

I tried a different tack. "All I want is time with my grandma. And maybe she'd show up if you weren't storming around arguing about money."

He had to understand that.

Only he looked like I'd just kicked his puppy. "You throwing me out of my own place?"

It wasn't his place. "It won't be for long," I promised. "I simply need some space."

"What did I ever do to you?" he demanded.

"Do you want a list?" It might take me five minutes. Ten tops. "I could do it alphabetically or in order of egregiousness."

Like the time he had me tracking down a psychopathic ghost in a haunted asylum. That was fun.

"That's it." His entire hat burst into flames. "I don't have to take this." He stalked for the wall by the laundry room, the quickest route to his shed. But before he got one foot through the wall, he spun to face me. "Whatever that key unlocks, your grandma isn't going to help you find it. She's either too weak, or she don't care."

"I refuse to believe that." It hurt to think it.

Frankie's mouth formed a grim line. "The only one who can help you is me. And we do it my way or not at all."

"Goodbye, Frank," I said, watching him pass through the wall and into the night, leaving only a faint hint of smoke until even that was gone.

Chapter Six

Grandma would be back. And when she appeared, she'd surely have more insight than a gangster ghost with the self-restraint of a cat at a fish market.

If she didn't, at least she wouldn't want to steal anything.

Or be bitter about saving me.

Or talk about locking people in lion's cages.

The key sat on the counter, taunting me. It had to mean something.

"But what?" I asked out loud.

The kitchen had never seemed quite so empty.

"It's okay," I insisted, if only to myself. I had a job to do. And feeling sorry for myself wouldn't feed my skunk.

I filled Lucy's bowl with fresh water, then grabbed carrots, green beans, squash, cooked brown rice, and roasted chicken from the fridge.

"Grandma will be back," I assured myself as I set to chopping the veggies.

Didi had taught me the art of the Southern drop-in. She was always the type to take time for a chat if she was in the neighborhood. She was Sugarland born and bred.

But what would she find when she got here?

I looked up from my cutting board. The kitchen was about the only intact room in the house, and that was because the counters were bolted down.

As for the rest of 12 Peach Orchard Lane? Well, I'd sold most of the furniture a few years ago to pay for a wedding that hadn't happened—the wedding where I'd almost married Ellis's brother.

I transferred the veggies to a small pan and added a tiny bit of water.

I'd dodged a bullet named Beau Wydell. Dating his brother, Ellis, several months later had caused quite the scandal.

That hadn't been part of any plan, but it had been worth it. I sautéed the veggies. I'd take on a hundred scandals and lose the clothes off my back if it meant I could be true to myself.

Still, it didn't change the fact I'd sold Grandma's prized stand mixer, her cookie jar, her well-loved table, and everything I could from the kitchen. Worse, I'd auctioned her antique sideboard, her china hutch, the parlor furniture she'd received as a wedding gift. I cringed. Even the hand-carved secretary desk where she'd lovingly addressed her Christmas cards.

All of it had reminded me of her.

I stirred the veggies harder.

I'd felt her when Lucy had curled up on Grandma's favorite rug in front of the fireplace. I'd felt her when I'd sat at her well-worn, well-scrubbed kitchen table. And I'd felt her when I'd checked my hair in the mirror above the mantel, the one she'd had in her room as a girl.

All of it was gone now, and so was she.

I lifted my spatula from the pan. What would she say about me scattering the legacy she'd left me? The one she'd entrusted to me.

Didi had left her money to my mom and my sister. She'd left her house to me because I'd loved it so much.

She'd believed I'd take care of it.

A rock formed in my stomach. Maybe that was why she hadn't returned after the library.

Maybe she'd taken one look at this place and fled.

I plated the veggies and set them down to cool. Then I popped the chicken and rice in the microwave.

How would I begin to explain it to her?

When the microwave dinged, I plated Lucy's dinner on a bone china plate I'd thrifted at the *New For You* store downtown. A year or two after I'd sold my family's fine dinnerware, I'd managed to find three bowls and five plates with lovely pink roses accented in gold. They reminded me of Didi, even if they didn't look a thing like the original plates she'd loved.

I placed Lucy's stir-fry along with a bowl of water on a silver tray—and did my best to feel posh, or at least proper, as I swept open the door for fine outdoor dining on the porch.

"Dinnertime, sweetie," I called, the screen door creaking closed behind me.

I'd expected her to dash out from under the porch, or perhaps from the nest she liked to make in the large pots of geraniums I kept at the top of the stairs.

Instead, her head poked from between the slats of the white-painted porch swing, her nose twitching.

"Stir-fry." I placed the tray near the edge facing the rose garden. "Your favorite."

But she didn't budge.

The swing rocked gently, which wasn't unusual on a breezy evening. But Lucy ignoring a meal? That was new.

She was curled up in the center of the seat, which was also odd. Lucy preferred the corners. If she jumped onto the swing at all.

Except when she was snuggling next to someone.

I gasped. Went numb. "You're not alone, are you, girl?"

I hurried for the bench, squinting desperately to see what my skunk so clearly did.

There, barely visible, sat a gauzy figure next to Lucy. My heart skipped a beat.

"Grandma?" Her name caught in my throat. "Grandma Didi?" She was here!

Tears pricked at my eyes as relief flooded through me. I'd been so afraid I'd never see her again.

Didi's form flickered weakly in the fading light, but it was her. It was her!

"Verity," she said warmly, rising from the swing, struggling a little as she did.

Lucy, ever the opportunist, claimed the vacated spot and spread out like a diva.

Didi chuckled. "This little girl was keeping me company as I gathered my strength."

"Sit," I urged, waving her back down. "I'll sit with you."

I'd been right. She'd come back!

The worn wooden slats of the porch swing creaked as I settled in beside her. The scent of roses filled the air, mingling with the earthy aroma of the garden. "I'm so happy to see you," I gushed, fighting the urge to hug her. "Remember when I'd sit here with you after school? You'd never let me get away without telling you every single detail of my day."

She shifted closer, bringing with her the faintest hint of sugar and vanilla. "I wish I had a homemade moon pie for you."

"I'd give anything for that." She made the best moon pies on the planet, filled with sweet gooey marshmallow and rich chocolate.

Melody and I would stop by after school almost every day. Mom worked, and our house was empty. It had felt good to come home to someone.

Didi's image flickered, nearly vanishing.

I instinctively reached out to steady her, glad I'd caught myself before I gave us both a shock. "Are you all right?"

Didi touched a hand to her chest, and her form solidified slightly. She looked good—her eyes bright, her hair done nice. "I'll be fine." She smiled at me. "It took a lot of energy to appear in the library. I hadn't planned to do that."

My heart stuttered. "You're not on fire, are you?"

"No," she said, surprised. "I felt my energy singe; then I lost my hold and ended up in the ether."

It was an in-between place where ghosts went to recover.

"I'm so glad you're okay." And that she'd made her way back to me. "Thank you for helping me find Melody."

She nodded gravely. "Melody was going to die." She clasped her hands tight. "The higher-ups asked me to prepare to greet her." She closed her eyes. "I went down to the library in order to be there for her when she passed, to help guide her to the light."

I sat speechless, stunned at how close I'd come to losing my sister. She was my only true family. At least the only family I could count on to always be here in Sugarland with me.

Didi's eyes caught mine and held. "Melody was lost. She couldn't see me. I felt so helpless. I was prepared to help her cross over, but I wasn't prepared to watch her die." Her form shimmered, weakening. "I tried to do something, anything to save her. I tried to break a window. Get her some air. But I wasn't strong enough. Then I saw you on the lawn, talking to a ghost!"

"Frankie surprised me too the first time he showed up."

"I thought if you could see him, you could see me. And together, we could save her."

"And it worked. She's alive and well."

Didi smiled at me, her eyes twinkling with mischief. "She's at her apartment right now with a handsome police officer."

"I know all about Alex Duranja," I said, directing a nudge her way. Being careful not to let it land.

She tilted her head toward me. "You know, I could always sense energies. I'm not surprised you can, too."

"I had some help," I admitted. The conversation lulled. That was when I noticed her shoulder beginning to fade. "Didi?"

"Oh, I'm all right," she said, patting it. It still stayed missing. "It's a side effect of my soul going to the light. You see, most of my energy isn't here. It's on the higher plane." She gazed out at the garden, a small smile playing on her lips. "I stop by from time to time. Do you remember your first night in this house, right after you'd moved in?"

"Melody brought me fried chicken and biscuits from the diner. Then we drank mint juleps out here on the porch."

We'd thought we were so fancy.

"That shooting star that streaked across the sky when you made your toast—?"

"It lit up the night. Right when I said I never wanted to live anywhere else."

She clasped her hands together. "That was me."

Oh, my word. "It felt so right."

"That's because it was." Grandma ducked her head. "Oh, and remember the time your car wouldn't start, and suddenly the engine turned over?"

Too many times to count.

"A little spare energy can crank an engine." She beamed. "I also send you the scent of roses on the breeze. I have to say, though, I never thought I'd be appearing to you like this."

She drifted to the pots of geraniums I kept near the porch stairs. "I missed these."

"I kept them up," I said, warmth spreading through my chest.

"I'm so glad." Their ghostly counterparts shimmered over the ones in the earthly realm. She plucked a gray, glowing bloom and tucked it behind her ear as her gaze swept across the yard. "And my rose garden. It's as lovely as ever."

"I've taken good care of it." For her.

Her brow furrowed. "What happened to the second bush from the left? That one was always so healthy."

"It still is."

She shot me a questioning look.

I shifted on the swing, tracing the familiar grooves in the armrest. "I'll take you inside later and show you." Though explaining Frankie would be a complication for another time. "Grandma, can I ask you something? Why did you have me grab the sash? I almost didn't make it out."

Grandma's hand flew to her mouth as she left the rail. "I'm sorry. I wasn't thinking. I became so emotional when I saw it." She sank onto the swing next to me. "I should never have sent you after my grandma's sash."

"Your grandma's?" It was my turn to gasp. "You mean Great-Great-Grandma Rose?"

Didi nodded. "Grandma Rose was a suffragette."

"I never knew." I smiled to myself.

I liked the idea of a suffragette in the family.

"I'm sure I told you," Grandma said. "Or maybe I didn't." She shook off the question. "In any case, she left her sash to me along with loads of papers for a secret society she led right here in Sugarland. They were dedicated to votes for women, among other things."

"What other things?" I pressed.

"I don't know. That was the secret." Grandma lowered her voice. "I think Grandma Rose's ladies may have done some things to skirt the law."

Frankie would be thrilled I had it in me.

Grandma continued, her form flickering in a way that worried me. "Grandma Rose left me boxes of papers and ledgers, but I couldn't see the value in them. It looked like old paperwork to me. I felt maybe they'd mean something to researchers or historians, so I donated all of the society's effects to the Sugarland Library for posterity."

"That's wonderful," I said, smiling.

"I thought so." Grandma's expression faltered. "But Grandma Rose was so angry at me for letting her society property out of the house."

How strange that a suffragette who'd fought for women's rights would object to sharing their history. "If you'd explained, I'm sure the library would have returned everything."

"They would have if I'd asked." A pained expression crossed her face. "Only it was too late. She was dead when I donated them. And I was dead when I realized."

"Oh, Grandma."

She brought a hand to her chest. "I didn't know she was upset until I met her on the other side. Turns out she'd come back to try to stop me. She was telling me no the entire time I packed up her things and drove them away. She said she'd screamed and cried and rattled the house to the foundation. But I couldn't see ghosts like you can. All I felt was a chill that made me turn the heat on." She squeezed her eyes shut. "I let her down."

"You didn't know," I said softly, resisting the urge to reach out and comfort her.

Grandma shook her head. "I should have. I wish I'd been paying more attention. I even tried her sash on in the mirror above the mantel."

"Did you feel the key in the lining?" I pressed.

"I didn't notice it." She deflated. "I gave it away."

"I found it," I assured her.

Hope flared in her eyes. "I'm so glad." Then she lost her spark. "I don't know that it will be enough. I still feel her on the other side, like an angry wall."

"It's not your fault." It truly wasn't. "You couldn't have known." The scent of roses intensified as a breeze rustled through the garden. "Grandma Rose?" I asked, feeling goosebumps erupt up my arms.

Grandma stiffened. "Is she here? You realize it was her garden first."

I stood and walked to the porch rail, watching the bushes, heavy with roses, rustle in the breeze.

"I don't see her," I said into the night. I leaned a hip against the rail. "Why is it so important to Rose?" So important she'd cut off her only granddaughter. "Surely, it's time to leave the past in the past."

Didi gazed at me, helpless, sad. "I wish we could." She joined me at the rail. "She says I ended her legacy by giving away those papers, by losing that key. But I wasn't privy to the details. I'm still not because she won't talk to me. She says she's bound by her obligation to this secret society. She says I failed her, I failed them, and there's no way to make it right." Grandma's form brightened slightly. "I mean, there *was* no way. Until I saw Grandma Rose's sash in the library and had you take it."

I stepped as close as I dared without touching her. "Do you want to stay with me?" I asked, feeling the chill radiating from the ghost. "You can have your old room back. We can find Rose's journals in the library. We can figure out where the key fits, what it all means. We can make this right for Grandma Rose."

"I—" She brought a hand to her chest. "I can try." She looked to the house, then to me. "Do you really think we can restore Grandma Rose's legacy? I don't want to make things worse."

I hated to say it, but losing Rose's trust, accidentally burying her grandma's legacy, was about as bad as it could get.

I only hoped Didi wouldn't feel the same when I showed her what I'd done with the treasures she'd left behind.

Didi glanced to the garden. "Maybe Grandma Rose can help. Although I'm not sure where she is right now."

"We don't need to know." We'd work with what we had. "It can be just us." I placed my hand on the rail next to her. "Let me do this with you. For her."

For Didi.

"You really think we can make it right, don't you?" she asked as if she were afraid to believe it.

I nodded firmly. "I know we can."

Chapter Seven

Didi's image flickered once more. Her shoulders sagged slightly, and the edges of her form blurred. "Stars." She touched a hand to her forehead. "With all this excitement, I think I might need to rest a spell."

"Of course," I was quick to agree. I'd been so excited to see her, it hadn't occurred to me I might be wearing her out. "You can use your old bedroom. I have it done up all nice." It was my bedroom now. Melody had even lent me one of the quilts Didi had left her, a beautiful double wedding ring pattern in blues and creams.

"Oh, Verity." She reached out to touch me, then thought better of it. "I appreciate the offer, but I don't think I'll be needing to borrow your bed."

"Nonsense." I wasn't going to kick her out of her own room. "I'd be glad to sleep in the parlor." Didi had always said we wanted every person who walked through our door to feel like family. And she wasn't only family, she was the queen of the castle.

Didi tilted her head to acknowledge my manners. "It's just that I'd be most comfortable in the ether."

"Oh." Naturally. "Of course. I mean, that makes perfect

sense." I stumbled over my words, desperate to make her feel comfortable while I grappled with how much she'd changed. And not changed. I was glad she had a place to take a break and recover her energy. I'd heard plenty about the ether from Frankie. All the same, I wished I could fetch her a blanket and a pillow to take with her. "You get some rest, and I'll be right here when you get back."

Her laughter rang out, warm and rich like honey. Oh, how I remembered that laugh. "You will not stay here. Go to bed. I'll be back before you know it."

She said it as if she were popping out to the market or down the road to borrow a cup of sugar. It felt familiar. Like home.

With a wink and a shimmer, she faded away, leaving behind only the faintest scent of roses.

"Goodbye," I said in the seconds after she'd gone.

I stood by myself for a moment on the porch under the stars. It was suddenly very quiet.

I'd never felt lonely in the big old house, not in all the years I'd called it my own. But I felt it then on the porch swing. Didi was barely gone, and I wanted her back. I wanted more time. More company.

"She'll be home soon," I declared. I meant every word of it.

Even so, I couldn't help but worry.

Seeing her tonight had been too good to be true. What if she'd used up her strength saving Melody and appearing to me tonight? We'd barely reconnected, and already she was struggling.

What if she couldn't make it back?

I sat down and tried not to think on that too much. Lucy hopped up on the swing, circled twice, then nuzzled in next to me. I scratched her behind her ears. "You always know exactly what I need, don't you?"

She snuggled in tighter.

The wood creaked gently as I rocked, looking out over my backyard at the tall apple tree next to the pond and the darkened shed nearby.

"Don't you fret," I told Lucy... and myself. "She'll be back before we know it."

This was meant to be.

From the very first moment Frankie crashed into my life, I'd hoped against all hope it would lead to this moment.

I'd endured the moonshine still Frankie built in my backyard, the ghostly horse he'd tried to stable outside my kitchen window, and the stinky, cute, did I mention loud ethereal goats that just had to be friends with the horse. I'd braved a haunted asylum, gone off the rails on a haunted train, and opened my door to the Chicago mob. And for all the ghosts I'd met, I'd clung to the hope that one day Didi would come home.

Frankie wanted to teach me to rob, cheat, and steal. I'd always maintained my real reward was the chance to connect with lost spirits, to set some things right. To do my best to leave Sugarland a little brighter than when I'd found it. And that was true. All of it.

But today, I'd discovered that was only part of it.

My real reward had been sitting on the back porch with Didi tonight, just like we always had. To have her back here, in my life.

And I'd lost her again way too soon. One minute she was here, and the next—blip—she'd retreated to the ether.

Lucy rolled onto her side, legs flopped out, her tiny snores a soothing backdrop to the night's symphony of crickets and bullfrogs. I took the chance to stroke her little tummy.

I was too keyed up to sleep.

Sure, Didi had promised to return, but she'd been so casual about it. She hadn't even wanted to see her old room.

She'd only come back because my sister was in trouble. Tonight, she'd proven she could leave just as easily as she had when she'd died.

Unless I gave her a reason to stay.

"I have to remind her she belongs here." That we could have a real relationship again. That it could be like it was...with a few minor changes. Like her being dead.

But that didn't matter. Not for me. I loved her and wanted her in my life.

And after she'd confided in me tonight, I had the chance to show her she could count on me to help fix her mistake, to spend time with her, to restore our family legacy.

It was more than I could ever have imagined, and I wasn't about to let this chance slip away.

She had to see she could count on me.

That she did right by coming back. And that she should stay here—that I needed her, and she needed me.

So that was what I would do.

I'd start first thing tomorrow.

"All right, girl," I said, folding Lucy in my arms. "Let's get you upstairs."

We had to at least try to get some sleep.

I carried my skunk up to our room at the top of the stairs. I nudged the door open, and as I paused on the threshold, memories washed over me. How many times had I curled up with Didi in her big mahogany bed while she told me stories about Sugarland?

She'd definitely want this room if she stayed, which was fine by me.

Her bed was long gone. Sold at auction with most everything else. My no-frills futon stood its place. Of course, on the ghostly side, Didi could make her room exactly like it was.

I placed Lucy atop the pillow next to mine. She turned a lazy circle and settled back down, asleep before I'd had the chance to crawl under the covers.

Even when I did, I was too excited to sleep. "It'll be wonderful," I said, stroking Lucy's little head. "You'll see."

After all, how could it not be?

Chapter Eight

I jolted awake to the blare of my cell phone playing "Here You Come Again" by Dolly Parton. Sunlight streamed through the curtains, stinging my eyes as I fumbled for my phone on the white skirted table by the bed.

It was the ringtone I used for Ellis. He was probably calling to make sure I was resting.

No telling when I'd finally fallen asleep.

The phone clattered off the table. Lucy grunted and scuttled under the covers. I practically fell out of bed trying to fish the phone out of my slipper.

I cleared my throat. "Hey, handsome," I croaked, wincing at the lingering scratchiness from yesterday's smoke.

"How are you feeling?" Ellis sounded way too serious for… whatever time it was in the morning. "I hope I didn't wake you."

"Don't be silly," I said, realizing my skunk had now taken my pillow. "It's—" I held my phone out to see the time. "Noon."

Panic seized me. I was late.

I hurried to the window overlooking the backyard, hoping to catch a glimpse of Didi on the porch swing, waiting for me.

She wasn't there.

I felt it in the pit of my stomach.

It doesn't mean anything.

Only it did, because she'd promised to return quickly. She'd been eager to get started.

I hoped I hadn't missed her.

"Verity? Are you all right?"

I turned away from the window. "My throat's sore." My hand was a bit throbby. "But otherwise, I feel good." I perched on the edge of the bed. My head was clear. Which was wonderful.

"Good." I could hear the relief in his voice. "I was going to stop by with breakfast but got called in to the library."

My chest clenched. "How bad is the damage?"

"Bad enough. But that's not the problem right now."

What could be worse?

"We found a body."

I stood so fast I startled Lucy. "Oh no." I gripped the phone tight. "Was someone trapped inside?" My stomach knotted. I thought I'd gotten everyone out. It didn't occur to me there could be someone else left inside.

Whom *I'd* left inside.

"It's not that," Ellis said quickly. "It's an old body. A skeleton. And according to the medical examiner, it was a skeleton long before the fire started."

I whooshed out a breath. "Thank heaven. Just a body in the library."

"Verity?"

"I know." That sounded weird even to me.

"We found it walled up behind what's left of the fireplace on the second floor. The one in the children's area. I'm on scene with the police right now. If you're up to it, I'm hoping you can come down and lend us a hand. See if there's a ghost hanging around. It would really help if we could get a positive ID on the victim."

"Sure thing," I said, attempting to locate my shoes. "Wait. You said *victim*. You believe it was murder?"

"Somebody walled them in."

Good point.

I fished my sneakers out from under the bed and slipped them on, then hurried to my armoire for a dress while Ellis filled me in.

"Right now we have no evidence the victim was killed at the library, but it's a reasonable assumption since they were buried in the wall. Do you know how hard it would be to sneak a body into the main library?"

And up the stairs.

"That means there's a decent chance the ghost of the victim is still haunting the space." I said it with a heavy heart. It was common for ghosts to haunt their death spots, but tragedy in particular could cause them to get stuck.

I put Ellis on speaker while I slipped out of my nightgown and into a pink and green sundress with a white lace trim. "We'll see who's around to chat." Even if the poor soul hadn't stayed to haunt the fireplace, many of the same ghosts had been lurking around the library for the last hundred and sixty years.

I smoothed my dress and grabbed a hairbrush to make a quick ponytail. The police couldn't take my findings to court, but I could at least give Ellis a place to start piecing together the evidence.

"Thanks, sweetie." His footsteps echoed on the wood floor, and I heard shuffling as he spoke to his colleagues. "Leave everything as it is. Verity is coming to take a look."

I fished a green bow out of the top drawer of my dresser. It warmed my heart that Ellis was proud of my abilities and that he'd publicly ask for my help. He'd played a big part in helping folks around here accept my abilities. People respected Ellis. They listened to him, and he counted on me.

"I'll be there as quickly as I can," I promised, tying a quick bow.

"It'll be good to see you."

He meant to fuss over me. Not that I minded.

"I just have to find my keys."

And pray Didi was downstairs. If she wasn't, well, I'd have to leave anyway. But I'd never forgive myself if I missed her, if she was called back to a higher place while I was off ghost hunting.

"Bring Frankie," Ellis urged.

"About that..." After the fit he'd thrown last night, I wasn't sure Frankie was in the mood to go back to the library. Or to do me any favors. Even if he wasn't still smoldering. "What would you say if I told you I had someone better in mind?"

"Better?" Ellis asked, incredulous.

If she was here, yes. "Let's just say I've got a secret weapon up my sleeve."

"You're going to ask your grandma."

It was very hard to surprise Ellis. I loved him anyway.

I located my hemp bag between my dresser and the armoire. "I'd rather not bring both. Frankie made it clear last night he isn't fond of working with her."

"Frankie doesn't always like working with *you*."

"Must you be so observant?" I asked, fishing Frankie's urn out of my bag and placing it on the dresser for safekeeping.

I'd accidentally grounded the gangster onto my property when I'd mistaken his urn for an old vase and rinsed his ashes out onto my grandma's favorite rosebush. It had been an honest mistake. The poor ghost.

I'd hosed him in good, too. Now Frankie couldn't leave my few acres of heaven unless I took his urn with me, with the smidgen of his ashes still left inside.

I told myself he wouldn't mind missing this one trip.

Much.

"Wait. You're going to use Frankie's power while you leave him at home?"

"Well..."

It was true I had no power of my own. It was Frankie who lent me his ability to see the other side.

"And you're going to play favorites with a ghost he doesn't like."

"Don't put it that way." Although I was pretty sure that was exactly how Frankie would put it.

Guilt niggled at me.

"He did save your life," Ellis concluded.

I'd be eternally grateful. Until the gangster reminded me too many times. He was never slow to call in a favor. "Fair warning, he'll probably want a second floor on his shed for that one." Or perhaps a circle drive.

"Maybe a secret underground lair."

"Don't give him any ideas." I fished around in my bag until I located my keys. "It's just that... He wasn't quite himself last night." I clutched my keyring and headed for the stairs. "I'm probably doing him a favor, giving him a chance to rest and recover."

Keep telling yourself that.

"I'm only saying you're about to step in it."

Ellis was honest to a fault. Usually, it worked in my favor.

The kicker was he was probably right. Sure, I owed the gangster my thanks. Maybe even a special shine and polish for his urn. But it didn't mean I had to take him with me today.

With any luck, Didi was waiting for me on the porch or maybe in her old kitchen. Wouldn't that be a blast from the past? Her frying up her famous buttermilk pancakes while the coffee percolated. I'd come down, and she'd ask me to put the syrup on the table. Though I couldn't touch a scrap of it—and I wouldn't want to since ghostly objects would give me a jolt—I still wanted that feeling. Most of all, I really wanted to see her, just her.

I wanted her to see me work. To know I was okay. To see me shine.

And bonus—while we were at the library, we could try to locate the secret society paperwork she'd donated. I needed her for that. I didn't know what it looked like.

"You're the one who has to deal with Frankie," Ellis concluded.

"I do every day," I said, rounding the banister and heading down the hall toward the kitchen.

With any luck, Frankie wouldn't even know I was gone.

"Gotta go," I said, signing off, picking up the pace.

But when I made it to the kitchen, there was no Didi.

"Hello," I said, flinging open the back door.

The porch stood empty.

My stomach squinched. No way should she still be gone. She'd promised to be quick. She'd been excited to begin exploring our legacy together.

More importantly, there was no telling when else I'd be able to get her into the library to search for the items she'd donated. No doubt it was closed right now to everyone except police and fire-fighters.

I chewed my lip. Maybe I should just ask Frankie.

Lucy had followed me down the steps, but I was on my own when I ventured toward the shed by the pond.

I almost tripped over my feet when Didi passed through the door.

"Verity!" She brightened when she saw me. "I love that dress."

"Thank you." She'd always liked me in pink. "It's wonderful to see you." She appeared more vibrant than before. And I could see her shoulder clearly. "You look fantastic."

"I'm getting my feet under me." She grinned, wiggling one of her trademark sequin-studded sneakers as she hovered a few inches above the ground. "Figuratively speaking, of course."

I was so glad to see it. "What were you doing at Frankie's place?"

With any luck, she'd won him over. Didi could charm the freckles off a spotted hound.

She stopped. "Your gangster lives there?" Her forehead crin-kled. "That explains the *Card Counting for Dummies* book on the table."

"Frankie has a book?" He really was growing as a person.

"And several fire extinguishers," she said, shocked. "Stolen from all over town!"

"His friends must have been by."

Didi wrung her hands. "I hope he doesn't mind I straightened up a bit."

It was too late to worry about that now. "I'm sure it's fine."

"He's not the picky type?" She hesitated. "I just thought it was your junk shed, and you know how I like to organize. Although I was going to have words with you about those extinguishers."

Maybe Frankie would think his girlfriend did it.

In any case, there was no fixing it now.

"We have more important things to think about," I said, ushering her over to the 1978 avocado green Cadillac I'd inherited from her. I opened the door for her, even though she could just as easily float right through. "Ellis needs our help. And this might be our only chance to get back into the library and find those files you donated."

"Surely, we can't just take them," she said, settling into the passenger seat.

I scanned the yard for Frankie as we backed out of my parking spot. "We'll see when we get there," I said, making a clean getaway.

A fire department van, several police cruisers, and the county fire marshal's SUV choked the circle drive in front of the library. The acrid stench of smoke hung heavy in the air.

Friends and neighbors huddled in quiet clusters on the lawn and in the square. Past the green space and the Colonel Larimore statue, Lauralee's food truck sat parked in front of the bank, serving up Southern comfort food.

I supposed we could all use some comfort right about now.

Plastic-wrapped flowers and teddy bears of all shapes and sizes crowded around the cannonball in the wall, forming a heartfelt memorial.

I pulled in behind Duranja's cruiser, barely squeezing my beast of a Cadillac into the last spot left.

Grandma's hand fluttered to her chest as she took in the shattered windows and streaks of soot marring the weathered brick facade. "It breaks my heart."

"Mine too." I could scarcely bring myself to look as I ka-chunked the car into Park. Still, losing my sister would have been indescribably worse.

Didi's lips formed a dainty O at the concert of pops and crackles under the hood as I killed the engine.

"It always does that," I said quickly. I'd treated her car like it was my own. "Whenever there's a problem, I take it straight to Billy Ray's Auto Depot off Route 4."

Didi used to say Billy Ray could make a car run smoother than a greased pig at the county fair.

"It's not that." She tugged at her earlobe, a nervous habit I remembered well.

"What, then?" I scanned the lawn, hoping to spot a ghost or two.

"We're not an official vehicle."

"Is that all?" I caught the eye of Officer Duranja, who stood guard at the front door.

From the way his fingers drummed against his holster, he seemed to be thinking the same thing.

"Don't worry," I said, grabbing my bag. "If I stopped to ask for permission, I wouldn't get anything done."

Grandma stared at me for a second too long.

Oh my. Was I starting to sound like Frankie?

I tried another tactic. "Think of it this way." I dropped the keys in my purse. "We're on official business."

Sort of.

At least I hoped nobody would tow my car.

"Ellis *is* waiting for us," Didi reasoned as I looped my bag over my shoulder and nudged the door closed.

"I knew you'd understand."

"Still," she said, hustling up the library steps with me, "the key to breaking the rules is you don't let anyone *know* you're breaking the rules."

I'd always thought subtlety was one of my strengths.

Then again, I hung out with Frankie.

"You'll have to teach me." I was always up to learning, and Didi had a way with people.

She shot me a quizzical glance. "Just how long do you think I'll be around?"

Forever, if I was lucky.

We sidestepped a cluster of ladies from the Sugarland Stitch 'n' Bitch Club. Their crochet-hook earrings and Mrs. Green's yarn-bombed walker looked out of place against the charred brick and broken glass.

Miss Eugenia clutched a half-finished afghan to her chest like a shield, while Mrs. Beeswax seemed to be sizing up Duranja for a new scarf.

"Excuse me," I said, almost tripping over a wayward ball of yarn.

They usually met in the library's cozy reading nook every Tuesday, but today they huddled on the steps, looking lost.

When I made it past, I spotted Melody near Duranja, deep in conversation with her assistant, Lucas, and Mr. Hartley. I closed the distance in three long strides.

"Melody!" My voice cracked.

My sister turned, her eyes lighting up. I crashed into her, hugging her so tight I felt the buttons on her dress. Her lavender shampoo mingled with traces of smoke.

"I'm so glad to see you safe," I said, chin on her shoulder.

"Thanks to you and Didi." Melody squeezed me back hard, then pulled away to whisper, "Is she here?"

"Yes!" I stepped aside, gesturing to Didi, who hovered right beside me.

Melody squealed, fixing her attention about two feet to Grandma's left. "Oh, Didi," she clasped her hands. "It's good to see you."

Didi zipped into the spot where Melody was looking. "You too, sugar." She reached for a lock of Melody's hair, passing through it. "I'm tickled to see you healthy and well."

"Ellis called me in on a police matter," I said to Duranja.

I had to admit, it was fun to say.

He gave a barely perceptible nod. "There's a parking lot out back."

Why did these people care so much about parking? Frankie wouldn't have cared if I'd left my car on the lawn.

Scratch that. He'd have been proud.

Melody looked from me to Duranja. "Ellis called? What's going on?"

"Can we help?" Lucas asked.

Duranja shot me a warning look. "I have strict instructions not to divulge."

I leaned close to Melody's ear. "I'll tell you later."

In a much less public place.

I stepped back. "Didi's here to see me work," I added, giddy at the prospect. "She's also looking for several boxes of papers she donated."

"In 1973," Grandma chimed in.

"In 1973," I echoed. "It's important."

Melody lit up. "I'm sure we have them somewhere. I can see where they're filed."

"I'll go too," Lucas stepped up. "I know the archives better than anyone."

"He does," Melody said with no small bit of affection.

A blond curl fell into his eye, but Lucas barely noticed. "Once I save enough money for grad school, I'm going to do my dissertation on an aspect of Sugarland history. I'm still deciding which."

I could see why she liked him.

"Let us in, too!" Miss Eugenia from the Stitch 'n' Bitchers bustled up, waving her half-finished afghan like a flag of truce.

"We need to salvage our yarn stash," Mrs. Bledstone said on her heels.

Duranja shook his head, his stance widening. "No one's allowed inside. Except for you, Verity."

"Truly?" I understood the yarn ladies. "But I could really use Melody's help." When he didn't budge, I added, "It's vital family business."

"For my dearly departed grandma," Melody said, catching on fast.

She flashed him a beautiful set of doe eyes.

I had to admit she had a talent for it.

"I have my instructions," he said with a warning look at the yarn ladies, who appeared ready to flank him. "Now, go," he said, cracking the door.

"Fine." I slipped in behind Duranja, who stood facing the crowd, arms crossed, every inch the gatekeeper.

He held the door a beat longer, and Melody, quick as a cat, darted in after me. I caught a glimpse of Duranja's lips twitching as he let it shut behind her.

Five stars for doe eyes. "Look at your man, breaking the rules."

Her cheeks flushed pink. "He loves me."

And he trusted us. He'd seen what we could do. This past spring, the three of us investigated a murder on a haunted pirate island.

Although it still surprised me that the officer I'd dubbed RoboCop had tossed the rules for us just then.

I turned to Melody in her flowing, floral-print maxi dress, buttons trailing from collar to hem. Her blond hair was pulled back in a messy braid, wisps framing her face like a halo. She looked like a garden fairy who'd stumbled into a film noir.

Okay, now I got it.

Both our faces fell when we saw the extent of the destruction in the historic library. The place reeked of soot. The once-pristine marble floors were littered with ash and debris. Sunlight streamed through the windows of the main reading room, catching the smoke that still hung in the air.

I spotted Didi bent over the original architectural map of downtown Sugarland, now a water-soaked, disintegrated heap on the floor. "Oh, no. No, no. This had been hanging since I was a girl."

The ghostly version remained on the wall, shooting off sparks like bottle rockets. Didi dodged one and retreated to the opposite wall.

"Why's it doing that?" I asked, ducking another.

Didi hugged herself, shoulders tensing. "The spiritual realm is still burning."

Oh no. "Is it safe for you to be here?"

"As long as I don't touch it." She gave the ghostly map a wide berth. "It's beautiful in a way. A lot of people in Sugarland loved that map."

"Still do." I counted myself among them.

Didi nodded. "It has a lot of emotions tied to it."

The thought of all those feelings burning made me nervous. "I just don't want you to catch fire like Frankie."

Her expression softened. I'd told her about him in the car. "Your housemate stayed in an active fire for too long."

"So he explained." None too kindly. "He's also a natural hothead."

"Has he been to the higher realms?" she asked sweetly.

"No, and don't bring that up with him." It was a sore subject with the gangster.

Melody's mouth formed a thin line as she stepped over a crushed Tiffany lamp, one of the originals from the 1920s. "The family history archives are in the basement."

I tried not to look at another broken frame against the wall, at all that ruined history. "We'll go down with you after I help Ellis."

She navigated half-charred books and scattered papers. "If we have any archives left."

"Don't," I said. That was when I saw how close she was to breaking. I couldn't imagine what it would mean to lose our town's entire history. "Don't borrow trouble." We didn't know anything yet.

She took a deep breath and stiffened her spine. "The family archive catalog is behind the reference desk." She squared her shoulders. "I'll see where your boxes are, Didi." She strode into the smoke-damaged reading room, past singed prewar study tables and waterlogged bookcases. To her left, a shattered window gaped, its frame blackened and warped.

"The boxes will be there," I said. "Intact." I had to believe it, or both Melody and I were going to end up in a puddle on the floor.

Didi gave a sharp nod. "In the meantime, I haven't seen any ghosts."

Me either. Not outside. Not in the lobby or the main reading room. There had been a trio of Civil War soldiers playing poker here since this building had been a field hospital in 1863—Owens, Gregson, and Stoutmeyer, who never let anyone else deal.

But now, they were nowhere to be found.

I watched Melody make her way to the polished reference desk at the back, its surface marred by soot. Behind it, the wooden doorway bore angry black streaks, as if fire had licked at it from the other side. I wished there was something I could do for her.

"Verity." Officer Jameson's voice startled me. I turned to find him standing in the main lobby. "Ellis is upstairs."

"Coming," I said, praying he wouldn't spot Melody.

He gave me an odd look as I hustled over, but he didn't pay any mind to the reading room. His grim expression made it clear he was still getting used to the destruction in the lobby.

"This way," he said, escorting me up.

Each step groaned under our weight, the lingering smoke growing thick enough to sting my eyes.

Didi ran a hand through the bubbled paint on the wall. "All of this is so much worse than I imagined."

Didn't I know it? I almost hadn't made it down these stairs.

At the landing, I paused at what was left of the display case. Glass shards carpeted the floor, catching weak sunlight. If I hadn't grabbed that sash, it would've been a charred ruin, along with everything else in the case. No one would have known where the mysterious key came from—if they noticed it at all. It would've likely been swept away in the cleanup.

Officer Jameson led me upstairs, past kids' crafting tables strewn with half-finished projects. Sunlight slanted through the windows to my right, stretching shadows across the floor. I kept an eye out for ghosts, but no dice.

So far.

And as we made our way past the rows of bookshelves, my stomach squinched into a tight ball. Little Olivia's pillow fort lay in ruins, cushions and blankets scattered.

Ellis stepped from around the corner. "Verity." The relief in his voice made me want to hug him.

"No ghosts," Didi announced, scanning the room. She popped her head through the wall to the other large room. "Are you sure this library is haunted?"

"Dead sure."

"I'll check the rest of the floor."

My heart lurched. "You don't have to—"

"I'll be quick," she said, disappearing.

She would be, but she'd also be gone. I tried not to let it bother me, even as what was left of my happy bubble burst.

It made sense there weren't any ghosts around. Not with items on the spiritual plane still sparking.

But I was hoping for at least one brave soul.

I dearly wanted to help Ellis, and equally important, I wanted to show Didi I could do this by myself.

Ellis planted a quick kiss on my cheek. "You okay?"

"Yes," I said. I really was. I should be glad Didi wanted to help. It wasn't as if she'd abandon me or disappear like Frankie always did.

"You have to see this." Ellis led me around the corner.

Police Chief Edmund Royce stood in the Children's Reading Room with two men in heavy-duty boots and jackets emblazoned with *Fire Investigation* across the back. Cases of specialized equipment lay open on the floor—cameras, sample collection kits, meters.

Royce kicked the nearest case shut when he saw me.

"Hi, Ed," I said, aiming for casual, wishing Didi were here. I was pretty sure she used to babysit him.

His eyes flicked in acknowledgment before he turned his back to me. "Do you think it was arson?" he asked the men, his voice low.

One of the investigators shook his head. "We don't know."

They knew.

I could see it in the set of their jaws, the way their eyes kept darting toward the identical fireplace on this side of the wall. A gaping hole marred the original wall beside it.

Ellis shot me a warning look. We'd talk later.

"Let me show you what we found downstairs," one of them said.

Royce nodded and joined them, shooting me a look like I was intruding.

He'd invited me.

Well, at least Ellis had.

As their footsteps faded, Ellis turned to me, voice low. "You ready to see what we found?"

"Always." He led me to the hole near the fireplace.

Fire had collapsed a section of the wall, revealing an opening behind the brick and marble. My heart raced as Ellis shone his flashlight into the darkness.

Nestled in the hidden nook lay a skeleton.

The bones, blackened by the recent blaze, curled in a fetal position. Scraps of charred fabric clung to the remains.

"Wow." I stared at the library's long-term resident. Empty eye sockets stared back.

Ellis ran his light over the brick-lined alcove. "We think this was a secret room."

The wall was thicker between the two big library rooms. I'd always assumed it was the back-to-back fireplaces.

"You don't think the poor soul was..." I could scarcely bring myself to say it. "Buried alive."

It had almost happened to me once in the basement of the Southern Spirits distillery. It had been terrifying.

Ellis had been there. We shared a glance. "I don't think the victim was walled in alive," he assured me. "Someone would have heard the screams."

I nodded, not sure how comforting that was.

Then it hit me. "The basement walls are just as thick."

"We believe one of the fires was started right here for a reason."

"One of the fires?" I gaped.

Ellis ran a toe over a scorched part of the carpet near the collapsed wall. "The tests aren't back, but it appears they used an accelerant."

My heart sank. "So definitely not an accident."

"No," he said grimly. "Did you see any ghosts?"

I ventured another glance around. "Not yet."

Ellis shone his light on a soot-stained circle of gold near the skeleton's hip. "A watch fob. Could be a man or a woman."

I noted paper fragments scattered among the bones. Whatever secrets they might have held had been reduced to ash.

"We talked to Mr. Hartley. There's no record of anyone disappearing in or near the library," Ellis said. "If they had ID, it's gone now. That's why I need you."

The pressure was on.

"All right. Just give me some space." I stepped back. "The good news—which is bad for helping me find the ghost—is they didn't die inside that wall."

"Yes, but my gut says it happened on this floor." Ellis scanned the room.

We'd covered that on the phone. It would be hard to drag a body up the main stairs undetected. And the Sugarland Library had no elevators.

I cleared my throat. "If you're here, sir or madam, can you come talk to me, please? My name is Verity Long, and I very much care about what happened to you."

A cold breeze whipped past my ear. I jumped, goosebumps racing up the back of my neck.

"What's your name?" I pressed.

Chapter Ten

Didi appeared directly in front of me, her hair frazzled and escaping her updo. "Sorry for the blast, hon. I forgot how fast I can zip around the mortal plane."

"Oh." My shoulders fell. Glad as I was to see her, I wished the fireplace ghost were standing next to her.

"Verity?" Ellis asked, catching my reaction.

"I'm not seeing any spirits," I told him. "Well, besides my grandma."

"I don't really count," she said, with a wave of a hand.

"I think you do," I assured her.

"It's got to be the fire that drove them away," she said, bringing a hand to her head. "And the aftermath keeping them out. No ghost in their right mind would stick around for this. I don't know if it's the sparks downstairs or the lingering zap in the air, but I can feel it draining my energy, sizzling over my skin. It's an awful kind of static electricity that bites down to the bone." She examined her hands. "I feel like I could erupt in flames any second."

Like Frankie. Fear shot through me like ice water.

"Okay, this is dangerous. You need to leave. Now," I warned. She'd gotten lucky the first time. And she'd been more tied to the heavenly plane then. We couldn't count on her losing power and ending up somewhere safe—especially now that she'd been down here longer.

We didn't need her smoking. Or burned. With embers flying out of her head like Frankie. "I can handle this. I promise. We can go ghost hunting another time."

Didi cast a wary glance around the room. "I don't think you're going to find your ghost. I checked every other floor, including the basement." She shuddered. "It's bad down there. Everything is burned and wet. Dare I say a lost cause. I'm sorry, but I may be going back to the light earlier than we expected."

"No," I said, too sharp. "I'll find those boxes." We'd figure out something real nice to do with them, some way to honor Rose.

I had to help Didi remember what she loved about Sugarland. Then she'd stay. Then everything would be fine.

"Verity?" Ellis asked. "Are you with us?"

"Always." My head swam a little. "I'm sorry. I don't see any ghosts."

I felt like I'd let him down.

I didn't want to let Didi down, too. "Let me walk Didi outside; then I'll check the other floors." Namely, the basement.

"I'm staying if you are," Didi vowed.

"No, you're not." It wasn't safe. "Frankie stayed too long. Last I saw, his finger was on fire. His body was smoking and kicking off embers, and his hair looked like he'd taken a thousand volts."

That last part was designed for true horror. In the South, a lady could survive almost anything—except a ruined hairdo.

I watched her waver.

"I'll be fine," she decided.

Argh. This wasn't like Didi taking the smallest piece of chicken at dinner or sitting in the uncomfortable chair when entertaining the neighbors. This was her ethereal body we were talking about, and if other ghosts had the sense to stay away, then she should too.

"How about this? You can wait outside while Melody and I

find what you need from the family archives." To sweeten the pot, I added, "Would you like to come?" to Ellis. "He'll keep me and Melody safe." Didi couldn't argue with that.

He could also help us carry out the boxes that I hoped and prayed were still there.

Ellis ran a hand through his hair. "I've got to stay with the skeleton. But go. Get what you need. I appreciate you stopping by to help."

"I'll try again soon," I promised, leaning in for a quick kiss on his cheek.

He caught me close instead, his body warm. Steady. "You look good. I needed to see that."

I wrapped my arms around his neck and gave him a longer, deeper kiss. "You worry too much."

"I do," he said, watching me head for the stairs.

"I'm glad," Didi said as we started down. "He's a good one."

"Yet you don't mind I'm worried about you?" I asked, charging to the lobby as fast as I dared.

"I'm always fine," she assured me.

Until she wasn't.

But there was no use trying to change her mind. If she was going to be ten kinds of stubborn and stay here with me, I'd make sure she didn't stay long.

She eyed me as if she knew what I was thinking. "I'm not leaving until I know Grandma Rose's legacy is safe."

And then—according to her—she'd be gone.

I had to find a way to keep her here until she realized she belonged.

Except I was about to complete the very task she'd set as her final goal.

We found Melody at the reference desk. She held up a Post-it Note. "According to our records, they're in the basement archives, row S, boxes 114.1 and 114.2."

"Let's go," I said, bursting through the rear door first.

I slammed straight into a wall of black jackets, a team of men who appeared as startled as I felt.

A man wearing aviator sunglasses—inside—held up a hand. "I'm sorry, miss. This is a restricted area."

"I work at the library," Melody said on my heels. "Mr. Hartley sent me for a file from downstairs."

"Absolutely no one is going downstairs," his colleague stated. "There's heavy water damage."

"And an ongoing investigation," aviator glasses added.

I turned to Didi. Maybe it was good she was here, although I swore her hair appeared a bit more frazzled than it had only minutes ago upstairs. "You can go down and retrieve the files on your side." Surely, that would satisfy Rose.

"Nobody's going anywhere," aviator glasses snapped.

"Not us," Melody assured him. "We're talking to our dead grandmother. Well, Verity is."

He and his team looked at her like she was a looney.

That was okay. They weren't from Sugarland.

Didi shook her head. "It doesn't matter if I take Rose's boxes back on the ghostly side. I need those records out of the public library, period. At least that's what Rose said." She shook her head. "One or both of you must find them and carry them out."

"I understand." She knew Rose better than I did. I tried another angle. "Can you at least verify they're down there? Give us a place to start?"

"If I could take a lid off to see." She fiddled with her earring, and I could swear I saw a sizzling ember drop. "Only I'm not strong enough for that."

Right.

"Leave. Now," aviator glasses snapped.

He didn't have to tell me twice.

"Come on," I said. "We'll come back later." When it was safe.

It would keep Didi out of harm's way and give me more time to convince her to stay with me for good.

"We'll go home," I decided when we'd made it out to the main reading room. Maybe we'd take a drive through old Sugarland to help her remember why she loved this town so much.

Melody lingered behind the reference desk. "I just want to grab a few things."

"Okay, but I'm getting Didi out." I didn't see any more sparks, but her hair and dress were starting to float like she'd been rubbing balloons all day.

I had her almost to the lobby, almost out the door, when she stopped cold. "Verity, look!"

She pointed to an area of tables to our left. Fiery shards floated down from the ceiling.

What the—?

Then it clicked. "There could be a loved object up there, like the map." Or... I shuddered to think. "That could be a ghost catching fire." Someone who didn't have a granddaughter to practically carry them out the door.

Didi studied the sparks. "If I'm not mistaken, it's coming from the fireplace area upstairs."

I groaned inwardly. She would have to say that.

And worse? She was right.

I closed my eyes briefly. "You're not going to leave, are you?"

Didi was already heading for the stairs. "Not a chance."

Jiminy Christmas. "Quickly," I urged, hot on her heels.

She had the self-preservation of a gnat.

"You're right. This ghost hunting is fun." Didi led the way without breaking a sweat.

I was glad somebody was having a good time.

"This way," I said, pulling ahead at the top, rounding the corner on Ellis, who stood guard over the body in the wall. "Did we scare you?" I asked, out of breath.

"Like a tromping buffalo," he said. With love.

Or at least that was the way I took it.

Didi scanned the floor. "I don't see any sparks up here."

We both turned to the wall at the same time. "We need to take another look inside."

Before I could say another word, Grandma walked straight through it.

"What am I looking for?" Ellis aimed his flashlight at the hole. "What did you find downstairs?"

"The arson squad," I said, skirting past him. "Also signs of a ghost in trouble up here."

I poked my head in gingerly. No sense sticking it through a spirit. That would bring on a world of hurt for both of us and kill any chance of polite conversation.

But I didn't see a ghost inside.

Well, except for Didi.

Only her head and shoulders were visible, off the skeleton's left side. The rest of her was in the floor. I tried not to let it bother me.

I mean, I knew she was a ghost. It was just that she was also my Didi.

No ghostly light illuminated the skeleton, no signs of a haunting. The skeleton appeared the same on the ghostly side as it did in my world.

Didi eyed me. "I think the sparks are coming from underneath."

"Where?" I didn't even see the sparks anymore.

"Look." She rested her cheek on the floor for a better angle. "There's a crackling glow under the pelvis."

She was right.

It was faint but there. "Ellis, can you shine your light on the body, near the floor?"

He traced his beam over the blackened pelvic bone and the spread finger bones braced against the singed wood floor. His light cast shadows on the cobwebs in the far corner. Lots and lots of cobwebs.

I didn't see anything unusual in our world.

"Wait." Grandma lowered down and tilted her head halfway through the floor. "Oh my word."

"What's she doing?" Ellis shoved his light deeper into the hole.

It wouldn't help.

"She sees something." Something Ellis and I couldn't.

Didi reached under the pelvis and pulled out a signet ring. The moment it cleared the bone, it lit up like the Fourth of July, throwing off sparks in every direction.

"Look!" Didi rose out of the floor with her prize.

"It's a ghostly ring," I told Ellis. Gray and glowing. "Put it down!" I added to Didi.

It sparked worse than the map.

"It's haunted," Didi said as a spark landed on her arm and her foot. "And it's hot." She tossed it from hand to hand. "Even now —" She winced as it tumbled out of her grasp.

"It's wildly dangerous," I finished for her as she began sucking on a finger. To Ellis, I added, "It burns them. It can set them on fire."

Didi pretended not to hear.

"Who does it belong to?" Ellis prodded.

"Probably the skeleton." But I wasn't sure. I ducked my head in the hole as far as I could, straining for a better look.

"Someone who cherished it," Didi said, nudging the ghostly ring back where she'd found it.

At last.

"See? That wasn't so hard."

She chewed her lip. "I should have looked at it closer."

"Let me handle that." I reached a hand back to Ellis. "Can I see your light?" Maybe I could spot it on the mortal plane.

I aimed the beam directly at the spot where Grandma had found the ghostly ring.

There, in the ash, under the pelvic bone, I could almost see a hint of gold. "Take a look," I said to Ellis after explaining what we'd found.

"Let me be the one to disturb the body." He scooted past me, stepping up over the wall. "But don't get your hopes up," he added, easing into the narrow alcove. He crouched over the body as I shone the light. "We had forensics in here. They're very thorough." He fished a penlight from his pocket and twisted cheek-to-floor. "Well, I'll be damned." He fished a gold ring out of the ash with the end of his penlight.

It was the same ring!

A gold signet identical to the one Didi had found in her realm. The ghostly ring over the real one made the entire thing glow gray.

He stood, showing me. "Verity, I'd say you've done your job."

The face of the ring was caked with ash on my side of the veil. But the ghostly image glowed underneath, revealing an inscription. "It's carved with the initials DNW."

"DNW," Ellis repeated. "I'm not sure what that means."

I wasn't sure, either. Although I could always learn more about Sugarland history.

Then I caught a good look at the crest below the inscription. Swirling vines surrounded a flower bud under a star.

My heart skipped a beat.

"Didi," I urged as Ellis stepped out of the hole. I felt the chill as she materialized beside me. "See this? We found the same crest on the key from the sash."

"Wait. Sash?" Ellis asked.

"I'll explain it later."

"Incredible," Didi said, dodging a spark. "Yes. Yes, I recognize that crest." She took the ghostly ring and held it up to the light, ignoring the sparks raining down into her hair. The one that settled there and grew into an ember.

"Didi!" My heart jumped as the ember caught fire.

"Oh, my goodness, Verity." She clutched the ring to her chest, either not noticing or not caring about the whisper of a blaze spreading through her hair. "I know where that key goes."

Chapter Eleven

I ignored the sideways look Didi shot me as I drove a little—okay, a lot—too fast down Highway 9.

"Verity—"

"I'm fine, thank you," I said in a rush. I wanted to be respectful of my grandma. I was brought up right. But I'd also been through the wringer in the last twenty-four hours, and I had to see what was in my house.

Her house.

Our house?

She patted her hair as if the wind from the open window could muss it. "I thought I taught you to drive better than this."

"You did." My mother had left it to Didi after I mixed up the brake and the accelerator. Twice. "I learned well." I looked over my shoulder and saw nary a speck of traffic. "Blind-spot check. Avoid a wreck."

She instinctively stepped on a brake pedal that wasn't on her side of the car. Just like old times. "I was thinking more like 'slow your pace, it's not a race.'"

"Sure, sure." But when I saw an ember escape her updo, I eased off the gas.

I should have gotten her out of the library sooner.

Logically, I knew Didi was a ghost and, therefore, unlikely to ignite with a strong breeze...even if she was smoldering. But it still felt irresponsible to take the chance.

Was it terrible I found it strangely comforting that Frankie had been more on fire than her?

I spotted our exit up ahead. "Tell me more. Where does the key fit?"

Didi winced as we plowed over a pothole. "You have to see it to believe it." She fiddled with her earlobe. "If it's still there."

"It is," I assured her despite having no idea what I was talking about.

The thing was, I had to believe. I needed this. Not only did I want to understand what the key meant to my family, I was tickled I had more to learn about my ancestral home. I thought I knew every nook, cranny, brick, crack, and dust speck in the place.

We'd uncover it together. Didi and me.

I wouldn't have asked for it to happen this way—with a fire, with Melody in mortal danger—but I couldn't help but be thankful to have Didi with me now.

Even if she didn't approve of my driving.

I'd have to show her how much better I'd gotten.

Later.

Our exit was coming up. There weren't too many drivers out, which made it easier to hit the gas.

Frankie would be proud.

He would have also spotted the police.

"Whoops," Didi said as we blew past a police cruiser waiting at the intersection of Route M.

I cringed. Froze. Kept my foot on the gas. No point pretending I'd been five under the limit.

I really needed to hang out with Didi more and Frankie less.

She shook her head. "Traffic school didn't do a lick of good, did it?"

She'd made me go even though Judge Forbes told her not to worry about it.

Bling! A text alert came through.

"Hmm…" Didi eyed my phone on the console. "Melody's handsome fiancé sent you a note." She cocked her head. "He says *'Don't Push It.'*"

He'd said worse things over the years. "Why does he always have to be the one to catch me?" I slowed a hair as we exited onto Rural Route 7.

"Park in the front," Didi said as we rumbled up the long drive to the house.

"I usually park out back—"

"Right here is fine." She steered me with a finger to a spot in front of the large hydrangea to the right of the brick steps leading up to the house.

I cut the engine and eyed the weathered front columns, standing since Jonathan Long built the house in 1834. Ellis had given the covered front porch a new coat of white paint this summer with sky blue on the ceiling.

"Is it in the porch?" I asked. It was the most logical assumption, since the yard lay open, bare save for some flowering plants and several rows of gangly peach trees.

The entire lawn had once been a thriving orchard. I'd planted a half-dozen rows of trees on either side of the driveway to recapture that history. They were still young and had yet to blossom, but I could picture them heavy with fruit.

"I thought I knew everything about this house," I said, taking in the weathered front steps, the white-painted latticing under the porch, and the two rows of windows overlooking the front yard.

"Me too," Didi said, headed toward the side of the house. "I suspect we're both wrong."

"Wait. Why'd we park out front?" I hurried to keep up, gravel crunching under my sneakers. A wispy trail of smoke floated in her wake. "Are you all right?"

"Oh, don't worry about me," she said, swatting an ember on her sleeve.

How was I just remembering how she always said that?

"You're on fire." I watched an ember drift from her shoulder this time. "And it's getting worse. That's about as far from all right as it gets."

"I know," she said, dropping the act.

"How bad can it get?" I jogged next to her. "Be straight with me."

She sighed and kept her eyes straight ahead. "If I burn too badly, I'll incinerate and die. Forever."

"Then why would you mess with this?" I pleaded. It was unthinkable. Irresponsible. "You need to take better care of yourself. If not for yourself, then for me and for everyone else who loves you."

"If it gets too bad, I'll go to the ether," she promised, picking up the pace. "It's such a light, breezy place. It'll extinguish the blaze. I'll be fine."

"So go. Now." I'd seen the way Frankie had been able to recover there in the past. "I can handle things here. Just tell me what to do."

"That's the trick. I can't. You need me." She shook off another ember without even looking at it. "And I don't know how long I'd be gone. Time doesn't mean anything when you're in the ether. If you're injured, you're stuck until you're healed. I could be gone days, months. We can't afford that."

That was all well and good, but... "We can't afford for you to burn up, either."

"I can contain it for now," she vowed. "I'll take care of myself after I make this up to Rose."

"Can you?" It almost felt like this was her way of punishing herself. "This is not your fault."

"It is." Smoke was curling off her shoulders now.

"It's not worth the risk."

She waved me off. "I'm more concerned the garden is gone."

"It's not." I hoped the embers weren't impacting her mind. "You saw it last night." Sure, I hadn't mentioned dumping a gangster's ashes into her favorite rosebush and moving it into the parlor, but—"I take good care of it."

"The old garden," she corrected as we rounded the corner to the backyard. "The way it used to be."

I stopped dead in my tracks.

In my world, I could see my gravel parking spot and a single row of roses against the house. But in the ghostly realm stood an elaborate rose garden that would make Martha Stewart swoon.

Roses climbed and twisted and bloomed in a carefully cultivated, free-standing garden stretching back almost to the pond.

She touched a hand to her heart. "It's here. Just like I remember it."

"I have a feeling you're the new dominant ghost." Places appeared on the ghostly plane the way the strongest spirit on the property saw them.

Frankie had ruled the roost since he'd come to live with me, but it made sense Didi would control how her home appeared.

I shuddered to think what the gangster would have to say about that.

The garden stretched from the back of the house, bound by tall roses climbing white iron trellises. Vines as thick as my finger wound through delicate scrolls and fleur-de-lis patterns.

"This is how Rose kept it when I was a little girl," Didi said, reaching for a petal.

It was beautiful. Breathtaking.

And I hadn't begun to see all of it.

"I want to go inside."

She led me to an arched entryway near the pond, dripping with roses that shimmered as we passed underneath. A path of crushed oyster shells led us past a small gazebo. In the center stood a tea table set for two.

My heart fluttered when I recognized the pattern on the dishes. "That's the bone china you left me."

The china I'd been forced to sell.

"Follow me," Didi said, leading me into the heart of the garden.

Each bush was prettier than the next. Weathered statues peeked from hidden alcoves.

"This was my grandmother's pride and joy," Didi said. "I used to love playing here."

I wished someone had preserved it. "What happened to it?"

Didi's shoulders fell. "She died."

The path opened onto a concrete fountain. Water cascaded from tiered basins into a shallow pool. The path circled the fountain and set off in new directions.

"I wish I'd taken pictures," Didi said.

"I never knew..." I stopped to admire a series of spiraling hedges. Between them, rosebushes of varying heights created a tapestry of textures. Blooms ranged from tiny, delicate buds to lush, fully opened flowers as wide as my palm. "What are we looking for?"

She stood very still with her back to the fountain. "I'm getting my bearings." She held up a finger. "It's been a long time."

Two paths broke off, one right, the other leading to the left, toward the house.

"I'll see what I can find," I said, venturing left until I hit a trellis wall.

In a secluded corner, half-hidden by a weeping willow, stood a gray ghostly statue of a young woman. Her stone dress featured a high collar and fitted waist, while an elaborate hat perched atop her upswept hair. A secretive smile played on her lips, and at her feet, a plaque bore an indecipherable inscription.

"Didi," I called.

I couldn't touch it, or it would give me a terrible shock. Worse, my touch would cause it to disappear.

She knelt and brushed the dirt away.

It was a crest, like the one on the ring and the one on the key.

Didi gave a small nod.

"You're not surprised."

"I know where we're going now," she said simply. A narrow dirt path led through an overgrowth of bushes. "This way."

"Um." I hesitated. "I can't touch the ghostly roses."

She held the bushes back, and I stooped over, following her to a small clearing with a birdbath. A ghostly sparrow dipped its beak into the pool without a ripple.

"We dig here," Didi said, pointing behind the base.

That was real dirt. Real grass. My actual yard.

"How deep?" I asked. I didn't have a trowel, but I did spot a flat-ish rock.

"Not far," she assured me.

"We'll try it this way, then," I said, going for the rock. "What am I looking for?"

A memory box? A trove of family artifacts? I plunged the rock into the soil.

Luckily, it had rained a few nights ago, and the ground was soft.

Didi stood over me. "When I was a child, I found something in Grandma Rose's garden. Got into heaps of trouble for it, too," she huffed. "She made me promise never to speak of it again."

"But now you're showing me," I said, glancing over my shoulder. I dug harder.

A mischievous grin spread across her face. "I suppose I can, seeing as I'm already breaking all sorts of rules by being here."

"You are?" I tossed a big chunk of grass and dirt.

"I was supposed to help Melody cross. Then I was supposed to head back. I'm supposed to stay out of Grandma's garden, but now I'm showing you how to dig it up."

"What's here?" I pressed.

"I don't know," she said, watching the hole get bigger. "This was Grandma Rose's pride and joy. She'd disappear in here for hours."

"Gardening," I assumed, digging deeper.

"Day and night."

Wait. "Night gardening?"

"She'd bring her friends, too."

My rock struck metal.

"I think you found it."

Didi hovered while I cleared the dirt as quickly as I could. "It's a hatch," I said breathlessly, unearthing one hinge. Two.

"I knew it!" Didi said. "Grandma Rose said I'd found trash, but I swore it was a door!"

"And I'll bet we have the key."

My fingers shook as I cleared away dirt, revealing an etched symbol in the center—swirling vines surrounding a flower bud under a star, and the letters DNW.

But there was no keyhole. Only a latch.

I flipped it and dug under the hatch. The hinges groaned as I dragged it up, up.

"This is it," Didi said breathlessly.

Cool air wafted out, along with the scent of wet earth and mud.

"What is it?" I asked, scrambling to fetch the flashlight from my bag. I shone it down and saw a rusted metal ladder leading down into the darkness.

Didi pressed her lips together, barely containing herself. "Let's find out."

Chapter Twelve

I shoved the Maglite under my arm and started down the rusted ladder. It shifted precariously with each step as the smell of wet earth grew stronger.

Didi hovered in the opening above. "Be careful," she urged, her voice tight. "It's hanging on by two screws."

"Oh boy." I sped up, the ladder lurched right, and I held on for dear life. A shudder ran through the metal—or maybe that was me. "I'm fine."

As if saying it would make it true.

My flashlight pierced the darkness below, revealing glimpses of rough stone walls.

There was no telling how far down this went.

I slowed, palms scraping as I gripped the rungs hard.

"Don't worry," Didi called. "If you fall, I'll—" She stopped.

She'd what? Call for help?

No one could see her.

Call Frankie?

He had the exact same problem.

"I've got this," I said, my voice sturdier than I felt.

I had to believe that, even as my foot stretched lower with no rung to catch it.

Oh, geez.

Down.

Down.

My toe touched rock. A wave of relief washed over me.

"I made it." I let out a shaky breath. Damp, musty air filled my nose. "I'm at the bottom." See? It all worked out.

Didi flickered into form next to me. "You take too many chances."

"You're one to talk," I said as a sizzling ember drifted from behind her ear, coming to rest on her shoulder.

She patted it out. "What is this place?"

"It looks like a cave." A real cave. In my own backyard. Unbelievable. "I wonder if Frankie knows about this place."

If he did, he hadn't told me.

It was about as big as Frankie's shed, with wet stone walls. The ghostly version layered over it like a double-exposure photograph, shimmering silver.

My foot struck metal, sending a hollow clang through the cave. I shone my light down onto an old lantern, its brass frame dulled with age, its glass panels clouded and cracked.

Didi ran a hand through it, as if she'd forgotten she couldn't touch it. "That's been here a while."

I placed it near the wall by the ladder, next to a half-dozen ghostly lanterns of the same size and style. "Why did they need so many?"

The space wasn't that big.

Across from us, on the ghostly side, stood a sturdy wooden coat rack draped with an assortment of ladies' outerwear. Two pairs of leather gloves hung from pegs, one long and one short. Two wide-brimmed hats perched on the topmost hooks, and a single silk parasol leaned in the corner.

"Look at this," I said, moving in for a closer look at a silvery purse with a beaded peacock design. "It has to be turn of the century." The vintage clothing store on Main would kill for this piece.

A tarnished mirror hung next to the rack. Well, tarnished in my world. Its ghostly counterpart gleamed like new. I gazed at my reflection in it. And then at Didi's reflection behind me.

"I recognize this mirror," she murmured. "There was an identical one in Grandma Rose's bedroom."

We shared a glance.

"There's more." Her eyes flicked to where the ceiling dropped in the far corner. A heavy velvet curtain concealed a doorway. "Let's check it out."

"Careful," I warned. We might want to at least listen first. But Didi was already lifting the curtain and walking through.

At least she'd held it open for me on the ghostly plane.

The fabric on my side of the veil was stiff and brittle. I eased it aside and ducked under the low ceiling and into a small passageway.

The air changed—a faint fruity scent mingled with the earthy smell of the cave. And as I turned a sharp corner, I froze.

A round-faced woman sat at a long, narrow table in the center of the second chamber. Candles on the walls and on the table scattered light and shadows, but I could see the glowing ghost as clear as day, peeling peaches. She wore a high-necked blouse with puffed sleeves, cinched at the waist by a fitted jacket. And over it, an apron. Her skirt pooled around her ankles, with sensible boots peeking out.

Didi gasped. "It's a ghost," she hissed, "a real ghost!"

The woman's head snapped up at the sound of her voice.

Didi went two shades paler.

I gaped at her. "You're a ghost," I pointed out. In case she'd forgotten.

"Right." Didi stiffened. "She's looking right at us."

She was stalking straight for us.

"Let me handle it." She could learn as we went.

"Am I that pale?" Didi murmured.

I hated to break it to her...

But before I could, the ghost was upon us.

I mustered my brightest smile. "Hi, my name is Verity Long, and this is Didi." The woman didn't blink, so I swallowed hard and kept going. "Sorry to barge in on you like this." I couldn't imagine she got many visitors. "With this being your underground lair and all, but we have this key—"

"What's the password?" the ghost demanded.

"I—" Oh my.

My gaze swept the room. Peaches shared the wooden table with scattered pamphlets and papers. Behind it, along the wall, stacked signs read *Votes for Women* and *Come see Mrs. Blackwell at Sugarland Library*. Separate signs read *This Saturday at 8 p.m. FREE ADMISSION*.

"Oh." Didi snapped her fingers. "I know the password."

No, she didn't. She hadn't even seen another ghost until a minute ago. "Let me handle this—"

"It's votes for women," Didi said as if it were obvious.

No, that was too easy.

But then, to my shock, the round-faced woman's shoulders relaxed, and the knife disappeared from her hand. "Correct." She smoothed a few stray hairs back into her bun. "Whew. I wish you'd have answered sooner. You nearly gave me a heart attack. My name is Madge. Are you two here for the meeting?"

"Yes," Didi said.

"No," I said at the same time.

I wasn't used to her help.

We needed to get our stories straight.

"We're here for the cause," I said, eyeing the curtained barrier to the next room.

Rose's cause.

I didn't see any place in this room that would fit our key, but we might find more in there. I took a deep breath and decided to come clean. "Rose Landry Long gave us a key, but we're not sure where it goes."

It was technically true. Rose had tried to give us the sash, which contained the key.

I would have inherited it if Didi hadn't given it away.

Madge tilted her head. "If Rose Landry Long gave you a key, she'd tell you where it goes."

Fair point.

"Let's just say she didn't get the chance." I dug it out of my pocket and held it out for her to see. "Does this look familiar? We're trying to learn where this goes and what DNW means."

Madge cleared her throat like she'd seen a ghost. "Who are you really?"

"I'm Rose's great—"

"Great," Didi added.

"Granddaughter," I finished.

Madge looked at me like I'd sprouted two new arms. "Rose has a daughter," she ventured.

"And me." I withdrew the filigree necklace, passed down from Didi, who'd inherited it from her mother. How far back, I wasn't sure. But when Madge's eyes went round, I had a pretty good idea. "She gave me this. It's my most treasured possession."

"Hers too," Madge said.

It was done in gold and silver and shaped like a cross. The delicate metal caught the candlelight, sending lace-like reflections across the cave walls.

Didi had begun exploring. "We'd assumed Grandma Rose's key was for the trapdoor that led us down here," she said, inspecting under the table. "Now we're thinking the key fits something else in the cave."

"I suppose you can look," Madge said, stepping aside as Didi took a gander behind the signs.

All in all though, the chamber didn't leave much to the imagination. Aside from the table and the stacked signs, it lay bare.

"What's behind the next curtain?" Didi asked, not waiting for an answer as she pulled it aside. "Oh, wow."

"What?" I asked, on her heels.

She stood in a larger cavern than the last, narrower. It smelled of earth, mud, and peaches. Ghostly shelves lined the walls on both sides, loaded with baskets of fruit. They glowed, providing plenty of light as we ventured past the shelves to a large scale next to a rack with fruit-picking tools.

"Get a load of this," Didi said, checking out a pulley system belonging to a rough version of a dumbwaiter. It went all the way up to a pair of cellar doors in the ceiling.

"It can't go into the house." I'd never seen those doors before. I didn't see a keyhole, either.

"I don't think we're under the house," Didi said, doing a quick visual survey of the chamber we were in. "I think we're under the orchard."

"I can't believe this has been under me the entire time," I said, inspecting the thick ropes that led up to the pulleys. They were as real as day on my side and glowed ghostly gray in the other realm.

"I had no idea, either." Didi surveyed the room, frowning. "I understand the idea of a peach cellar considering we have a peach orchard. But shouldn't it be under the house?"

"Maybe the caves are better at preserving the fruit." The peaches in those baskets had appeared ripe and whole.

Didi planted her hands on her hips. "So it's a peach operation that hides the suffragette operation."

"It sure looks that way."

"Hidden in Grandma Rose's garden."

I had to hand it to Rose. "It would be the perfect cover for secret meetings."

"Nobody would think to look down here," Didi said as the double doors overhead flew open on the ghostly side.

A hook-nosed ghost above us let out a cry, dropping her basket of fruit. Didi zipped out of the way. I wasn't as quick and caught a silvery peach to the shoulder. The icy wetness of the other side seared me.

"Ow!" I cried as it plowed straight through me and rolled across the cave floor.

The hook-nosed woman appeared directly between us. She

wore men's work gloves and an apron smeared with dirt. "What are you doing in my storage room?"

"Madge let us in," I said, rubbing my shoulder. "We're looking for the lock that fits this key."

She studied the key I held up. "You won't find it here," she said grimly.

"Then do you know where?" Didi pressed.

Her lips thinned. "That's not for me to say."

"They're with Rose," Madge said, shimmering into existence next to me. "I've been keeping an eye on them."

The ghost looked us up and down. "They're not even wearing corsets."

"It's a new day," Didi told her.

She frowned at that. "I say we leave this up to Liberty Brown. If she wants these ladies involved, she'll tell them what to do."

"Liberty Brown?" I'd never heard of her.

"She'll be at the meeting," Madge said. "You can wait with me."

"When does the meeting start?" Didi asked as Madge led us out of the storage cellar.

"Ladies will be showing up any minute," she assured us. "In fact, I hesitated to leave the meeting room, well, until you startled Viv."

"I think we all did our fair share of startling," I said.

"So what's with all the peaches?" Didi asked. "I can understand meeting down here, but actually helping with the harvest?"

"It's...complicated," Madge said, holding the curtain for us. "But you might as well help me peel a few while we wait for the meeting to start."

I fought off a cringe. "That might be difficult." Objects on the ghostly plane felt like ice against my skin and fire in my veins. And anything I touched would vanish within minutes.

But if we played our cards right, we could try to learn more from Madge.

Didi seemed to be thinking the same thing.

She commandeered an apron. I skipped that part and dredged up a rickety stool from the corner. It slanted sideways and looked like it'd crumble in a mild breeze, but it was the only seat I could find that wasn't glowing gray.

My rule when it came to the ghostly plane was definitely more of a *look, don't touch* approach.

The table appeared real enough despite the ghostly sheen. The peaches were on an entirely different plane.

"Ready?" Madge said, placing a shimmering silver knife down onto the table next to me.

"Sure," I ventured.

Oh, who was I kidding? I was never ready for this.

The ghostly knife would be freezing cold. It would make my teeth chatter and my hand go numb. And if I dared touch it, we could kiss it goodbye.

Same with the peaches. The basket.

And while nuking all the unpeeled peaches would no doubt speed things along, I'd rather stay under the radar.

Learn what we could.

I made a show of flexing my fingers.

Didi grabbed a knife and a peach. "So, seriously, why are we peeling fruit for the vote instead of marching or making ourselves heard?"

She was right. I could think of a dozen more effective ways to be heard and inspire change.

Madge wiped her hands on her apron before grabbing her knife. "Bake sales are important fundraisers."

Oh, come on. "You have to give us more than that."

"That's it," Madge said, not fooling anybody.

"We're in an underground cave," I pointed out. "This isn't a baking party. What are you really working on down here?"

Madge stiffened. "We've been ordered to keep the fundraising going."

"With peaches?" Didi asked, slicing into her first one.

"It's no secret the movement is in danger."

And it was clear they weren't telling us everything.

She eyed me. "Keep at it, and Viv is going to kick you out."

"Let's not get hasty," I said as Didi placed a half-peeled peach in front of me. I could pretend it was mine.

Madge dug into a peach with her knife. "Let's be honest. I know everyone in Sugarland, and I don't know you."

How strange to be on the other end of that one.

"You should, right?" I agreed. "I mean, if you don't go back five generations, are you really from Sugarland?"

"I'd say the true test is whether you've put a raft down on Devil's Bend," Didi said.

"Or gone to Roan's for a hammer." I nodded. They'd been in business since 1843.

"Or stared up at Rockhill Mansion and wondered what the heck goes on up there," Madge added.

"It's haunted, that's what," I told her. I'd solved the case.

"I knew it!" Madge gushed. "If I've said it once, I've said it a million times." She shook her head. "This is fun. I missed chatting. And working together," she added, eyeing my knife on the table.

"Do you really have to worry about spies?" Didi asked, while I wondered if I was brave enough to reach for the knife.

At Madge's raised brow, I did, gritting my teeth as I felt the bracing chill. I stabbed into the skin of the peach without picking it up.

"Didi has a point," I said to our host. "We're women." I ignored the goosebumps erupting on my arms. "Why wouldn't we want the vote?"

Madge cocked her head as she ran a knife around the peach, skinning it with swift strokes. "You have no idea the lengths some women will go to in order to give up their power." She eyed me. "They leave chicken feet on my husband's desk at work and call him henpecked." She returned her attention to the peach. "They say he's not a man because he stays home with the baby while I volunteer."

"My man takes care of my little Lucy while I work," I said, flicking the peel and stabbing the peach before tossing it into the metal bowl. "Why shouldn't your partner take care of his family? It's what good men do."

Madge placed her peeled peach next to mine. "He has been quite wonderful. I'm lucky."

"You are," Didi said. "My husband pretended he didn't know how to work the washing machine. For fifty years."

Madge barked out a laugh. "Mine can take apart a carburetor but needs me to make his toast." She pursed her lips. "Although I do cut it into hearts for him. He likes that."

"You're lucky," I said, making note to try the heart toast with Ellis. "Mine can't cook to save his life. The bacon is either raw or burned to a crisp, but he keeps trying."

"Pretend you like it, and he'll get better," she said, placing another peach in front of me. "That's been my plan now that my husband has been fixing dinner every night for the kids. He saves a plate for me." She brought a hand to her head. "I've been gone so much."

"Doing important work," I assured her.

"It may not look like it, but it is," she assured us. She flicked her knife toward the peach she'd laid out for me.

"I already did one," I said, looking to the metal bowl.

The entire bowl had begun to fade.

Oh no. It was disappearing! Fast.

I hadn't touched it.

But I had touched my peach, which I'd tossed in with the other peaches, which set off a chain reaction of disaster.

"What the—" Madge stood, her chair falling backward as the entire bowl evaporated.

Oh my goodness. I stood quickly. "I'm so sorry."

She shrieked, pointing as my knife began to disappear from the table.

"I'm sorry about that, too," I cried.

Viv dashed into the room. "What's the matter?"

"They're—" Madge pointed at me. "I—"

"I'm alive." There. I'd said it. "I messed up the peaches because I'm alive."

Viv rested a hand on her hip. "Of course you're alive. Everyone is alive. And peaches don't disappear."

"I saw them," Madge said breathlessly, staring at the table.

Didi placed her knife down and rose from the table. "What year do you think this is?"

Viv rolled her eyes. "It's 1919, of course."

They didn't know they were dead.

Or that I was alive.

"And when is the meeting supposed to start?" I asked Madge. "Tell me. What date? What time?"

She looked at me funny. "June 20th. Two o'clock."

"1919," Didi finished.

That poor woman really had been peeling peaches for a century.

"I don't think we can wait around anymore." Liberty Brown wasn't coming. Nobody was. These poor ghosts didn't realize their time was long past. And if they hadn't noticed by now, I wasn't sure how to convince them. "Is Liberty the only person who can help us?"

"The only one who'll be at the meeting," Madge maintained.

"Rose and Hope were the only ones trusted with keys," Viv said from the door.

"Where is Hope?" Maybe we could track her down.

"Hope died last week." Madge's voice broke. "She died in jail."

"How awful," I said, rubbing my hands on my dress. They were still tingling.

"They locked her up for disturbing the peace," Viv said. "In truth, it was to scare us. To keep us from organizing."

"Or asking questions," Madge added.

"About what?" I asked.

They both clammed up.

Viv's hands formed into fists. "Now Rose is locked in the same jail. I feel so awful for her. No one is allowed in, and she's in the same cell where Hope died."

The musty air clung to my skin, and I could hear water dripping somewhere in the distance. I stood as primly as I could, fingering Grandma Rose's filagree necklace. "I'm dating a police officer. I might be able to help."

Viv gritted her jaw. "We can't trust the police."

Not again. Not in Sugarland. "Why would you say that?"

Madge drew a hand to the button brooch at her throat. "Eleanor Blackwell has vanished. She's slated to speak at the rally tomorrow. It's crucial to our cause."

Didi crossed her arms. "When did she disappear?"

"Two days ago," Viv said. "She left the Sugarland Hotel after dinner. We thought she was coming straight here to the house, but she disappeared on the way. Several of our members went to the police, but they've done nothing."

"At least that's kept it out of the papers," Madge added. "If we have to cancel the rally, we'll lose a lot of support."

For now. But I could offer some comfort. "The good news is I do believe it will all turn out in the end."

Viv scoffed.

Madge's cheeks flushed gray. "How can you say that?" she demanded. "Our vice president died in her jail cell. Our speaker has been kidnapped. Our president has been arrested. Our lawyer is trying to get her out, but she's on a hunger strike. She could die in there, just like Hope."

"Grandma Rose will make it," Didi murmured to me.

"But at what cost?"

From the way she'd treated Didi in the afterlife, it was safe to say Rose had been through a lot.

Didi nodded. "Grandma Rose is alone in the world. Her husband, Grandpa Jack, died in 1915."

"We already lost Hope. If we lose Rose and Eleanor both,

we'll have no shot at the grand plan," Viv added. "We'll never stop, but that doesn't mean we'll succeed."

"Or live." Madge wiped her eyes.

"I'm so sorry." I'd had no idea.

And they might be more right than they knew, seeing as they were still trapped down here a century later.

Didi had the same idea. "Hang tight and stay where you are. We'll see what we can find out."

Would we?

"If Rose is in jail, we can talk to her about the key," Didi said.

She was right. Even if Rose had moved on, Hope might still be haunting the place where she died. She'd be able to tell us about the key as well.

Viv brought a hand to her head. "Rose is the one we trusted to keep the key safe."

"It's safe," I insisted. And soon we'd secure Rose's legacy as well. "Which jail is she in?"

The ghosts shared a meaningful look before Viv answered, "Occoquan Workhouse."

I nodded, committing the name to memory. I turned to leave, pausing at the curtain. "Stay here. Have your meeting. We'll be back with news," I promised, my voice barely audible as I ascended into the world above.

Chapter Thirteen

"I remember the Occoquan Workhouse," Didi said as I clambered out of the cave. "I can take us there, but we'll have to be careful. From what I've heard, it's a rough place."

"Let me feed Lucy, and we'll go straightaway," I said, keeping an eye out for my little skunk. She liked to sun herself on the pavers that lined what I now realized were the few remaining bushes from Grandma Rose's garden.

But I didn't see her there.

While I was at it, I also wanted to google the disappearance of Eleanor Blackwell and perhaps check to see if the suffragettes in Sugarland had really sold peach pies.

I still wasn't buying it.

"What I don't get is if Madge and Viv have been down in the cave for the last hundred years, why haven't any of the other suffragettes stopped by to tell them they're dead? Friends don't let friends peel peaches for eternity."

"Maybe they moved on," Didi said, leading the way down the path toward the pond. "Coming back from the higher plane isn't always simple. Same for the ether. You can get stuck there and not know decades have passed. Centuries. It's very pleasant."

My gangster buddy seemed to like it, too. "Frankie has gone

to the ether to rest, but he always comes back, sooner rather than later."

Didi plucked a dwarf rose from a bush and set to peeling the thorns. "I've noticed Frankie makes his own rules. But you also have to remember Frankie is grounded to your property."

"He never lets me forget."

She tossed a thorn. "Frankie has something pulling him back. Most spirits don't have that."

I stuffed my hands into the pockets of my dress. "So these other suffragists could be in the light or even in the ether for a century?"

"Easily," Didi said as we reached the end of the garden. "Spiritual injury can keep you in the higher planes longer than that. Or if you're hurt too bad, you might never come back. It's hard to explain, but when you're dead, time doesn't matter so much."

I supposed I'd have to wait and see.

Then I did a double take as we left the garden.

The old tire swing hung from the apple tree by the pond. It glowed ghostly gray, but other than that, it looked exactly like it had when I'd played on it as a child. Same weathered rubber, same frayed rope that made my palms go red. It even had that wonky tilt that had inspired Billy Ray's dad to give it to Didi in the first place.

The swing had fallen into the pond two decades ago when Melody and I had the brilliant idea to see how many of the neighborhood kids could swing over the water at once. We were up to seven before the rope gave way and we all got soaked.

"Stars!" I mad dashed to get a closer look. I'd give anything to climb on that swing again, to see how far I could get it over the water. The faded markings were still there from when Melody and I had written our names in nail polish. "Thank you."

"What did I do?"

She saw her home the way it had been all those years ago.

Then a little striped head popped up from a patch of grass

under the tree. I'd been so enamored with the swing, I'd missed the ball of fluff curled up in one of her favorite napping spots.

"How would you like some tuna fish?" I asked my skunk, who danced a circle and dashed straight through one of her training tunnels and up the steps to the back porch. "I'll take that as a yes."

She deserved to feel as happy as I did right now.

And wouldn't you know it? The back porch held another surprise.

"My jade is back," I said, pausing near the kitchen door to admire the potted plant nestled in the mosaic stand I'd made in sixth-grade art class. I'd gifted Didi with the stand and a jade clipping wrapped in a paper towel. The wonky tiles—originally blue and green—glowed ghostly gray.

"I can't imagine the porch without it," she said, just as she had the day she'd given it a place of honor.

I'd been so proud. I couldn't get over it. Then or now.

"It's wild to see my own work immortalized on the ghostly plane." And I loved the special touches now that she was back. Frankie never changed a thing about my actual house. Not that I would have wanted him to. But Didi?

This was perfect.

She slipped the rose bloom behind her ear. "I can't wait to see what you've done to the inside."

No, she wouldn't. I crashed back to earth in an instant. In less than a minute, she'd see I'd failed her. I'd lost almost all of it. Everything she'd held dear.

"About that," I began. I wouldn't make excuses for what I'd done—selling our heirlooms, wrecking the legacy she'd left me. "I tried my best."

And I'd let her down.

She breezed through the back wall.

I cringed and opened the door, ready for her disappointment, her hurt. Her questions. I deserved them all and only hoped I could make it all right.

Instead, I walked into the kitchen and found her standing by the island, smiling.

Wait. I stopped cold. "What's happening here?" The sunny, yellow space was bathed in glowing gray.

Didi's floral flour, sugar, and coffee canisters were lined up on the counter next to her trusty stand mixer—a wedding gift from her parents. Her chrome and Formica dinette set gleamed, set with a floral lace topper and Tupperware salt and pepper shakers. Like the jade plant and mosaic stand outside, everything glowed ghostly gray.

Unbelievable. The kitchen looked exactly as it had the day before I'd put everything up for sale.

The day before my life—and my house—had been ripped apart.

Except—hold on. She'd made improvements.

Didi's avocado green rotary phone hung on the wall, same as it always had. Only the cord on the ghostly side looped in a perfect spiral.

It hadn't done that since before I was a teenager.

And the parlor! The ghostly restoration continued there too. Her floral-print sofa was back. It sat proudly next to Grandpa's leather armchair, both angled toward the fireplace. His, a bit crooked, like he'd preferred when he'd read the paper and watch her knit. Above it was the portrait of Jonathan Long, in the same place it had hung since he'd hammered in the nail.

And the original chandelier—my favorite thing in the house.

It was one of the few things I'd managed to recover and set right, but it seemed even grander now, surrounded by Grandma's treasures. Crystal teardrops caught the light and scattered it across the room like a frozen fountain.

"You brought it all back together." Right here in my parlor.

She'd made this house a home again.

I turned a slow circle as I took it all in. "The house is exactly the same as it was when you left it to me."

"It is," Didi said, as if she didn't quite believe it herself. "I'm sorry. I don't know how that happened. Let me fix it." She waved her arms as if she could turn it all to mist.

No, no, no. I rushed to her. "What are you doing?"

"It's just how I see it. Your poor purple couch." It was buried in the middle of the floral sofa. "I'll try to stop."

"Don't stop. I love it. You don't know how long I've wanted this back. All of it." And this was the next best thing. I'd wanted this since I'd lost it all. "You've given me my wish."

"Hardly." She planted a hand on her hip and surveyed the perfect, lovely, homey decor. "You won't be able to fix your meals, sit on the couch, do anything without interacting with the ghostly plane, getting a terrible chill and having your furniture disappear."

Her furniture, but who was I to quibble? "It'll be fine," I said. I'd figure it out.

She shot me a look. "I saw what happened with the peaches."

That had been unfortunate. "But with you here, it'll come back." I headed to the kitchen to fetch Lucy's dinner. "I can get used to a ghostly house," I said, yanking the cabinet door open with my pinkie, gritting my teeth at the cold shock.

I'd promised Lucy tuna. At least I wouldn't have to touch the silverware. Grandma's silverware! I pried open the drawer just to see. Sure, the shock ricocheted up my arm, but my reward was the sight of her Evening Star Oneida. "I've always loved this pattern."

Didi slid the drawer closed. "This isn't healthy."

I left it open on the earthly plane. "Tuna is good for skunks," I said, pretending that's what she meant. I decided to forget the fork and instead dumped the entire can into one of the mismatched china bowls I'd bought to replace what I'd lost.

See? I could definitely live like this.

Lucy also appeared to be adjusting well, weaving in and out of the ghostly table legs as she waited for her supper.

I set the bowl down for her, and she came running.

While she ate, I grabbed my laptop from the hall table—now

with Grandpa's cowboy hat displayed above it—and returned to the kitchen to try to find a place to set it up.

One that wouldn't give me a shock.

It would be fine.

"You're afraid of your own kitchen table." Didi tsked.

"It's not that." Although it would be nice if there were a sliver that I could use.

"I promise I'll figure out a way to fix this," she said, running a hand over the ghostly table standing over it.

That was what I'd said to Frankie when I'd trapped him.

It had been three years and counting.

But we'd made it work. Mostly. And, really, I'd do whatever it took to keep Didi here and happy.

"It's perfectly fine." I popped out the back door to the porch. "I like working on the swing." It was a pretty afternoon, and if you didn't count the glowing gray jade plant, the ghostly geraniums, and—oh my, her wrought-iron patio set—well, then the porch was ghost-free.

See? This could work.

I settled on the swing and fired up the laptop. And first things first, I typed *Eleanor Blackwell*.

Dozens of newspaper articles popped up. She had been something else.

Born to a wealthy banking family in New York, she'd given up her fiancé and been shunned by her family for her beliefs, but it hadn't stopped her. She'd known she was part of something bigger than herself. "She was an eloquent speaker," I said, skimming, "able to inspire men and women alike for the cause." Until she disappeared in Sugarland on June 18, 1919.

"Didi?" I turned to get her opinion, only to realize she'd stayed behind in the kitchen.

She'd better not be changing anything back.

I heard Lucy scratching on the back door. I cracked it open to let her skip out onto the porch while I peeked inside. Whew!

Didi's kitchen table was still there, her mixer, all of it. I returned my attention to my computer on the porch swing.

The search for Eleanor Blackwell had lasted weeks and upturned the whole of Sugarland. But she was never found.

"She could very well be our skeleton in the library," I mused to Lucy, who had stopped to chase a butterfly before frolicking after it, down the porch steps and into the yard.

I searched for peach pies next, as they related to fundraisers and the suffragette movement.

As I'd suspected, I came up empty. Of course the suffragettes hadn't been holding bake sales. Madge had been lying.

But why lie about pies while pointing us toward Hope?

Unless she was lying about Hope as well.

We'd find out soon enough.

I was about to go tell Didi the news when a blood-curdling scream erupted from the shed by the pond.

"Frankie?" I deposited my computer on the swing and started down the steps as he came blazing out like his hair was on fire.

"Aaargh!" He zipped straight for me. His hat was gone. His hair was gelled up like Elvis. And he wore a striped sweater and rolled-up jeans. "What is this?" he demanded. "What is that?" He flailed his arms toward the shed.

It looked the same to me.

"Frankie, I—" I didn't know what to think.

He didn't look bad. Just different. Like he'd stepped out of *Happy Days*.

"I was tired. I was on *fire*."

"I remember." It would be hard to forget. "You should go to the ether," I said quickly, remembering Didi's solution.

"Not a chance," Frankie snapped.

"As long as you keep it under control—"

"I'm always in control," Frankie seethed. "I retreated to my lair. I sat in my leather chair to plot my revenge."

"Naturally."

"I fell asleep. I woke up, and my chair was a *recliner*. My shed is full of tools. And my bar is a workbench!" He spun a circle. "What is the meaning of this?"

Oh my. It seemed Didi's power had reached farther than we'd imagined. "Whoops."

"Whoops?" He sputtered. "Whoops?"

Good thing Frankie didn't own a mirror.

He ran a hand down his face. "I think I fried my circuits in that fire."

"Not exactly," I hedged. How to explain? I didn't want to send Frankie and his gangster friends after my grandma.

But he was on a roll.

"It's weird." His eyes bugged out. "I mean, this is my place. My stuff. I tried to change it back, but it won't change. My poker table is gone. My girlie magazine turned into the *Sugarland Gazette*."

"Why would you have that anyway?" Sure, he was a ruthless killer and had the grace of a glitter bomb, but still, I'd expected better.

"You don't get to tell me what to do." He punctuated every word with a jab of a finger.

"Your finger is on fire."

He didn't seem to care.

"This is a disaster," he said, pacing. "I've got the guys coming over any minute, and my gold stash is a compost pile, my Wanted poster is a seed calendar, and my gun is a water pistol!" He drew his revolver and shot a weak stream of water in the air. "It's over. I'm broken."

"It's not you," I insisted. At least I hoped it wasn't. "It's only —" Oh boy, how to say it? I just had to spit it out. "You're not the dominant ghost anymore."

He dropped the water gun. "What?"

This was going to be fun. "Well, you see..." I ventured the last couple of steps down the stairs. "With my grandma in the picture—"

"What?" he ground out.

I held my hands out to the sides. "She's the dominant ghost." There. I said it.

He stood stock-still. His chin wasn't supposed to vibrate like that.

I hoped I hadn't broken him.

"I. Am. The. Dominant. Ghost!" he roared.

It would have been easier to believe if he wasn't wearing a sweater.

And penny loafers. Yikes. It was not a good look for him.

"Where is she?" He blazed toward the house. "Is she in there? She can't hide from me."

At this rate, she might want to. I was no expert, but I had to assume hell hath no fury like a gangster in penny loafers.

Chapter Fourteen

"Stop!" I barreled after him. There was nothing either of them could do.

When I got to the kitchen, I found him looming over Didi, eyes blazing, flames sparking from his ears, fit to be tied. "This is my house!"

"Actually, it's Verity's house," Didi countered.

"How about both of you go to the ether?" I suggested.

"I'm not abandoning my house to this crazy lady," Frankie gritted out.

"Then I'm not leaving, either," Didi shot back.

"You both need to calm down." Or else the flames would get worse, and we'd be in big trouble. I inserted myself between them. We could talk it out. "In all fairness, I think he's simply mad about the sweater."

"The *what?*" Frankie looked down and shrieked.

"And the fancy hairdo," I added.

Frankie slapped a hand to his head and gasped in horror at the pomade on his palm.

"And the gun and the shed," I added.

"How?" Frankie shrieked, tearing open the buttons of the sweater. "How are you doing this to me?"

It was a fair question. Ghosts were usually stuck wearing what they'd died in. Luckily for Frankie, it had been a dapper look.

Well, until now.

Didi opened her mouth. Closed it. "I don't know why this is happening," she said, watching the sweater land on Grandpa's old chair. "Except I've always liked penny loafers on a man."

"What?" He stumbled, staring down at his feet.

"My late husband had a pair exactly like them," she added gingerly while the gangster stood fuming in a white T-shirt.

"It's different from his normal look," I explained. After all, she'd only just met him. "In fact, where are my manners?"

"Where is my gun?" Frankie demanded.

"Oh, I don't like guns very much," Didi admitted.

Frankie tossed his arms out, embers cascading down onto the hardwood. "Who *are* you?"

"Let's start over." After all, Didi liked guests. Frankie had manners. When he felt like it.

Maybe this could work.

I kept it civil. "Frankie the German, meet Delia Ida Jane Franklin Long. She got Ida Jane from her mom. Franklin from her husband, and Long because it's a tradition in our family."

"Going back to Catherine 'Kitty' Stevens Long, who married Jonathan Long back in 1820." Didi beamed.

Frankie really did have smoke coming out of his ears. "That. Doesn't. Answer. My. Question!"

He didn't have to shout that last part.

He pointed a finger at her. "You're going to get my stuff back. Now."

"I have no idea how," she snapped, then looked to me. "Do you?"

Not a clue. They were the ghosts. I didn't know all their rules. "I didn't start this. I just live here."

Frankie stalked toward me, and for the first time, I could feel the heat radiating off him. "Oh, you started it, babe. You started it all when you *hosed my ashes into the dirt.*"

We were still paying for that one.

Didi inserted herself between me and the gangster. "Let me get this straight. He's grounded here. I control the land. Maybe try separating his ashes from the dirt."

If only it were that simple. "We've tried," I told her. We'd tried it every which way to Sunday, and it had never worked. "He's stuck here."

"To be tortured for eternity." Frankie yanked off a penny loafer like it was about to eat him alive and tossed it into the parlor. "I got news for you, babe. This is not how it's going to be." He launched the second shoe.

Should I tell him he'd grown a pair of bushy old-man eyebrows?

Didi noticed. She did a double take, but to her credit, she didn't say anything that would stoke the flames. "So you've been the dominant ghost on this property since you arrived."

Frankie spread his arms wide. "This place is the only thing I have left that's *mine*."

Didi's voice hitched. "I'd let you be dominant if I could."

He looked at her like she'd just stolen his puppy. "My afterlife is not yours to give! This is My. Life. Mine. My house. Mine!"

Then I really wasn't going to tell him he was wearing the sweater again.

He followed my gaze down and shrieked.

"Hold up. I think I know what's happening," I said before he noticed the pipe sticking out of the pocket. "Didi's controlling the house and the yard and everything in it. Unfortunately, your ashes are part of the yard, so that includes you."

He turned an icy glare on her. "Then. Stop."

She met his glare with one of her own. "I. Can't." A flame erupted at the crown of her head. "And I don't appreciate your attitude."

They stared each other down.

A flame licked her ear.

Oh no. Strong emotions weren't good for quelling the flames. I had to try to keep them both calm.

"There's nothing she can do," I insisted.

Didi had lived on this land her whole life, had loved it. This property was hers more than his. And there was no way to change that even if she'd wanted to.

To her credit, Didi blinked first. "I'm sorry I messed up your outfit and your shed. I didn't do it on purpose. Being home reminds me of my late husband and what he liked. He's in the upper realms, you see. It's where I was before."

"Rub it in, why don'tcha?" Frankie snarled, backing down a little.

She notched up her chin. "Can I ask you something?"

He stiffened. "You can try."

She took a step back, giving him the once-over. "Is that a bullet hole in your forehead?"

Frankie slapped his hand over it. "You took my hat."

"Dang." Didi planted a fist on her hip. "I'm not sure where it went. Or how to get it back. But if you'd like, there's a cowboy hat on a peg over the hall table."

Frankie's jaw dropped. "When is she leaving?"

Never, I hoped. "This is her house."

Didi cocked her head. "It's your house, Verity."

Technically. But it had been Didi's longer than I'd been alive.

"I'm hoping she stays," I told him.

"For the time being, at least," she added. "I've been helping Verity ghost hunt."

His face fell, and his jaw slacked. "You went without me?"

Well, sure.

But from the way he looked at me, I didn't think that was the right answer.

"You don't always want to go," I reminded him.

I'd had to beg him, bribe him, and practically stuff him in the car at times.

Most times.

Frankie drew his shoulders back. "Did you even think to ask?"

"I—" I'd been busy.

"Of course not. You only ask me when you need me. When you don't need me, you set me on fire, make me pass out, and leave me to wake up in a striped polyester recliner with a broken hinge!"

"I can fix that," Didi said.

Frankie slapped a hand over his heart. I could swear I saw his last nerve twang.

And the sweater was back.

It looked good on him.

Although I didn't think he'd appreciate me telling him that.

"Okay." I held up my hands, trying to defuse the situation. We could all get along. Maybe. "Didi and I are going to a haunted prison," I said before he tried to set fire to the recliner, the shed, and everything in it. "Do you want to go?"

He looked at me like I'd asked him to join the Russian ballet. "I do *not*."

There. I asked.

He shook an ember from his elbow. "Need I remind you I've spent my life and a good portion of my afterlife trying to stay *out* of prison?"

"And you're doing a bang-up job," I said.

"Now this place is worse," he added, flopping his hands to his sides.

"Excuse me." Didi stiffened. "This is how my home used to look."

He gave her a long look. "Did you have a shed?"

"No." She squared her shoulders. "I didn't plan what happened to your shed. I may have thought, 'oh lookie—that would be a nice potting shed.' But I didn't plan any of it."

"Obviously," Frankie gritted out.

Tires squealed outside. I looked out the window as a ghostly Lincoln Continental blazed down the side yard, cornering past the rose garden.

"Oh no." Frankie's eyes grew wide. "They're here." He began shooting sparks. "Quick." He furiously beckoned to Didi. "Give me a white tuxedo with a Panama hat, a box of Cubans, two cigarette girls, a full bar, and a band by the pond."

Didi blanched. "I thought I'd start by trying to get rid of the sweater."

"Now," Frankie gritted out.

"I'll try." Didi clasped her hands, squinted hard, and stared out the window into the yard like she could shoot lightning bolts out of her eyes.

A gray mist swirled.

"Faster," Frankie urged, whipping off the sweater, kicking off the penny loafers.

Three wiseguys in suits and ties got out of the car.

The mist swirled brighter, giving off flecks of light.

Frankie fisted his hands. "Do it. Do it. Do it. Gah!"

A clothesline cropped up in the backyard, with granny panties fluttering in the breeze.

"Not that way!" Frankie heaved.

"I—I always wanted a nice clothesline." Grandma waved her arms desperately, trying to wipe it out. Instead, it sprouted a second line full of very large bras.

"Cover it with a bandstand," he ordered, like he was in charge of anything. "Then give me one cigarette girl. A table of booze. A —what is that?"

A gangster with no neck stumbled up against the car as a wiry old woman appeared in front of him. "Ma?" he garbled like he had a mouthful of marbles.

"I'm sorry. I'm sorry!" Didi waved her hands harder. "I can't make myself believe a cigarette girl belongs in my yard, and do those boys' mothers know what they're up to tonight?"

In a flash, two more mammas in aprons appeared in the yard. The wiseguys froze, caught between their tough-guy poses and shrinking from their mothers' disapproving stares.

"My life is over. Again!" Frankie wailed. "My reputation is dead. I hope you're happy!"

"Let me fix it," Didi urged, doubling down on the hand-waving, the smoke, the sparks.

"No!" Frankie's entire being twanged like a snapped rubber band. "You're just like Verity. You think you can fix everything, and you only make it worse."

"Hey—" I began. Yes, sometimes I made it worse, but then I always made it better.

But he was on a roll. "I may be stuck with you, Verity. But I'm not stuck with her."

Technically, he was stuck with both of us.

"That's it! I'm out of here." He retreated toward the wall that led out to the rose garden. "Now's the time to make a clean getaway. Verity, get my urn. We're leaving."

Well, that was fine and dandy. "The car's out front." We were going anyway. "I'll get my purse and your urn."

"We'll meet you there," Didi said, zipping down the hall toward the front of the house.

I charged up to the bedroom to grab what I needed. As I stuffed Frankie's urn into my bag, I peeked out the back window. Three gangsters cowered in my yard, being dressed down by their ghostly mothers.

This would be the last party Frankie held for a while.

I slung my bag over my shoulder and headed down the stairs.

Poor ghost.

He was stuck here. At least before, he'd been able to make it his own, but now he was stuck in Didi's world.

They'd have to work it out.

Right?

Frankie stood fuming at the bottom of the stairs. The sweater was back. So were the loafers. "You don't get it," he said as I hurried down the final steps. "When a dominant ghost settles in, they become more...them. It's going to get worse."

"You don't know that." After all, my grandma had never

taken over the property before. "It could get better." I had faith she would try her best.

"Mark my words," he said, as we headed for the door. "This isn't going to end soon, and it isn't going to end well. She's going to ruin my afterlife. She'll ruin your regular life. We can't live like this," he said as I paused at the gray-glowing door.

The whole foyer was lit in a ghostly light.

"We'll work on it," I said, getting a shock as I twisted the knob.

There was no helping it.

I shook out my icy-cold hand and decided I was okay with leaving the door cracked behind me.

It wasn't like I wanted to touch it again.

Frankie waited for me on the porch. "What do I have to do to get her out of here?"

"Nothing," I said, waving to Didi. She was already in the car. "At least not until we can save Grandma Rose's legacy. And hopefully not for a long time after that."

"Is this what the prison is about?" he asked, trailing me down the stairs.

"As a matter of fact, yes."

"Good," he grunted. "Then we're going to solve your grandma's problem."

"We are." I smiled.

"She's going to want to go back to the light. Back to guys who wear sweaters and penny loafers." He sneered the words as if he couldn't imagine any man who would.

"She might." My smile faded. If Grandma Rose was happy, if all Didi's problems were solved, she might leave to go enjoy her afterlife. She deserved that. So did Grandpa. I wanted that for her, and I didn't.

She could be just as happy here, right?

And he could visit.

Hey, maybe he could stay too. That would be even better.

Frankie went to straighten his tie, then dropped his hands

when he realized he didn't have one anymore. "You need me to help navigate the other side."

"You always make it easier." Well, some of the time.

He halted outside the car. "She's in my spot."

"It was my car," Didi said from the front passenger seat. She was also the dominant ghost. Although he wouldn't want to hear that.

"Don't worry. This will be fun," I said, sliding into the driver's seat and depositing my bag on the seat between us.

The gangster scowled. "I refuse to get in the car unless—" He gasped as a wiseguy tore headlong into the front yard, chased by his mother. Frankie dove head-first into the back seat. "Drive."

I fired up the engine and took off.

"Oh my. Are we making a getaway?" Didi asked, craning to watch the wiseguy try to hide behind a tree.

"Don't you start," Frankie warned.

"Who knew life with a gangster could be so exciting?" Didi mused as the house grew distant behind us.

Exciting was one word for it.

Rather than turn on the radio, which would no doubt spark another round of debate, I filled Frankie in on what Didi and I had found. I also told them both what I'd researched on my laptop. Didi listened intently. Frankie pouted. But at least they weren't fighting.

And when my phone rang, I was almost relieved to have something else to think about.

I pulled over to the shoulder of Route 7 and plugged in my headset before answering.

It was my sister, Melody. "How are you feeling?" I asked.

"Are you going to act like I'm broken every time?"

"Pretty much, yes." She'd scared me half to death yesterday.

"Then how are you feeling?" she asked, turning it around on me.

"My throat is better." Still raw, but not as bad as yesterday.

"I've been so busy I've hardly thought about my hand," I added, pulling back out onto the road.

"Anyway, I'm glad I caught you. After you left, I went back in with Lucas to see if we could bring up the records Grandma donated. Turns out Alec's police academy buddy is on the arson investigation team. He and Alec went down with us."

That was wonderful. I turned onto the highway. "Did you find Rose's things?"

"They were stolen."

I jerked my head so hard I almost came unplugged. "Are you sure?"

"I wish I weren't. Grandma's boxes were there during the fire. The whole shelf was covered in soot and water, but the spot where her records should be was clean. That means the boxes didn't burn. Someone took them after it was all over."

Wow. But why?

"What?" Didi asked.

I waved her off.

Melody kept talking. "The worst thing is we found pieces of one of the boxes stuffed behind the shelf. It looks like somebody tried to incinerate it all over again, and when that failed, they took it."

To destroy it later?

I hoped that wasn't the case. I hoped they'd wanted the box. "What did the arson team say? I'm thinking whoever set fire to the library stole the boxes."

"Correct." She sighed. "Can Grandma give us a list of what she donated?"

I relayed the message to Didi, who shook her head. "Papers. Stacks of them. Meeting notes. Club records. I skimmed a few things, but none of it appeared valuable. At least not to anyone but researchers."

"Lucas found it all fascinating, but he also likes to talk my ear off about how the town's first traffic light caused a three-day protest in 1948."

"You know you love it."

"I do." She let out a breath. "I have him working on a list of the boxes' contents, but he's having trouble remembering who donated what for the suffragette exhibit, and I don't know because I was putting together the activities for the festival. Anyway, we have a list of what each family donated, but Mr. Hartley isn't letting anyone in the archives or the record room. He bit our heads off when he learned we went down there with Alec."

"Why? It's your job to maintain the collections."

"Among other things." She huffed. "He says his concern is safety and security."

"Or he's trying to hide something."

"That's what I'm afraid of."

"We can't rule out Lucas either," I said. He'd had plenty of access, thanks to Melody.

She sighed. "Lucas has been volunteering to prep for the festival after hours. If he'd wanted to steal anything, he'd have done it then."

There was another thing I didn't get. "These records have been in the library for decades. Why steal them now? And why set a fire to get rid of them?"

"They wouldn't have been allowed outside the library," Melody said. "That section of the stacks is closed to everyone but approved researchers. We log IDs, and after they check out the materials, they can only study them in one of our research rooms."

"And if someone walked out with them, you'd know who it was."

"Without a doubt," she said. "And get this. I went to the catalog to see if anyone checked out the boxes, and if so—who."

"And?" My stomach fluttered.

"The logbook page was stolen."

Wow. Wait. "You keep paper records?"

"It's a clipboard. We're not exactly the Library of Congress."

"Okay." Let's think. "Someone might have checked out a box.

They saw what was in it and set a fire to destroy it." I glanced to Didi. "So now we're chasing an arsonist."

"And a thief," Frankie added.

I didn't even realize he'd been listening.

"At least the records survived the fire," Melody said.

If the thief hadn't destroyed them already.

"Speed," Grandma said as I blazed past a patrol car at the intersection right before the turnoff for Main. "I really taught you better."

"I promise this is unusual," I vowed. The fire, her being here, Grandma Rose's documents... It all had me in a tizzy.

As I spoke, a text came through on my phone.

Didi bent her head to check it out. "Alec Duranja says you're on very thin ice."

"He says that a lot." I turned off the highway.

"Who says what?" Melody asked. It was easy to forget not everyone could hear ghosts. "Never mind." Alec would take great joy in filling her in later. "We're headed to the Occoquan Workhouse."

"Really?" Melody asked. "That closed down in 1934."

"We're trying to find one of Grandma Rose's friends. If she's there, we'll ask if she knows anything about Rose's papers and what they might have contained."

And we'd ask her about the key.

And if I could work it in, I really did want to know about those peach pies.

"Good luck," Melody said.

"Thanks for going down into the stacks for me," I told her, making a left toward downtown Sugarland.

"For us," she corrected. "For Grandma Rose and her legacy."

"Of course." We were in this together.

Chapter Fifteen

I drove south on Main and over a few blocks toward Fifth Street, where the old workhouse building hunkered next to the Sugarland Police Department.

"Park there," Didi said, pointing to a spot in front of Pickler's Fine Shoes.

The shoe store sat between J&B Meat and Roan's Hardware, in the same quaint two-story brick building it had occupied for half a century. Most businesses on this block could say the same.

I parallel parked in front of the metal carousel ride that had been there for as long as I could remember.

Melody and I had always loved going to Pickler's because Mr. Pickler would hide a silver dollar inside one random children's shoe box every morning. If you found it during a fitting, it was yours to keep.

I'd spent years hoping to be that lucky kid, sampling more shoes than my mom had ever planned to buy. I never did find a dollar, but somehow Mr. Picker always had a butterscotch candy for me "just for trying."

I missed getting candy just for trying.

Didi slipped through the passenger door while I killed the engine.

As I was stashing my key, Frankie propped his elbows on the back of the bench seat. "What's the deal? I'm feeling transparent here, and not in a fun way."

"I have no idea what you're talking about," I said, grabbing my purse with his urn.

"You never listen to me. You never do what I tell you." He threw off a spark. "But Hurricane Holier-Than-Thou blows in and you're all, 'Yes, Your Majesty.'"

Hardly. "Notice none of Didi's suggestions involve robbing, shooting, or stealing." I stepped out onto the sidewalk.

"You're just mad because my way works," Frankie said, joining me. "I get things done. I can fix any problem you have."

"While you create two more to replace it," I said, joining Didi on the sidewalk.

"Is he always like this?" she asked.

Yes. "No." I slung my bag over my shoulder. "He's usually not on fire."

"Oh, there's Fred Pickler." Didi brightened and waved.

Of course, he couldn't see her, but rather than remind her of that fact, I waved as well. He smiled and returned the gesture.

"Come on," I said, "let's head across the street."

The Sugarland Police Department stood on the corner across from us, dominating the block. Its limestone trim and tall windows gave it a stately, official air it had maintained since 1902. Next door squatted its plainer cousin, the old workhouse.

Frankie shoved his hands into the pockets of his jeans as he trailed behind. "I should be able to wear my own clothes now that I'm off your property."

That would have been nice. "Except Didi controls the dirt, and you're in the dirt, and—"

"I don't want to talk about it," he said, aiming a glare at her back.

Frankie shrank into an orb as we passed the police station, going incognito, no doubt. Still, I didn't see any ghostly officers. Or anything supernatural at all.

"Coast is clear," I said as we reached the humble brick work-house building. Painted a dull gray, it had served more functions than I could count. The first floor alone had been a records room, a temporary lockup, evidence storage, and for one memorable month in 1997, an impound lot for seized motorcycles.

We headed for the entrance, but I stopped short.

The doorway was filled with brick, laid so precisely it looked like there had never been an entrance at all.

"Oh my." My stomach dropped. Even the windows were painted over.

"Don't worry. I'll look for Hope," Didi said, stepping through the door. "You keep watch outside."

Wait. "No," I said, a little more forcefully than I would have liked. "It could be dangerous," I pointed out when she stuck her head back through the brick. "We have no idea who might be haunting the place."

It had a dark past.

"Ghosts like me," she said as if that was the solution to everything.

"You haven't met the mean ones yet," I warned. "Besides, I'm the ghost hunter."

"Now I'm one, too," she said pleasantly. "Only I can pass through walls. Let's make the most of it."

And then she vanished through the wall. Without me.

"Frankie." I turned to him, aghast.

She really thought she could do this without me. I mean, maybe she could, but I doubted it.

We were supposed to be a team.

"I never would have left you behind," the gangster vowed.

"You wouldn't." He was right. He hadn't ever tried to investigate without me.

Of course, half the time he didn't want to investigate with me, either.

"Quick," I said, "circle the building. Find us another way in."

In the meantime, I made a beeline for the bricked-up door.

"Didi," I hollered, rapping on the wall. "Come back out. We'll find a way in together." I kept at it, my knuckles going raw. "You can't do this without me." It was reckless and wrong and—dang it, kind of mean.

Logically, I knew she was only trying to protect me. She for sure wanted to help me.

But she'd *left* me. Standing in the dust.

She hadn't even bothered to help me find a different way inside.

And now, she was either ignoring me, or she was knee-deep in adventure without me.

I felt the chill as Frankie materialized directly behind me. "The door at the back is bricked up as well."

"It still doesn't give her an excuse," I said, abandoning the door, knuckles stinging.

There had to be another way in.

"Dang, I miss my cigarettes," he said, digging around in his pocket and coming up with a pipe.

He tossed it over his shoulder.

"Come on." I swallowed my pride along with my hurt as we headed for the front door of the Sugarland PD. "Maybe Ellis can tell us how to get inside the workhouse."

At least he wouldn't walk through any walls and leave me behind.

I yanked open the heavy wood door, setting off the electric chime overhead.

The place smelled like old bricks and coffee.

I made my way to a massive wooden desk that had been witness to small-town drama since the '50s. Joshua Carter, eternal college student working on his victory lap between years six and seven, perched on a tall chair behind it, thumbs flying across his phone screen.

"Hi," I said as he demolished a battalion of orcs. "I need to see Ellis Wydell. It's important."

"Just a minute." Josh didn't even blink.

I planted my elbows on the desk, which had been sanded and scarred so many times the surface dipped like a poorly paved country road.

"I don't have a minute." Didi could be getting into all sorts of trouble in that workhouse. Ghost hunting was delicate work. If we were lucky enough to find Hope still haunting her death spot, one wrong move could send her running. I knew how to handle spooked spirits. Didi did not.

If she scared Hope off, we might never learn what Grandma Rose's key unlocked.

Frankie materialized next to Josh. "Watch this," he said with unholy glee, bracing himself as he stuck a ghostly finger straight through Josh's ear.

Josh yelped and toppled sideways, his phone clattering across the desk.

"Hi, Josh." I smiled sweetly. "About Ellis?"

Josh scrambled up, tugging his uniform straight and trying to tame his static-charged hair. "Ellis is with the team at the library."

"Then I need...him!" I said, spotting Duranja on his way down the hallway in the back. "Yoo-hoo!" I waved like a maniac to get his attention.

Was he ignoring me?

Frankie rubbernecked with me. "Nice to see you got a plan."

"A what?" I asked, belatedly hoping Josh didn't see me talking to thin air.

"A sure-fire way to one-up the fuzz," the gangster said as Duranja halted and began muttering under his breath. "You can get yourself arrested. See the workhouse from the inside. May I suggest the classic hotwiring of his squad car? Or you could never go wrong with stealing the cannonball out of the wall at the library."

"I'd never," I gasped. That cannonball was an artifact.

"I tried once." He shrugged. "In any case, sometimes the best way to break people out of jail is to get nicked yourself."

"I'll keep that in mind." I shot him a look. "But nobody's

getting arrested. Duranja and I have a new understanding," I explained as the detective strode into the room, taking the longest, most judgmental sip of coffee I'd ever witnessed.

"Verity," he drawled. I had been pushing my luck lately. "Haven't I done enough favors for you today?"

Yes. But one more wouldn't hurt. "You see, when I was saving Melody from the fire, I found a hidden key from a secret society of suffragettes who met under my house."

He stared at me. "This would only happen to you."

I didn't see where that was the issue. "The point is Grandma Didi is working with me to learn what the key unlocks, but now she went through a brick wall into the workhouse because she somehow thinks she's a ghost hunter by association, and now I have to get in there before she scares off the dead suffragette who may or may not be haunting the place, or worse—runs into any spooky ghosts."

"Because dead suffragettes aren't spooky," Duranja said dryly.

"Not the ones I've met," I said in all honesty.

Duranja pinched the bridge of his nose and took a deep breath. "Sure, I can get you in there. Come on back. And be glad I love your sister." He muttered that last part as he led the way past reception and took a left down the hall.

If he was going to be that way about it... "You could just point us to a door. Any door that isn't bricked over."

"There isn't one anymore," he said, handing me his cup of coffee to hold. "But I can do you one better."

He led us down a set of worn concrete stairs that ended sharply at an old metal door. He worked the padlock and swung it open. The air grew thick with decades of dust as he revealed a narrow passageway.

I handed back his coffee. "People have sworn this place was haunted for years," he said, flicking on the lights, illuminating a series of hanging bulbs that disappeared down the shadowy passage.

"Everywhere I go is haunted," Frankie said, although I noticed he wasn't going first.

Duranja led the way. "This used to be the drunk tank, then a records room. Some say they still hear chains rattling."

Our footsteps echoed on the concrete floor. "What do you use it for now?"

The hanging bulbs cast weak pools of yellow light, leaving the corners in shadow.

Frankie whistled low, pointing at scratch marks on the wall.

I saw. And I didn't like it at all.

"We use it for storage. Nobody works in the building anymore." Duranja ducked under a low pipe. "Even still, people report lights in the windows after dark." He glanced back at me. "Never saw anything myself. I never believed any of the stories. Well, until you showed me a few things on that haunted island."

"Thanks for bringing me down here." I shuddered as a cold draft whispered past. "There was a time you'd have rather locked me up."

"I do that when people break the law," he said as something skittered in the darkness ahead. Probably a mouse. Hopefully a mouse. "I caught you twice today, in fact."

He had me there. "I keep getting distracted. A lot has happened in the last twenty-four hours."

"I know. How are you doing?"

"Same as usual."

"That bad?" He chuckled.

Har-de-har. "How's Melody doing?"

He sighed. "She woke up with nightmares last night. We made hot chocolate and watched infomercials until she fell asleep on the couch. My plan is to hold her extra tight tonight."

I couldn't help but smile. Despite our earlier issues, I had to admit he was a solid guy.

The passage opened into a cavernous room. Light filtered through grimy windows near the ceiling. Stacks of old computers and dusty monitors clustered hodgepodge across the concrete floor, their dark screens like empty eyes.

I didn't see Didi anywhere.

My elbow nearly caught an old mop leaning against the wall. "Will you check upstairs for my grandma?" I asked Frankie.

He gave me a long look.

"The sooner we fix her problem—"

"The sooner she scrams," he finished.

Although he didn't have to put it that way.

"You stay here," he ordered, gliding through the ceiling.

Where else was I supposed to go?

The jail cell loomed before us, eight feet square with bars as thick as broom handles. Black paint flaked off the iron like dead skin, revealing corroded metal underneath. A century of Southern humidity had eaten into every joint and seam, turning the hinges red-brown and oozing black stains on the red brick wall.

And the whole thing glowed silvery gray.

"This was the main holding cell." Duranja stopped several feet short of the bars, as if he could sense the ghostly energy. "Take your time. But don't let that door close behind you. The key is long gone."

"Thanks," I said, brushing past him.

Most people can sense ghosts, even if they don't realize that's what they're feeling. It's that gut-level certainty something's lurking behind you in the dark. That hair-raising wrongness when a place just isn't right.

Duranja shifted his weight. "The thing is I have to get back to work."

He didn't want to leave me here. Smart man.

"It's okay. I'm not alone." I had Frankie.

And Didi, wherever she'd wandered off to.

"Right," he said, clearly fighting his instincts. "Call me if you need me."

"Always," I said. And I meant it.

With a tight nod, Duranja retreated down the passage, leaving me in the damp silence of the old workhouse.

The cell door stood open an inch, maybe two. The lock plate bore deep scratch marks around its keyhole. I grabbed the old mop, hooked it past the corroded metal and pulled, hinges screaming in protest.

"Hope?" My whisper felt tiny in the oppressive silence. "Are you in here?"

I slipped inside and stood alone at the center of the cell.

A pair of discarded leg cuffs lay on the floor, glowing ghostly gray. I stepped over them and toward a crumbling wooden bench jutting from the back wall.

"Who's haunting this cell?"

The bench had to be newer than the ghost—it didn't glow. I lowered myself onto it, trying to ignore its ominous creak.

"I don't mind waiting," I said, then winced at my words.

How many prisoners had languished here, counting days into months into years?

The air reeked of rust and decay.

I traced initials carved into the wood, too worn to read. The cold from the bench seeped through my dress.

"Hello." A voice echoed through the cell.

I whirled to find Didi in the doorway, glowing faintly in the dim light.

I slapped a hand over my galloping heart. "Where have you been?"

"Trying to locate Hope." She drifted toward me. "I didn't know when or if you'd make it inside." She settled onto the bench next to me. "There's a lot of junk upstairs."

"Down here too. Any sign of her?"

"No, but I'll bet this is her death spot," Didi said with a shiver. "It appears you found the only jail cell."

Good.

I didn't want to think there were more places like this.

A cold wind swept past us, sending shivers down my spine. I

scrambled to my feet as a woman appeared in the blink of an eye. She wore a long skirt, a high-necked blouse, and a frantic expression. "Call the guards. Now." She jabbed a thin, gray finger at me. "You have to get out of here before she sees you."

"Is your name Hope?" Please be Hope.

She waved Didi away. Frantic. "You too. Go now. Quickly."

Didi glided toward her, hands out. "You don't understand—"

"We need your help," I added. "We came here to talk to Hope."

"I'm trying to help." The ghost's voice crackled with panic. "Don't you see?" Her gaze darted past us as if she expected someone or some*thing* to materialize any second. "You're in danger."

"From whom?" I stiffened, checking over my shoulder.

If this was Hope's death spot, she should be the dominant ghost. Then again, plenty of people had died in and around the old workhouse.

And not all of them good.

"We're not going anywhere until you talk to us," Didi vowed.

"She's right." I lifted my chin.

For better or worse, we were in this together.

The ghost pressed her hands against her head. "If that's what it takes." Her gaze darted to the doorway. "But if she sees you, you might never be rid of her."

Then we'd make it quick. "First things first. Introductions." We were Southern, after all. "I'm Verity Long. This is my grandma Delia, and we're looking for a suffragette named Hope."

"I'm Hope." She smoothed back a loose strand of hair. "Hope Taliafero."

Well, wasn't that something. "I think I know your granddaughter, Adelaide." She lived down the street from me and kept the most gorgeous bird feeders. "Named after your daughter, of course." I calculated quickly, and yes, the math worked. The Adelaide I knew was in her early eighties.

Hope appeared startled for a moment. "My Adelaide is just a

baby." She reached for the locket at her neck and opened it, revealing a black-and-white image of an infant. "She's so small. I miss her so much."

Oh my. Hope didn't realize she was dead.

Poor thing. She'd been stuck here a long time.

I wished I could hug her. Instead, I'd do my best to help ease her out gently. "I hear you died in this cell."

She closed the locket with shaking fingers. "I might, but not yet." She pressed a hand to her stomach, laughing with an edge of hysteria. "Though, I am feeling rather weak."

I exchanged a look with Didi. Ghosts often haunted their death spots. It was a common way of dealing with what had happened to them in their final minutes.

But to deny death completely?

"The hunger strike is difficult." Hope drifted toward the bars, her hand still pressed to her middle. "But that's not even the worst." Her form flickered. "It's this cell. It's haunted."

"By you?" The words slipped out before I could stop them.

"What? No. By something horrible." Her voice dropped to a whisper. "It comes at night, filling the cell with rage. I can feel it, dark and desperate, pressing against me, suffocating me." She hugged herself, her gray form trembling.

"How awful." Didi touched a hand to her shoulder. "How can we get you out?"

"You could unlock the door." Hope's laugh was bitter.

It was then I realized the door now stood firmly closed on the ghostly side. I let out an involuntary shudder. Grandma was trapped. It would be no picnic for me, either. I could pass through the open door on my side of the veil, but it would be a heck of a shock.

Hope had to be creating this. The door had been open when we'd walked through.

"Pass through the door," Didi urged me. "You can make it disappear."

Hope stared at her blankly. "Stop teasing." She broke away. "It's cruel."

"No." I said, and not just because it would sting down to my teeth. Hope was afraid of ghosts, and if I scared her by making the jail disappear, she might poof out of here, and we'd never find her. "Let's handle something else first." I reached into my pocket. "We came to ask you about this." I held up Great-Grandma Rose's key.

Hope clawed at the air between us. "Where did you get that?" She lunged for it. "Give it to me. Now."

"I can't." I tucked it away and stood my ground. "Rose left it for us to protect. But we need to know what we're protecting."

She retreated, shielding her throat.

Didi stood still. "Where is your key, Hope?"

Her form flickered violently. "I hid it, but he took it." Pain twisted her face. "Then he held a pillow over my face."

"Who?" Didi pressed.

"My lawyer." Hope's voice shook. "People will kill for the key."

"What people?" I stepped toward her, and she flinched. "You have to help us. We're on your side."

"We'll keep it secret," Didi promised, though my stomach sank.

I'd already shown everyone at the library when we'd found the body. And according to this morning's Google search, it was in the newspaper. Dread washed over me. If someone set fire to the library to steal the key, would they kill for it as well?

A sound like breaking glass pierced the air. Hope vanished as darkness welled up through cracks in the concrete floor. It twisted upward like smoke, blotting out the dim light from the high windows.

The temperature plunged. The cell door slammed closed on my side with a thunderous clang.

I choked out a gasp as frost crackled across the bars. I scrambled back until I hit the corner by the bench, heart hammering.

"Leave," Didi ordered. "This instant."

A deep rumble filled the cell, rattling my bones as the metal cage hummed with energy.

Didi surged forward, hitting an invisible wall. Disembodied yellow eyes fixed on her. "Watch out," she cried as the shape coalesced in front of me.

"Verity!" She fought to reach me while misty tendrils reached for my throat.

The wall pressed cold against my back. There was nowhere left to run.

"Who are you?" My voice wavered as the mist stretched closer. "My name is Verity Long—"

The tendrils brushed my skin, and pain shot through me—ice cold, stinging, wrong.

My throat closed. My lungs refused to work. The claws dug into my skin.

Didi's screams faded to nothing as black spots danced in my vision. So cold.

The mist traced my gold and silver filagree necklace, its touch burning like frostbite.

Through the churning void of its face, I saw *her.*

My blood froze.

Then she vanished. The poltergeist disappeared, leaving me ice cold and shaking with the bitter taste of copper in my mouth.

"Verity!" Didi rushed to me. "Are you all right?"

"I saw it." I could barely form the words as my knees threatened to buckle.

"You couldn't miss it," she said as I crumpled onto the bench.

"No—" I traced the ice-cold skin of my throat. "The photograph on your hall table of Rose in her wedding dress with the high lace collar." Each word felt like glass in my throat. "It was her, Didi. It was Grandma Rose."

Chapter Sixteen

Didi staggered back, her hand flying to her mouth. For a moment, she looked as vulnerable as I felt.

Then her jaw set. "Hope was right." Her gaze flicked to the cell door. It stood open now that the poltergeist had fled. "We have to get out of here."

We made a hasty retreat down the shadowy passage. It was her. Grandma Rose.

I'd seen her clear as day.

And poor Hope, tortured like that. She was a good person. A suffragette. She'd fought for a better Sugarland.

And Grandma Rose... A chill swept past, carrying the metallic tang of old chains. "Grandma Rose can't be a *poltergeist*." My voice cracked on the word. I didn't want to believe it. I couldn't. "She's moved on. You've seen her. You've talked to her on the higher plane. She's in a happy place."

Didi's mouth formed a thin line. "Grandma Rose is scared. She's angry."

The hanging bulbs cast weak pools of yellow light that barely reached the walls.

But *that* angry? "All I'm saying is—"

"It makes sense." Her words came out sharp, brittle.

Maybe. "Let's think about it." A bulb ahead sputtered and went dark. I pressed on, a full-body shudder passing through me. My body was still catching up, but I had to think. "How can Grandma Rose be in two places at once?"

"She's not always in the higher realms," Didi said cryptically as my ankle brushed something furry in the dark. "She disappears quite a lot. Even I know that, and she refuses to have anything to do with me."

"Okay." Not the best news. "But poltergeists are ghosts who let their rage take over until there's nothing else left." It was terrible. Unthinkable. Rose had a beautiful garden. She was a suffragette. She was related to me. She had to be all right. "If Grandma Rose is still allowed in the higher plane—"

"I haven't seen her in a long time."

The pipes overhead groaned, a deep sound that seemed to come from everywhere at once.

"Maybe she isn't fully gone." Maybe we still had a chance to save her.

"If she's not gone, she's close," Didi said, not even trying to sugarcoat it. "Did you see her?" She ran a hand over her eyes. "It's my fault. All of it. I put her legacy in jeopardy. I made this happen."

"You didn't do it on purpose."

"But I did it." Didi's voice splintered. "I had no idea a few old things in a box were so important. Why is it so important?"

"I don't know." I ducked under the low pipe, moving faster now. "That's what we're going to find out." This wasn't only about Grandma Didi anymore. "We'll recover Rose's legacy." Not just to atone for Didi's mistake, but to save Grandma Rose's afterlife. "We'll make things right for her. She won't go full poltergeist."

"I'm scared," she whispered as we reached the stairs.

"So am I."

We burst out of the police station into late afternoon sunlight. My hands trembled on the strap of my bag, my heart hammering against my ribs.

Didi kept swiveling her head to look behind us. "What do we do next?"

"That's the trick. Hope didn't tell us where the key goes, only that it's important."

"Her lawyer killed her for it."

Good point. "Let's start with him." I pulled out my phone and saw Melody had called. I halted and quickly called her back.

It rang six times, and I was about to give up when Lucas answered. "Hey, Melody says don't hang up. She needs to talk to you."

"About?" I asked, eyeing Didi.

"It's her story to tell. But I did want to talk to you about your peach orchard."

The what? "Did something happen in 1919?"

"I'd be glad to look," he offered. "No, I was going to say—did you know the large orchard that used to take up most of your front yard was planted by Lucy Hollis Long? She used a brand-new variety she created herself."

No kidding. Lucy was my four-times great-grandmother. I'd named my skunk for her after finding Lucy's personal notes on the animals she'd rescued and rehomed.

She was one of my heroes.

"She spent years grafting different varieties until she created one that was just right—sweeter than Georgia peaches but hardy enough for our winters. She called it the Sugar Peach. The agricultural department even came out to study them in 1884. I found their report in the archives—they said they'd never seen anything like it."

"That's amazing, Lucas." It was.

"You know, when Matthew Grayson proposed to wild Bessie Lou Fairfax with one of Lucy's peaches in 1893, it started a trend.

The newspapers said no boy ever got turned down when proposing with a Sugar Peach."

I loved that. "You don't know how much I needed to hear something good today."

"I can show you more of what I found once the library is back in shape. I'm going to specialize in stories like this. People don't pay enough attention to small-town history."

And I had a feeling he could talk my ear off.

"Hey." Melody came on the line. "Did Lucas tell you about the ring?"

"I was too busy telling her about peaches," he said in the background.

"I showed him a picture of the signet ring you found, and he recognized the crest. It's from a society of suffragettes who used to meet in secret in Sugarland!"

We were a step ahead of her on that one.

"But the organization broke up right before women earned the vote," Lucas added.

That was weird.

"Good work, Lucas."

"It's what I do," I heard in the background.

I glanced up to see Didi eyeing the workhouse. "Hey, I called to see if you could help me with something else. Hope Taliafero was killed at Occoquan in 1919. She told us her lawyer did it. Can you try to learn his name? Also, if Hope was killed for her key, I'm thinking Eleanor Blackwell may have been targeted as well." It was a longshot. We'd already searched, but... "If she's our skeleton in the wall..."

"It might be here in the library," Melody finished. "I'll go look right now. I might need to call in Alec. I'm not sure what I'm allowed to touch, but I'll do my best."

"Be careful."

Hope had said people might kill for it. Even today.

Didi stood frowning as I hung up. "I don't like where any of this is headed." She glanced back at the workhouse. "And where's

Frankie?" she added as I started for the car. "We can't go without him."

"He'll be along soon," I promised, hitching my bag over my shoulder, his urn knocking against my hip. He'd leave the property as soon as his urn did.

The instant I stepped off the curb—whoosh. Frankie appeared, and I nearly ran him over.

"What the—" The gangster stumbled, cigarette dangling from his lip, his hat tilted sideways. "Why?" He threw his arms out, catching up with me in two long strides. "Why do you always mess it up right when I'm about to score?"

Because I wanted distance between me and the poltergeist, and my car was dead ahead.

"We're glad to see you, too," Didi said, waving to a Jeep that had slowed to let us cross. "Your gangster needs to work on his manners."

We'd add that to the list.

"Nice to see you got your cigarettes back," I said, fishing for my keys as he blew out an angry cloud of smoke. "See? Grandma didn't do you dirty. You're going back to your old self."

He shot me a glare as he yanked off the old-man sweater and tossed it in the street. "My smokes aren't back. There's candy in my pocket. And I'm wearing tighty-whities!"

"Grandpa Jack said those were the most comfortable," Didi supplied.

She wasn't helping.

The gangster also wore a plaid button-up shirt with short sleeves. That was new. He took a long, shaky drag. "This," he said, clutching his smoke until it bent, "is keeping me sane. I stole a pack from a locked desk drawer."

Didi stopped dead. "How'd you get into a locked drawer?"

Frankie gave her a flat look, smoke trailing from his nose.

"He's a thug," I reminded her, opening the driver's door and tossing my purse in. "Where were you?"

"In the records room, snooping through the ghostly archives

for a file on Hope." He slipped through the passenger door, shooting Didi a triumphant look when she realized he'd swiped her spot. "I was wondering if Hope had her key on her when she was arrested."

Oh my word. "Frankie, that's brilliant."

He rested an elbow on the door and sucked his cigarette down to the nub. "I know."

"Except the police didn't discover it if it was stolen after someone smothered her in jail," Didi said from the backseat, her elbows on the bench seat between us.

Frankie dropped the grin. "Yeah, there was no mention of it on the intake, and that girl was found dead in her cell."

Murdered. I started the car. "That means what we're searching for could have been stolen in 1919. But if so, why the fuss now? Why would someone be stealing Grandma Rose's mementos from the library?"

And then try to burn the place down?

Frankie drew another cigarette from the front pocket of his plaid shirt. "If somebody nicked the prize in 1919, dear old Grandma Rose would have figured it out a long time ago."

"Agreed," Didi said as I turned left toward Main Street. "Grandma Rose is obviously protecting something, even today. We still have a chance to find it and save it."

Yes, but whoever had stolen her boxes might have gotten a head start.

And all we had was our key.

I knew it was asking a lot but... "Frankie, did you find anything else?"

He grinned as he lit up, tossing the match out the closed window. "I did." He reached behind his smokes and drew out a folded paper that glowed ghostly gray. "Want to see?"

Oh my goodness. "Yes," I said, pulling over into a parking spot on South Main. Far enough from the police station to breathe but close enough to the library to keep me on edge.

Frankie unfolded the stolen paper like it was the Magna Carta, smoothing the edges where the creases had started to tear. *SUGARLAND'S MOST WANTED – MARCH 1919* blazed across the top. Dark water stains bloomed over the bottom corner.

"Read it and weep." He jabbed the page. "Isn't it glorious? I'm number eight." He took a hard drag. "I was barely getting started and already in the top ten. Right behind Sticky Fingers Sullivan—who nobody should get within ten feet of—and Three Time Tommy, wanted for running the same con on three different banks at the exact same time."

Didi sucked in a breath. "You realize what this means."

"It means I'm now number six at least," Frankie crowed, smoke curling from his nose. "'Cause Sticky Fingers moved to Chicago to join the North Side Gang, and Three Time Tommy thought he could con his way into the light. Nobody's seen him since."

He laughed himself silly and took another drag.

I locked eyes with Didi. Unlike Frankie, I knew exactly what this list meant. "The whole workhouse is stuck in 1919."

Didi stiffened. "I'm thinking Grandma Rose is the dominant ghost in that jail."

"Poltergeists wield immense power." I'd seen it first-hand.

Frankie looked at us like we'd stopped for tea. "You're missing the point of the list."

Didi shifted. "So Hope's own lawyer likely stole her key in 1919, but he didn't uncover whatever the suffragettes were protecting."

It made sense. "If he had, there'd be no reason for someone to look for the key now."

"If that's what they were searching for," she cautioned.

We just didn't know.

I tapped my nails against the wheel. "So they had the key but were in the same situation we are—trying to figure out where it fits."

Frankie slapped the Most Wanted list onto the seatback between us. "Can't you be happy with me for one minute?"

"I'm very happy for you," I assured him. We just had more pressing matters. "If we only had a top criminal mind to help with this..." I mused, aiming for his ego.

He dropped the smirk. "I know what you're pulling, but you do have one thing right." He took a healthy drag. "I am one of the top criminal minds of my generation." He waggled his fingers. "Let me see that key again."

I dug through my bag until I touched cold metal. The key was heavy, with intricate scrollwork woven into the brass. Dark patches of age spotted the surface.

"Twist it around." Frankie squinted at the elaborate handle. "That's not factory made. See how the metal's braided instead of cast? Those turns in the shaft? Someone crafted this baby by hand."

"I'm not sure I care about the key itself," Didi said with a frown.

"You should," Frankie scoffed. "This isn't just a key. This is art." He took a drag. "You want to know where this key goes, you talk to the top artist in town." He blew out a steady stream of smoke. "Fingers McGee. He's a genius safe cracker with the instincts of a god."

"Do you know this Fingers McGee?" I asked. I hoped.

"You know him too." He pointed his cigarette at me. "You told him to stop teaching Lucy how to pick pockets while he played poker on your porch last week."

Him? I remembered him. "The cockeyed mustache guy who keeps picking the lock on my jewelry box even though he isn't strong enough to take anything?"

"What's the matter with window-shopping?" Frankie demanded.

"It's creepy," I insisted.

"Hey!" Frankie tapped ash out the window. "Fingers McGee is

the Michelangelo of safecracking, lock picking, and sticky fingers." He rested an elbow on the seat back. "When the mayor tried to lock himself in his office to hide from Ice Pick Charlie? Fingers picked it blindfolded. When the Third Street Bank installed their 'uncrackable' vault, Fingers opened it by ear and replaced all the cash with Monopoly money." He leaned closer. "That man broke out of jail with nothing but a bobby pin and his gold tooth." The gangster huffed. "Heck, I wouldn't be surprised if Fingers tried to pick the safe this key opens. He might tell you where it is if you let him tag along."

He sounded perfect. "Please tell me you know where to find him."

"I do." Frankie tilted up his chin. "I'll even invite him over to the house. *If* Grandma Didi here does something for me." He shot her a withering glare.

She twisted her hands together. "I have a feeling I know what you want."

He leveled his cigarette at her. "Stop your antics."

"I'm only being myself." She winced.

Frankie waved her off. "You clean my place up. Put it back to how it was."

"Her place," I corrected him.

"Your place," Grandma Didi corrected me.

Frankie gritted his teeth but didn't argue. "You give me my shed and my life back. Get my clothes and my gun back. And my cigarettes. All of them. And I'll put Fingers on the case."

She shot me a worried look. "I'll try."

"I'll help," I promised. Though I had no idea how we'd pull it off.

We arrived home to find Frankie's shed transformed into a ghostly garden paradise, complete with a creaky metal glider sporting floral cushions. A hand-painted sign declared *Welcome to Grand-*

ma's Garden, Where Visiting Hours Are 9-5 and Weeds Get Time Off for Good Behavior.

"This is a disaster." Frankie stormed through the side door, tangling himself in a clothesline strung with vintage aprons and doilies. "You promised to make it better, and you made it worse."

"I just got here," Didi protested, her eyes catching on a flowered daybed under a canopy near the pond. "Oh, this is lovely—" She spotted a basket overflowing with yarn.

"Focus," I reminded her. "It'll be fine, Frankie."

"It will," she promised, turning from the dream knitting spot and screwing up her strength. "What do you want?" She faced the gangster. "A Tommy gun rack? Brass knuckle displays? Bullet holes for ambiance?"

"You think I live in a cartoon?" Frankie looked at the knitting hut like it might rear up and bite him. "Although I will take the Tommy gun rack. That would make the boys jealous."

"I can do that," she vowed and began waving her hands.

Blue sparks crackled around Grandma as she worked.

This felt different than before.

Better.

"Come on, Didi." I crossed my fingers as Frankie's shed shimmered into...a hopscotch court.

She dropped her hands. "Oh, that's darling." She caught herself. "No." She slammed her eyes shut. "Think gangster. Tommy guns. No brass knuckles."

"No whammies," I supplied as the court vanished, replaced by another knitting tent.

"Sorry," she said, wiping the air. "I just really love that knitting tent."

At Frankie's slack-jawed stare, she steeled herself. "This time. This time for sure."

She set her jaw hard. She waved her arms. She doubled down on the love and the energy and the determination like only she could.

This time, she had it.

This time, she'd make it right.

This time, an ear-shattering boom echoed across the yard. Orange flames shot up behind the hydrangea bushes on the far side of the pond, briefly illuminating a shower of copper pipes and mason jars.

Didi clapped a hand over her mouth.

"My still!" Frankie clutched his heart. "You torched my still." His eyes bugged out. "Betsy Sue the Fourth."

"Hey, what happened to the Third?" I demanded.

He sank to his knees. "Handcrafted. Perfectly calibrated. Do you know how long it took me to get the temperature just right?" He collapsed into the grass.

"I'll fix it," Didi promised. A contraption materialized next to the apple tree. It looked like her old pressure cooker connected to her favorite tea kettle by a line of garden hose. "Right?"

"That is not—" Frankie's jaw dropped. "Is that a doily under the collection jar? And potpourri sachets hanging off the condenser?" He threw up his hands. "You're making me look like an idiot."

"There's nothing she can do," I pleaded. There was nothing any of us could do except halt the crazy train before it got worse. "Face it. We're done. We're over. We tried. Now can you please introduce us to Fingers McGee?"

"Never," Frankie vowed, climbing to his feet. "Fingers McGee is dead to you and so am I."

As he spoke, a thin man in a gray suit materialized behind him, sporting an uneven mustache that twisted up on one side and drooped on the other. The man's eyes were sharp, his smirk sure, and his fingers were impossibly long and delicate.

Fingers McGee.

"Ready for tonight's poker match?" he asked as Frankie locked his jaw.

My head was going to explode. "He was coming anyway?"

"I always drop by early to help stack the deck," Fingers said.

Frankie smoothed his wrinkled grandpa shirt. "It's not my fault you never pay attention to my social schedule."

Just then, Lucy burst from the ghostly rose garden, making a straight shot for Fingers McGee.

Her tail fluffed and her eyes sparkled as she happy danced a circle around him. "How's my girl?" Fingers crouched, and Lucy cuddled up next to him, almost touching. "You want to play?" the safecracker cooed.

She really could charm anyone, alive or dead.

Lucy stood up on her hind legs as he pulled a ghostly peach from his pocket. "Fetch!"

I was a little shocked when she scampered after it. She wasn't a dog. And that was technically my peach. "What are you doing?"

"Practicing our new trick." Fingers laughed as Lucy dashed for the peach and leapt right over it, making a wide arc before barreling back to him. "She's a natural. I should enter her in the pet festival next year."

Impossible. "You're dead."

"A technicality."

A big one.

Besides, that was our contest. "She's my skunk, not yours."

"Show him the key," Didi urged.

Right.

I pulled Grandma Rose's key from my pocket. "Seeing as you've made yourself at home—in my home—I was hoping you could look at something. Do you remember who owned the safe that matches this key?"

"Well, isn't this interesting?" A criminal sparkle lit his eye.

We didn't have time to play games. "It may hold something dear to my grandmother...of sentimental value only."

No sense sending a thief after it.

His mouth tipped into a grin. "I recognize the style." His fingers hovered over the key, chilling the metal. "Custom work. Very specific." He tilted his head. "Only two types ordered these

—the wealthy and the criminal. Usually both." His mustache twitched. "Matter of fact, I made this one myself."

I stared at him. "*You* made keys?"

He shrugged. "For the right price. I designed and crafted the only safes I couldn't break, as a favor to criminal enterprises I found interesting."

"My grandma Rose was not a criminal," Didi huffed.

"Because all the nice ladies have a hideout under their house," he smirked.

"Excuse me. What?" Frankie dropped his cigarette.

"You wouldn't last a minute," I told him. "It's filled with dresses. And doilies."

"And half-finished needlepoint projects that say things like *Live, Laugh, Love,*" Didi added.

"Is this my life now?" Frankie groused.

I locked eyes with Fingers. "Can you tell us who ordered the safe and this key?"

He pulled another peach from his pocket. "Maybe I don't remember," he said, turning it over. "You going to let me play with your skunk? Teach her tricks? Get her to swish her tail?" She wound around his ankles. "Me and her got a connection."

"Lucy likes everybody," I said.

Frankie frowned.

"Well, except for him," I amended. And frankly, I didn't want any strange gangsters around my skunk. Ever.

"That's unfortunate." Fingers cracked his knuckles while Lucy looked up at me with big black button eyes.

I supposed I trusted her judgment.

"Don't play chase too close to the pond," I warned. "I don't want her falling in."

He held his hands out. "As the lady wishes," he said, letting the peach fly.

Lucy let out a happy grunt and dashed for it.

"Tell us who you made the key for," Didi pressed, drawing close.

He watched Lucy go, then turned back to us. "One of my night clients. We met in the dark. A hush-hush deal. He wanted a waterproof vault that could withstand a solid rock wall. Nifty, huh? He wouldn't give a name, only a billing address." He glanced at Frankie. "The Crow's Nest."

Frankie huffed, then sputtered out a laugh. "If that's the case, you'll never find it. The Crow's Nest was a ghost story, even in my time. A speakeasy that never existed."

Fingers shrugged.

"Maybe it didn't exist for you," I said, "but this man knows about it."

"Not where it was," Fingers hedged, pausing to smile at Lucy as she scampered back. "Or where it might be now. But it was a fun job. I set him up real nice."

"Well, then, the Crow's Nest has to be somewhere," Didi said.

One would think.

"I know every inch of Sugarland, and I—" Then it hit me, and I couldn't help but smile. "I think I know where it is."

Chapter Seventeen

My headlights carved through fog as we wound up the narrow road to Crowe Manor. My late father used to tell stories about this place, how he and his friends would canoe past it, holding their breath to ward off ghosts.

If only it were that easy.

Twisted oaks lined the drive, their gnarled branches twining overhead. Rocks popped under my tires, echoing off the riverbank below, mixing with the sound of rushing water.

"This is the perfect place for a speakeasy," Frankie said, rubbernecking from the backseat. "Remote location, easy river access, and just the right amount of terrifying. Plus, if anyone asks what those screams are, you can blame it on the tortured ghosts instead of the drunk politicians."

"Your practicality knows no bounds," I said dryly. "And notice I'm the one leading you for a change."

The manor loomed ahead, a Victorian shadow against the starless sky. Vines had claimed the walls, crawling up three stories of peeling paint and rotting wood. At the peak of the highest tower, a black iron weathervane creaked—a crow frozen mid-flight, wings spread wide.

"The Crowes died out decades ago," I said, watching shadows

play across the wraparound porch. "But their descendants, the Hartleys, still own the property. They run a trucking company out past the drive-in."

"They were the library's biggest donors in my day," Didi murmured, her gaze rapt out the passenger window.

"These days, too," I told her. According to Melody, it was how Mr. Hartley had gotten his job. And while I appreciated their support, I'd stopped believing in coincidences. "They sponsored the suffragette exhibition at the library." The one that had burned.

Or rather, been set on fire.

I grabbed my flashlight and double-checked my pocket for the key.

It was chilly on the bluff.

A crow's call cut through the night. Another answered, then another, until the air filled with their cries. The weathervane groaned, tracking the wind's shift toward the river.

"Great," Frankie muttered. "Murder birds. Because this place isn't creepy enough."

The crows took flight, black wings beating against the night sky as they circled the tower. Their shadows cut across weathered stone, dancing over warped glass. One perched on the widow's walk railing, tilting its head to study us. The tower loomed just beyond.

I gasped when I saw a warm yellow light flickering in the window.

"Someone's up there," Didi said as we crossed the overgrown lawn.

A living person.

The crow cawed and launched into the night.

"I don't believe it," I said, straining to see. "This place has been empty for decades."

I flicked off my flashlight.

I'd rather not meet any living souls inside the mansion.

The dead were trouble enough.

Frankie pulled ahead. "I'll break us in." He glanced back. "Old-school style, seeing as your grandma made my lock-picking kit disappear with my favorite suit coat." He glared at Didi, who rolled her eyes.

"How long can this guy hold a grudge?"

"Pull up a chair," I said. "He's still mad about losing a card game to Baby Face Nelson's grandmother in 1924."

Frankie glowered from the porch. "You had to bring that up. She cheated, by the way. No one's that good at gin rummy."

"So forever," she concluded.

"Thereabouts," I agreed, reaching the porch before Frankie could make a door out of a window. "I promised Ellis I'd obey the law when I investigate," I said, rattling the brass knob. The thing felt like it would come off in my hand.

But it didn't.

It was locked.

"Break it off and toss it through the window," Frankie ordered. "Or just kick down the door. Dry rot is not your fault."

Didi leaned through the window to get a look inside. "I think it's sweet you keep your word, Verity."

"Sweet?" Frankie dropped his head back. "I'm surrounded by amateurs. Windows were invented for a reason, and that reason was crime."

"I'll keep that in mind," I said, hopping off the porch to find a servants' entrance. As we rounded the corner, I noticed something odd. While vines choked the front of the house, this side had a clear path.

The door hung loose on rusted hinges. I eased it open.

"Where's the style? The panache? The property damage?" Frankie groused as I clicked on my flashlight. Dust and cobwebs draped the corners like tattered lace.

"Let's get to the tower," I said, keeping my voice down. Fresh footprints marked the dust ahead. Large ones. Someone had been here recently.

I hoped they weren't here now.

I stepped inside the prints, concealing my movements. And my presence.

Didi paused at the servants' stairs. "The only way to go is up."

"Agreed." That was where the footprints ended.

The narrow staircase wound up through the house in tight spirals, each step groaning under my weight.

Past empty halls with shadowed bedrooms.

Past a crumbling ballroom.

Past faded portraits.

The stairs ended at the servants' quarters.

"Follow me," Frankie said, passing through the stained-glass window overlooking the widow's walk. The glass showed a crow in flight, its head and wings forming an arrow toward the tower.

I took the French doors next to it, noticing how easily they opened despite decades of neglect.

I cut my flashlight. No sense drawing attention.

The evening air bit through my sundress and sent goosebumps up my arms.

"There it is," Didi urged, leading us toward the tower.

The iron railing swayed beneath my grip as we inched along the path. Thirty feet below, the river churned black against the cliffs. Wind howled up from the river, whipping my hair across my face.

"Look." Frankie's voice barely carried over the rushing water. He pointed to the tower window, where a dark shape crossed the yellow light, too tall and too thin to be human.

"I don't like it," Didi said as I opened the tower door.

The steps were so narrow we had to go single file. "I'll go first."

"Do I have to go at all?" Frankie shuddered.

He wasn't fond of hauntings.

"Do it for the speakeasy," I said, venturing inside.

"This had better be magic booze," he said, sticking close.

Didi brought up the rear. "Now I wonder if we should avoid whoever's luring us up to a decrepit tower in the dark."

"For once, I'm with your grandma," Frankie muttered.

"It's our best shot at finding the speakeasy," I said, bare shoulders brushing the walls. "Besides, we've come too far to turn back now."

The stairs ended at a door. Yellow light spilled beneath it.

"She never learns," Frankie said to Didi as I pushed it open.

The tower room glowed ghostly gray, with windows on all sides looking down on the river valley and on the woodland beyond. Moonlight filtered through warped glass, casting strange shadows.

A large oak desk dominated the space in both my world and the ghostly realm. Leather-bound books secured the curled edges of a hand-drawn map. Behind the desk, an oil lamp burned steadily in both realms, its flame reflected in the dark glass.

"Hello?" Didi called.

I saw no ghost. No person. The flickering lamp was the only sign anyone had been here.

The last living visitor certainly hadn't disturbed much.

It troubled me that anyone would visit this place.

"Why lead us up here if nobody's here?" Frankie asked, making a stiff survey of the room.

I moved to the desk, studying the river map. It detailed the bend where we were, downstream to the Jackson tributary.

"Verity." Didi's voice sharpened. "Come look at this."

I stepped over an art deco mosaic where geometric patterns flowed from the center like ripples on a river, all in deep blues and silvers.

Didi hovered by a section of curved wall behind the lamp, running a hand along the wainscoting. "See how the pattern changes? These panels are birch, but this section's oak. And the molding doesn't match. No self-respecting Southerner would allow that."

Frankie shoved his hands into the pockets of his jeans. "You, of all people, shouldn't be giving decorating tips."

"I think she's onto something." I pressed the mismatched section. It clicked. "Someone altered this room."

The panel swung inward, revealing a brass lever.

"That looks like trouble," Frankie muttered.

"Then you should love it," I said, pulling it.

Gears ground beneath us. The mosaic separated into concentric rings, rotating and descending into stairs.

"Amazing," I gasped. The pattern had hidden the seams perfectly.

"I've never seen anything like it," Didi breathed.

"Now this is a speakeasy," Frankie said, bouncing on his toes. "Quick. Give me cash."

A wad appeared in his hand. "Yes!" he hissed, descending straight through the floor.

"I did it!" Didi smiled and clapped.

We had bigger fish to fry.

My flashlight revealed little beyond the spiral. But the mosaic steps felt solid enough. I followed Frankie down.

Below stood an elevator cage wrapped in antique wood with ornate iron doors guarding the chamber. Faded red silk wallpaper lined the interior in my world. It glowed gray in his. Ghostly gas lamps flickered to life as we approached.

Frankie stiffened. "It feels like a trap."

"Or an opportunity," I said as the ghostly door slid open on its own.

Speakeasies liked paying customers. He had cash. And I needed to save Grandma Rose.

He retreated into the wall. "I've set up enough ambushes to know one. When people want you somewhere, it's time to run."

And when anyone locked him out, he had to break in.

Only the world didn't always operate according to the Law of Frankie.

"Think how you'll brag about finding the white whale of speakeasies." I pulled the physical door open, rust flaking like snow. A cable overhead creaked ominously.

Frankie looked like I'd asked him to walk the plank. "There'd better be dancing girls. And crystal champagne fountains. And tigers on diamond leashes."

"You never know," I said, not one to dash his hopes.

I stepped inside and grabbed the railing as the cage swayed. The floorboards groaned under my feet, and I tried not to think about water damage, termites, or how many decades it had been since anyone had inspected this death trap.

"I want caviar on gold plates served by men in top hats," Frankie said in a clipped voice as he slid in next to me. "A room where it rains money. Everyone drinking brandy from Ming vases."

"Why stop there?" I asked. "Maybe they've trained monkeys to serve drinks while riding tiny motorcycles."

"Now you're talking," Frankie said, rubbing his hands.

Stranger things had happened.

Usually to me.

A brass button gleamed in the ghostly light with a swirling crow's head etched on its surface.

I pressed it, praying the cables would hold.

The elevator shuddered to life with a groan that seemed to come from the earth itself. Metal shrieked against metal. "So far, so good," I said, trying to sound more confident than I felt as Didi joined us.

"It is unique," she managed.

Frankie kept quiet.

We descended past rotting wooden walls, their boards warped and stained. Then stone replaced wood—rough granite like the river cliffs.

This was it. "When Fingers McGee made the safe, he made it to withstand rock walls."

We were close. I could feel it.

The temperature dropped with every floor until the elevator shuddered to a stop.

I pried open the door and stepped into what must have been

the height of Jazz Age luxury. Tattered peacock-patterned velvet clung to the walls, and a broken chandelier dripped its guts onto cracked marble. On the ghostly side, everything gleamed new—pristine velvet, sparkling crystal, and polished stone.

At the end of the hall stood a door that made Frankie whistle. In my world, weathered mahogany bore a carved crow, with tarnished brass letters spelling *The Crow's Nest*. In his realm, it glowed gray and perfect while hot jazz blasted through—trumpets wailing, drums pounding, and a piano playing hard.

We did it.

We'd found it.

"What do you think?" I asked the gangster, who'd slipped into wiseguy mode the second he'd passed through the elevator doors.

"Stick with me," he said, leading the way.

"I suppose he has done this before," Didi said, hanging back with me.

"You have no idea," I told her.

Frankie whipped off his grandpa sweater, tossed it on the floor, and knocked three times.

The slider scraped open. Dark eyes peered out.

"Password?" The voice was dusty.

Frankie stiffened.

Didi and I exchanged looks.

"Crow—" I began.

The eyes narrowed. "No password, no entry."

The slider slammed shut.

Chapter Eighteen

"Gah!" A flame shot from Frankie's head, the brief flash illuminating the crow etched on the locked speakeasy door. "I almost had us inside, and you jacked it up."

"Your head," I gasped.

He frowned. "What about my—" His hand found the flame. "This is your fault, too!"

For once, he was right. I felt a twinge of guilt. The poor ghost had been burning since he'd rescued me from the library fire. I hadn't meant to set him off.

In any case, the solution to our newest problem was clear. "You're a ghost. Just walk through the door."

He looked at me like I had bees in my brain. "I don't want to get shot."

Please. "They'd hardly fire on you for bypassing the guard."

"They'd shoot me for wearing this sweater," Frankie said, shrugging it off and tossing it onto the floor again.

Then we needed a new plan.

A bullet wouldn't kill him. Not when he was already dead. But it would knock him out cold and keep him from searching for the safe.

"How about this?" Didi stepped between us. "Verity and I

will hide around the corner. You wait five minutes to get your sweater back—"

"It's not my sweater," he ground out.

"Ditch the cigarette and smoke the pipe instead," Didi added.

"Maybe I do want them to shoot me," he growled.

Didi pressed on. "You'll look like a different man, and then you'll give them the password."

He pointed his smoke at her. "Love the disguise and the lying. The only trouble is I don't know the password."

She gaped. "Then what was the fit for? You said you could get us in."

He stamped out his flaming head and smoothed his hair. "Watch and learn." He knocked three times, same as he had before.

This time, the slider didn't budge.

"Argh!" Frankie kicked the door, leaving a scuff in his realm and a shower of sparks in his wake.

That was helpful.

"We're not getting in without a password," Didi said.

Which might mean we weren't getting in, period.

"Lookie here." The gangster beckoned us from the door. "I don't need a password. I just need to get 'em to open the slider again." He dug past the cigarettes in the pocket of his shirt and pulled out a ghostly silver lighter. "I found this on the desk upstairs."

"Swiped it," Grandma corrected.

"I didn't see either one of you bothering to case the joint." He turned the lighter over to show the engraving. *To Mayor Rich Chrismer, President of the Anti-Saloon League, Happy New Year 1919.* "Isn't it a beaut?" He grinned. "Nothing opens a door faster than threatening to tell Sugarland their honorable mayor is boozing it up at a secret speakeasy."

Sugarland did love a good scandal.

"But you didn't find it on him," I said. "Anyone can engrave a lighter."

Frankie spread his hands. "Hey, I agree. Would've been nice to steal it man-to-man. But up-close crime isn't always necessary when it comes to threatening people."

"He's right." Didi looked far too happy about it.

Whose side was she on?

She touched her chin, thinking. "The lighter alone would start tongues wagging. Tennessee passed prohibition in 1909. Mayors like Chrismer were heroes for enforcing it."

"And hunting people like me," Frankie smirked, pocketing his prize.

But as usual, he hadn't thought it through. "We can't prove he's inside unless we get past the door."

"Not with you guessing at passwords," he groused.

Unless...

I faced the gray-glowing door, screwed up my courage, and knocked. The cold shock of the other world hit my gut, but I knocked a second time. A third.

Frankie lit a cigarette with the mayor's lighter. "If they ignored me, they'll ignore you."

Oh, ye of little faith. "I'm hoping my touch makes the door vanish on the ghostly plane."

I'd still be locked out in my world, along with the key, but at least Frankie and Grandma could look around.

"Hate to break it to you," Frankie said, exhaling smoke. "They'd snap it right back with all the power in there. But I'd love to see their faces first."

"You don't know that." I'd never zapped a ghostly door before.

"Think about it." He dragged hard on his cigarette. "Prohibition is in full swing in Tennessee. Security is everything." Smoke trailed from his nose. "Especially for the swells who hang out at the uber-secret speakeasy." He fiddled with the stolen lighter. "My gang's getting shot up and arrested doing the dirty work. Meanwhile, they're making booze illegal and partying in secret." He took another drag. "The only good news is they've got a vault in there."

"It makes sense," I admitted. And he appeared to be right about the door, too. It hadn't so much as flickered.

"I am a brilliant criminal mind." Frankie twirled the lighter between his fingers like a magician with a coin.

I turned to Didi. "If this place is stuck in 1919, like the suffragettes in the cave, like Hope at the jail—"

"It's all connected," she said low under her breath.

It sure looked that way.

Frankie ashed his smoke. "I'm betting whatever is in that safe is from 1919 too." He glared at the door.

Nothing riled Frankie more than a locked door, vault, or armored car.

"Maybe there's another way in," I said.

It was a speakeasy. It had to have a back door.

"All we know is there's a vault embedded in rock. Some-where." Didi planted her hands on her hips. "Come on. Let's check the rest of the basement."

Frankie crushed out his cigarette. "You know how I feel about poking around in dark corners."

"It's the best way to find something," I said, leading the way.

Ghostly gas lights flickered on both sides, casting dancing shadows. Didi drew up beside me.

Frankie slinked behind.

The hallway curved right. Water stains marked the ceiling, warping the paneling below. The deeper we went, the stronger the musty smell grew—like river mud and old wood.

"Hold up," Frankie ordered.

"What?" I froze.

"You hear that?"

A faint splash echoed ahead.

"The river's close," Didi said low under her breath.

We crept forward until the hall turned a corner and dead-ended.

"Look." Didi traced the wall, catching on something in the shadows.

I shone my light. A narrow passage broke left. Moldy carpeting gave way to a natural stone tunnel. My light caught rusty tracks embedded in the floor.

Weird.

The tracks disappeared into the darkness, but fresh scrape marks scored the dirt. Someone from my world had been here recently.

"Let's check it out," I whispered.

I wished I'd told Ellis where we were headed. Or left a message with Melody. If we ran into someone dangerous down here, I could vanish without a trace.

Frankie glanced toward the Crow's Nest. "We need less exploring, more breaking and entering."

"If we're lucky, we'll do both," Didi said.

What the what?

I let it go. For now.

I led the way down the stone corridor barely wide enough for two. The walls pressed closer with each step. Green-black lichens dotted the ceiling like constellations. The tracks were swallowed under decades of mud as the passage sloped down, down, down.

Cool air brushed my face, carrying the scent of the river.

Twenty steps later, the passage opened onto a sand and pebble beach. The sight stopped me cold.

A covered dock rose from the darkness, glowing ghostly gray. Dark water lapped at weathered planks, sheltered by a canvas, draped canopy. I drew closer, squinting to see past the ghostly illusion to my side of the veil, where rotted beams crisscrossed overhead like ancient bones. Splintered posts jutted from warped wood, and rusted iron cleats clung where boats once moored.

The river slid past like black silk, its surface broken by moonlit ripples. Cypress trees hunched on the far bank, their branches draping into the water, swaying with the current.

Frankie whistled low. "Now this is a beaut." He tested the

boards with his shoe. "False panels for hiding weapons." He stroked a ghostly chain hanging from the canopy. "Strong pulley system for heavy loads." His attention locked on an iron-banded cart frozen at the end of the track. "A rail system to move it all quick and quiet." His voice held a cathedral-like reverence. "Whoever built this, I'd love to buy 'em a drink."

"If they'd let you in the speakeasy," Didi said.

He scowled at her. "Don't rub it in."

Meanwhile, I puzzled over the setup. An illegal speakeasy with a dock. The river made it impossible to hide.

The Hartleys ran a shipping business in my day and age. Their ancestors, the Crowes, might have owned a legitimate distribution operation. But something felt wrong.

I left the dock and followed the tracks toward the tunnel.

The underground hall and narrow passage seemed built for secrecy, not commerce. Why would the Crowes run shipping from their private home? Right beside a speakeasy?

Then I spotted it. A second set of tracks split from the main line, curving along the bank. They glowed gray through generations of sand and rock.

I followed them to a dark cut in the limestone. The rock face swallowed the tracks whole.

"Guys!" I called. "Over here."

At the dock, Frankie wrestled with a ghostly harpoon he'd pried from a hidden panel. Didi watched, arms crossed.

"Hey," he grunted, nearly dropping it, "it's not my boat sinker, it's theirs."

"Yet you can't leave it alone." She tossed up her hands.

Welcome to my world.

I turned from them. Water dripped ahead, each splash echoing off stone. My flashlight caught rotted lumber scattered across the ground.

Three steps in, I found what remained of a wooden door. Time had eaten most of it, leaving rusty hinges clinging to the frame. But in the spirit world, the ghostly door stood pristine, as solid as the day it was hung.

Frankie arrived first. "Nice work, kid." He kicked the door open. "What?" he asked when I eyed his harpoon.

A storage chamber opened before us, carved into the limestone. Water pooled in the low spots, reflecting my light off rough-hewn walls.

I swept my beam across the rock, hoping the safe would be here instead of in the speakeasy. Natural hollows and crevices pockmarked the walls, but nothing manmade. No metal door, no combination lock.

Near the entrance, chisel marks scored a smooth section. My heart leapt—but no, just bare rock.

I stepped past stacks of ghostly gray crates clustered at the center of the chamber.

"There has to be a back entrance to the speakeasy," I said, following the curve of the walls. They narrowed toward the rear, ending in solid rock. No hidden passages, no disguised doors.

Frankie's harpoon clattered to the rocks. He didn't notice. "Slap me on the back and shoot me in the foot." His jaw went slack as he stared at the crates.

"What is it?" Didi asked from the entrance.

I wasn't sure.

But when I looked closely, it became clear. The ghostly crates each bore the same mark—a lightning bug burned into the wood.

Frankie dropped to his knees before a tall stack, his eyes going misty. "Firefly Moonshine. Cases and cases of it." He traced the brand like it was written in gold. "This is legendary shine. I haven't seen it since prohibition."

"What's so legendary?" I studied a bottle atop one case. Thick glass, old-fashioned, with a hand-dipped wax seal.

"It's smooth. Tasty. And one sip will set your hair on fire." He shot me a look. "In a good way." He flicked ghostly wax everywhere, prying at the seal. "This is the Dom Perignon of moonshine." The cork popped, echoing off the stone walls. He took a long swig. "Ahhh…" His hips wiggled.

Smoke curled from his body as his knees buckled. He plopped onto a crate, grinning. "We called this angel's milk."

"Did you make it?" It seemed unlikely. Frankie's idea of good moonshine involved a dirty sock as a filter.

"We claimed we did. The boss wanted it that way," he said, passing the bottle to Didi. "Truth was, we had an in with a guy. His alias was H. Artley. I never actually saw him. He liked skulking in the dark."

I fought the urge to bang my head against a rock. "Hartley? As in the owner of this house and the Crow's Nest?"

"Well, I'll be danged." Frankie took the bottle back from Didi, who fanned herself after a hearty swig. "Artley disappeared in 1919, and the recipe went with him. My gang tried cracking the code for years." Another swig made his hair stand up. "We never figured out the secret."

"Frankie…" Didi touched her shoulders, arms, and head, wonder spreading across her face. "I don't think I'm on fire anymore."

Frankie shot to his feet, patting himself down. "Holy smokes. You're right."

"Give me another swig." She reached for his bottle. He handed her a fresh one instead.

"I'm glad you're feeling better," I said, watching Didi attack the wax seal. This from the woman who nursed one sherry at Christmastime. "Really. It's a load off my mind." Frankie dabbed moonshine behind his ears. "But let's not start our own speakeasy."

"It's medicinal," he said, stuffing a second bottle in his shirt.

"You have good taste in booze." Didi saluted him with her bottle.

Frankly, I'd be willing to bet their newfound health had less to do with the booze and more to do with relaxing, getting out of their heads, getting along for once.

In either case, I was on my own. I turned back to the stone walls. There had to be something I'd missed.

We'd found a dock and a hidden cave, but no safe. And clearly, I'd been wrong about the Crow's Nest having a back door.

Now Grandma had snagged a bottle too. I'd never get them out of here.

"Didi—" I began, hoping to appeal to her sensible nature.

I followed her to the far corner, where moonlight leaked through a crack in the limestone, turning pooled water silver.

"Look," she said as I reached her.

She held up the bottle, tracing the label. A lightning bug soared above a crow perched on a rock.

The crow. The firefly. "What do you think it means?"

She handed me the bottle. "I think it means I know how to get into the speakeasy."

Chapter Nineteen

Drips echoed off limestone.

Frankie stood slack-jawed. "*She* has a plan?"

Didi sidestepped a puddle. "Yours didn't work."

"Oh, it'll work." Frankie pulled out the mayor's lighter, silver glinting in the beam of my flashlight. "Here's what we do—" He wedged another bottle into his waistband.

"Did he just say 'we'?" Didi drew up beside me. "He's growing."

"Don't point it out."

It would only discourage him.

Frankie was on a roll as we headed for the beach. His old-man sweater was back. Moonshine bottles clinked in his pants. But he didn't care. "We'll con our way into the speakeasy, find the vault, and crack whatever secret the suffragettes are guarding." He spun around, walking backward in the sand, nearly pitching into the river. "We'll use it to track down those boxes of loot Didi handed to the library."

"It was an honest mistake," I reminded him.

She felt bad enough.

"An honest mistake is why I'm wearing old-man underwear." Frankie snagged a ghostly pistol from the haunted dock. "But we'll fix this. Get it all back, preserve your family legacy." He pointed the butt at Didi.

"It's not so easy," she warned. "I tried."

"I'll succeed." He stuffed the pistol in with the bottles.

How did he have room?

"We'll make things right," he said, pocketing the lighter as he backed toward the tunnel. "We'll get Rose out of poltergeist mode and happy so she can go into the light with you." He jabbed at Didi. "Where you'll stay."

"Let's not go overboard." My chest tightened. Didi could be happy living with me. Sure, life had changed with Grandma around, but we had so much left to share. I loved having her here.

Frankie flashed us a smile before ducking into the tunnel. "Once Didi's in the light, I get my shed back. My suit, my cigarettes, my afterlife." His voice bounced off the walls. "Then I'll corner Mayor Chrismer with the lighter and bribe my way into an eternity of partying. It'll be me and the swells at the Crow's Nest. Suds can join me on Tuesdays."

He had it all figured out.

"You haven't even seen what it's like in there," I said, tripping on a rusty track.

He clapped his hands together. "Tigers on leashes!"

"Don't get your hopes up," Didi warned.

"I take it you've never seen a tiger on a leash." Frankie snorted.

I'd bet he hadn't, either.

"Just don't go gaga and embarrass me." He slicked his hair and reached to straighten his tie, realizing too late he wasn't wearing one anymore. "The life of a gangster can be quite glamorous."

"Right." I remembered the rusty still in my backyard.

The one Didi had torched.

"Is he always this delusional?" she whispered.

"We haven't even hit the speakeasy yet."

"I'm warning you now." Didi caught up to him as he entered the hallway. "It might not be all sunshine and roses. If this haunting holds true, the party ghosts will be stuck in 1919."

"It was a good year." Frankie adjusted his bottle-laden pants.

"It could get awkward." My flashlight traced moldy carpet. "You were alive then."

We'd managed the workhouse. The cave under my house, too, although Frankie wasn't there.

But what would happen when a dead Frankie met ghosts who knew living Frankie?

At best, it would be jarring. At worst? Well, I wasn't suggesting a *Back to the Future*–level catastrophe, but still. We were in uncharted territory.

As usual, Frankie couldn't care less.

He led the way. "It's not like I'm going to run into myself and explode," he said, proving my point. "This is a moment in time I wasn't invited to. Now I am." He glided down the hall, arms spread. "1919 me wants a seat at the table. 1919 me wants to swing from the chandeliers. Drink champagne from a silver fountain with mermaids spitting bourbon from their mouths."

"That's oddly specific," Didi said.

"It's my dream," Frankie countered.

If you can't fight 'em... "Sounds great. As long as we find the vault, use the key, and solve the mystery."

"If we get in," Didi hedged, trailing behind.

Frankie stopped, his bottles clinking like windchimes. "You said you had a plan."

She fiddled with her earlobe. "More like a hunch."

"I believe in you," I said, slowing to keep pace with her.

Frankie's head dropped back, and his eyes fixed on the ceiling like it might offer him salvation. "It was bad enough when there was just one of you."

"Trust me," Didi said as we reached the speakeasy door.

Frankie drummed his thigh. "This'd better work," he muttered as she knocked. Once. Twice. Three times.

The slider stayed shut.

"*That* was your plan?" His voice cracked. "That's it." He fumbled in his pocket. "I'm smoking my last cigarette."

"Hold on." She cupped her hands against the slider. "Hope burns bright."

We held our breath. The words hung in the stale air. I didn't know what she was doing, but I trusted her. I believed in her.

It would work.

It had to work.

"And?" Frankie prodded.

Nothing.

The slider might as well have been welded shut.

Water dripped in the darkness.

"That's it?" Frankie drew his last cigarette. "The master plan?" He tucked it under his lip. "We should have—"

Metal ground against metal, and the slider scraped open. Dark eyes peered through, shadowed by thick brows. Then the door creaked wide, revealing a bruiser in a black tux.

Frankie's cigarette fell from his lip.

The door guard stared us down. A fresh scar ran from jaw to collar. His gaze raked us, lingering on Frankie's sweater.

"Password checks out," said a thin guard behind him, spinning a coin through his knuckles. "Not our usual crowd, but..."

"Somebody wants 'em in here." The bruiser stepped aside.

"Yeeeees!" Frankie snatched up his cigarette and jammed it in his pocket. He yanked off his sweater and flung it down. "Watch and learn, amateurs."

He strode into cigarette smoke and jazz with pure joy on his face. The speakeasy sprawled before us, glittering and wild.

A mahogany bar stretched down the left wall, with white-jacketed bartenders spinning bottles behind their backs and catching them blind before pouring deep. On the opposite side, on a stage draped in gold tinsel, a jazz band wailed while a woman wearing strategic feathers swung from a perch in a giant birdcage suspended between crystal chandeliers.

The dance floor churned with flappers and suits. "Look," I choked out. "Tiger on a leash!"

A real, living tiger. Well, a dead one, glowing gray. But still! A blonde in sequins led it on a glittering leash like an oversized housecat.

Frankie spun in place, bottles clinking. "I told you!"

Okay, this was a party.

"Is this really what they did in 1919?" I asked, trying to take it all in.

"Not even close." Frankie's hips bopped. "See Tommy Bananas over there? He was in prison then. And this song? Fats Waller didn't come out with 'Honeysuckle Rose' until 1929. This is anybody and everybody from any time who can find a good party." He beamed. "And now, it's me!"

"Is that the mayor's wife on the bar?" Didi gasped. "Dancing the Charleston?"

"It is." I felt my jaw fall. She had more clothes on in the formal photos hung at city hall, but it was her all right.

"Chrismer's here?" Frankie yanked the bent cigarette out of his pocket and slicked his hair. "You keep her busy while I find him."

He zipped into the thick of it, not even noticing the peacock drinking gin from a crystal bowl.

I nodded to the man pouring Tanqueray for his bird as I scanned the place. "Where do you think they'd keep the safe?"

Didi's gaze flicked over the crowd. "Behind the bar? Or there's got to be a manager's office."

"I'll go left; you go right."

"Deal."

"Wait." I had to know. "How did you get the password?"

I'd been with her this entire time. She hadn't seen anything I hadn't.

She dodged a flapper racing past with a martini in each hand, her feather boa flying. "The Firefly logo on the crates and moonshine bottles. You didn't catch it?"

"I saw it." The firefly with its wings spread above the crow.

"In your attic," she said, "on the door frame. There's the same firefly, hand drawn. Underneath, it says *Hope Burns Bright*."

I froze. I'd seen that wobbly pencil sketch. "I thought a kid did it." We'd always had fireflies in the attic. "What if it also has something to do with the vault? Or with Grandma Rose?"

"Let's find out."

We split and went our separate directions, with me weaving through the tables, edging toward the bar. I'd make a circuit around the stone walls on the outside, keeping an eye peeled for the vault. Didi would do the same, and we'd meet in the middle.

The bartender lined up Firefly shots like dominoes. Men in tailored suits and women dripping pearls cheered as—match, flame, whoosh—he set the outlaw liquor on fire.

Nobody noticed me edge behind the bar.

I hugged the rock wall, searching. I saw crystal glasses, imported bottles, and enough Firefly to drown a horse.

But no vault.

I escaped the bar and kept to the wall.

At the back, three society women lounged on crushed-velvet couches, passing an ornate hookah pipe between them.

"Ladies." I nodded and kept moving.

Smoke curled toward the limestone ceiling.

A little way farther, a man in a silk top hat balanced a tray of glistening figs in one hand while his pet monkey, in a matching miniature hat, plucked treats from his fingers.

"Reminds me of my skunk," I said, one pet-owner to another.

The monkey tipped its tiny hat.

Lucy would approve.

I rounded the corner toward the stage.

A singer strutted to the footlights in an explosion of feathers and sequins, her voice honey-smooth over jazz. While the crowd pressed forward, I crept up the side stairs.

No one noticed as I ducked behind the tinsel curtain.

The backstage area was barely bigger than my bedroom,

crammed with steamer trunks and costume racks glowing ghostly gray. Feather boas and beaded dresses hung from hooks drilled into the limestone walls.

I squinted past the ghostly illusion. On my side of the veil, the room lay bare except for a section in the wall covered in wood paneling painted with black crows flying over a dark river. Half-rotted and ready to collapse at the center, the pair of panels made the tight space feel even more claustrophobic.

It was a strange decorating choice.

I squeezed past a tower of ghostly hat boxes for a closer look. I'd have given them a dress rack if anything.

Pure white caught my eye—a ghostly silk scarf, its edge trapped in the seam where the two panels met.

I hesitated to tug it free. Not if I could avoid the shock. Instead, I pressed both hands to the left panel and pushed.

It shifted.

I pushed harder. The wall rotated with a click, retreating under my hands.

"Heavens." My light revealed a staircase vanishing up into the darkness. A faint scrape of stone echoed from above, so faint I might have imagined it.

I had a feeling I'd just found the back door.

Didi needed to see this. And Frankie.

I hurried to the side of the stage and peeked out the curtain. The party was in full swing. I searched, but there was no sign of Grandma. She was probably skulking in the shadows. Frankie was easy to spot, sprawled on a velvet settee, wearing a society matron's tiara while two flappers and a minister poured him a champagne waterfall *Flashdance* style.

It looked like I was on a solo mission. Again. I glanced at Frankie holding court from his velvet throne. He'd be useless for the next hour at least. And Didi, well, she might tell me to wait, be careful, think it through.

But we were so close.

I hurried back to the secret passage. With one last glance

behind me, I slipped inside. The panel closed with a sharp click that felt unnervingly final.

The darkness pressed in, heavy and quiet.

It would have been nice to at least tell Didi where I was, but there was no help for it now. Ellis didn't even know I'd come to the abandoned house. Alone.

Or that I was underneath it now.

It wasn't as if Didi or Frankie could tell him if something happened. The thought settled like ice in my stomach, but I pushed it away. I was fine. I'd be careful.

Besides, how many chances would I get to unlock the suffragettes' secrets?

I crept up the stairs, dust tickling my nose. My light caught cobwebs shivering between the hollowed limestone walls.

The stairs ended at a wooden door outlined in a faint silvery light in my realm. On the ghostly side, it stood open.

Curious.

Decades of river air had eaten the finish off the brass handle. I turned it slowly, dreading who might be inside.

Persian rugs and leather chairs glowed gray. A ghostly bar near the desk was stocked with Firefly Moonshine. I scanned the room for an occupant. A narrow slit window had been carved into a natural gap in the rock. It overlooked the river, shielded by a rock overhang. Perfect for watching the river undetected.

I didn't see any ghosts.

Yet.

I glanced behind me.

In my world, empty moonshine bottles scattered across the bare rock floor like bowling pins.

Fresh footprints in the dust made my heart stutter. Someone had been here recently. My grip tightened on my Maglite. The tracks led to a massive desk at the far end. And there—in a porcelain frame—was Grandma Rose, young and fierce, staring out like a challenge. In this world and the ghostly one.

Behind the desk, a safe stood waist-high in the wall.

I'd found it! I hoped. This had to be it.

It had a slit at the top and two keyholes, like a bank safe-deposit box. An ancient key protruded from the left lock. The safe was shut tight in both realms.

I gave one last glance behind me before drawing the key from my pocket.

With shaking hands, I slid it into the lock on the right. It clicked home.

A perfect fit.

I wished Didi could see this.

The metal was cold against my skin, the lock stiff as I turned the key.

A chill crept up my spine. The temperature plunged so fast my next breath came out in a cloud. The shadows in the corners of the room deepened. Every instinct screamed at me to run.

But I was so close.

"Now what do we have here?" The words rolled like thunder, each syllable dripping quiet menace. Every muscle in my body seized, my hand frozen on the key.

"Nothing." I yanked the key and spun to face a ghost who filled the doorway. His charcoal pinstripe suit stretched tight across broad shoulders, a diamond tiepin winking at his throat. He cracked his knuckles, his scars rippling white. His eyes were chips of ice set in a granite face with deep lines etched from nose to jaw. A thin scar traced his upper lip, twisting it into a permanent sneer.

"This is a private office, little mouse." His voice was steel wrapped in silk. Each step he took made the shadows retreat and my spine lock up. "Want to tell me what you're doing here?"

Chapter Twenty

The cold hit my lungs like knives. My heart hammered so hard I felt it in my teeth.

I clambered to my feet. Sweat slicked my skin. "I can explain," I managed, my voice cracking only a little. Okay, a lot. "I realize it looks bad to break into your office and open your safe and—"

He skirted the desk and came straight for me.

The temperature dropped another ten degrees.

I forced a smile and used every scrap of courage to hold my ground. "My name is Verity Long, and this"—I held up the key like a shield—"was Rose Landry Long's."

He flinched like I'd struck him. "Don't say that name."

Oh boy.

"I'm on a mission. For good." I hoped. "For the suffragettes." That much I knew. "I'm not usually this criminally adjacent, I promise."

He was close enough now that I could see the exact moment his eyes narrowed, the scar pulling his lip from a sneer to a snarl.

But he hadn't attacked me, so I wasn't stopping.

"I'm trying to locate something for her. For them," I corrected.

Goosebumps skittered across my arms, my neck, as he leaned

close enough to touch. "And what exactly do I have that you want?"

My smile warbled, stuck. "Shall we find out?" My voice squeaked. "Together?"

The safe echoed with a boom that made my heart jump and my world shake. Frost crystallized across the metal.

He lunged.

I dove under the desk. *Ohnoohnoohno.*

He grabbed for my foot. I felt the cold swipe as I scrambled out the other side, leapt up, and bolted for the door. For freedom.

It slammed shut inches from my face.

I yanked on the handle, the ghostly touch searing my hands.

It didn't budge.

He chuckled under his breath. This was bad. Very, very bad. I felt him draw near. I could recover. Maybe. I wheeled and slammed my back against the door. The chill of it seeped through my dress, into my bones.

"Wait." The key dug into my palm. "Please—"

I had to think of something, anything to make him stop. Listen.

Or at least let me run.

He drew a silver revolver from his coat, the metal gleaming.

"Don't bother," I bluffed. "I'm alive."

"I know what you are." He raised it with practiced ease, aiming straight at my heart. "Thief."

"I'm not a thief!" The words burst out. "I'm with the suffragettes. Eleanor Blackwell and Hope, who's in jail. And Liberty." I forgot her last name. "And Rose Landry Long, who is my kin, and I love her and—"

"Lies." He pressed the barrel against my chest. The touch of the ghostly object was like ice through my veins, invasive and wrong. It would disappear for touching me, but not fast enough to save me.

I clung to the gold and silver filagree necklace Didi gave me and squeezed my eyes shut.

This was it.

I didn't know how to stop it.

His cold, wet fingers brushed my necklace. The touch made me jump, made my skin crawl.

"This belonged to Rose." His voice changed, grew tender.

I forced myself to look straight into his gray, glowing eyes. "It belongs to me now."

His outstretched hand hovered over my neck.

His face was all harsh angles, the scar slashing downward as he frowned. "She left it to her daughter."

I nodded. "Ida Jane Butler Long." I scooted away as much as I dared. "Who left it to her daughter, Delia Franklin Long. Who left it to me." My cold breath hung between us.

"Rose said it was still in the family." He stood straight, studying me with new intensity.

"You're dead," I told him. It sounded rude, but he needed to know.

The corner of his mouth ticked up. "I'm aware."

"Good. I'm Rose's great-great-granddaughter." I tilted my head, like Rose's picture in the hall.

If it worked, he didn't let on. "She's never mentioned you."

Okay, that hurt. "I haven't run into her. Much," I corrected, recalling the poltergeist.

But surely, she hadn't been herself.

"You know her well," I said as I inched off that awful, cold door.

"We've run into each other from time to time."

"Her picture is on your desk."

The ghost drew back his shoulders. "Her key was given away. Lost." He gestured with the muzzle of his gun. "Where did you find it?"

"In Rose's suffragette sash at the library." I straightened my spine, found my courage. "I'm trying to reclaim what my grandmother accidentally gave away."

"Didi." The name fell from his lips with a sneer.

My breath caught. "You know what happened." I ignored his narrowed eyes and pressed on. "That's what I'm doing now. I'm trying to make it right. For Rose."

He slammed his gun back into his side holster. "There's not much time for that."

"I know. I saw." The words tumbled out. "She's turning poltergeist." It was scary and terrible and quite possibly permanent if we didn't hurry. "But she's not gone yet. We can save her."

He stared at me.

"I know how," I said, doubling down. "I just need to get into that safe."

His gaze flicked over me. "Nice try."

"I'm not lying," I insisted. "I'm Rose's great-great-granddaughter."

His eyes swept over me. "That, I believe."

Thank heavens.

I surged. "Then believe this. Whatever she left in your safe was important. She was furious with Didi for giving away the key. Now someone's actively after her history. She's going mad right now, thinking her legacy, the legacy of the suffragettes in Sugarland, might be gone, compromised."

He scoffed, but I caught something else. Interest? He flicked a hand toward the safe. "You don't even know what's in there."

I lifted my chin. "That's true." I'd admit it. Honesty was all I had left. "But I know this. Rose needs what is in that safe. I need to find it so I can understand how to help her, how to make this right. How to save her."

The corner of his mouth twitched. "When you talk like that, you sound exactly like her."

I gasped so hard I nearly choked. "Tell me how you know her."

He ran a hand behind his neck. "I know her from before we died." His expression grew wistful. "She was my fiancé. Still is, I suppose."

That one took me a second. "Er."

"Speechless?" he prodded.

"Are you my grandpa?" I managed.

The boom of his laugh made the windows rattle. "She'd birthed Ida Jane the year before," he managed. "Rose was a widow."

Thank goodness.

"Don't look so relieved," he said dryly.

"I'm not." I brightened.

So much for honesty.

He strolled toward the desk. "Rosie—that's what I called her —was my secret love. Quite unexpected, really, how these things happen. We were in business together, and then it was more than business." He ran a hand along the wood. "But we could never marry." He glanced at me. "She was a proper widow with a cause, and I—" He waved a hand. "I'm a smuggler. A criminal. A thief," he added with a meaningful look at me.

"I'm not—"

"You say it like there's something wrong with it," he said, sitting on the desk.

Now he was starting to sound like Frankie.

He shrugged a shoulder. "I had the contacts she needed. I was the one who kept bailing her out of jail. Through my lawyer, of course."

"Hartley?" I asked.

"You've been asking around."

Just paying attention. "What was he, your cousin or something?"

"A distant relation."

"What kind of contacts did Rose need?" I asked, trying to understand what my upstanding suffragette grandmother would want with a criminal.

He merely smiled.

Seriously? I mean, Frankie came in handy, but I'd never date someone like him.

"How did you help her?" I asked, trying another tack.

He lost the smile. "Someone was targeting suffragettes. I did what it took to keep her safe."

"She lived—" I began.

"Longer than I did," he finished.

A sharer he was not.

I strolled toward where he sat on the desk. "So, can I see what's in the safe?"

He watched me carefully. "Be my guest." He'd said it casually.

The man was anything but.

I skirted around him, around the desk to where the footprints, along with mine, left deep impressions in the dust. There were two identical sets, and large ones at that. Made by men's shoes, size eleven or twelve at least. The tread pattern was distinctive, a chevron design. Whoever had made the prints had been here very recently, based on how clean the edges still were.

This was bad.

I felt the ghost's eyes on me, but he didn't stop me. Not even when I knelt and inserted Rose's key into the lock.

I hated to turn my back on him, but I didn't have a choice.

The metal was ice cold as I turned it.

But the safe refused to open.

Maybe I had to turn both keys.

The key in the lock next to mine was the same size, filigreed, with a crow symbol instead of the star and vines.

"Is this one yours?" I asked the ghost.

His eyes narrowed. "It was. Rose kept it after I died. The thief must have stolen it from her possessions."

"From the library." My heart lurched so hard my head went light. "I'm not the only one tracking Rose."

"You're not," he said plainly. "He left it when I scared him off."

Oh boy. "Can I use it?"

The ghost nodded slowly.

He didn't need to tell me twice. I pinched a fold of my dress and wrapped it over the handle in case the thief had left fingerprints. Then I twisted both keys. This time, they turned easily.

The safe swung wide.

Stacks of money glowed gray, filling the interior, bundles of hundred, five-hundred, ten-thousand-dollar bills, stacked neat and pristine.

The safe was packed to the gills with cold, hard cash.

"That's it?" My shoulders slumped.

There was that grin again. "Sorry to disappoint."

I squinted hard to see what might be there on my side of the veil.

But in real life, the safe stood empty.

A gaping void.

After all that work.

After nearly getting *shot*.

I plunked my forehead onto the top of the door.

"Are you getting the vapors?" my former assailant asked from above. "If you faint, I can't help you."

Like I wanted to keel over in his arms.

"I'm fine." I kept my head on the door for a second longer, anything rather than face the fact I'd failed.

I'd been sure, so sure I'd find what I needed in there. That was the plan—open the safe, find what Rose had hidden, make things right.

Now?

"May I?" I gestured to an old handkerchief on the desk.

The ghost nodded, and I wrapped the key I'd found before placing it in my left pocket. Rose's key went in my right.

After that? "I'm not sure what to do next," I said, rubbing the indentation in my forehead.

He pressed his lips together. "How about you find the living soul who stole the cash from my safe?"

I dropped my hand. "Did you see what he looked like?"

His lips thinned. "He wore a ski mask. I chased him off. Twice."

"But he got the money."

The safe slammed shut, and I nearly jumped out of my skin.

"But that's all he got," he thundered. "The last thief got even less. I died protecting this safe from Rutledge!"

"Who?" I stammered.

"The snake who stole Hope's key."

He turned away sharply, his shoulders tight. When he faced me again, he wore a steely glare. "The real prize was with Rose." He stalked straight for me, but I held my ground. "She had a safe, a smaller one. A much more valuable one."

I gasped.

"Our thief already knows about it. He was carrying the receipt for the installation."

"How?" But I knew.

Rose's box.

"Oh yes, little miss," he said, stopping inches from me, the icy chill radiating off him, his gray eyes like steel. "If you're as loyal as you say you are, you'll find it."

I would. "Where is it?"

The ghost eased back a fraction. "Number 12 Peach Orchard Lane."

My stomach dropped. "My property."

Of course. She'd need it to be handy. She'd want to watch over it.

But I knew every inch of my property, and I didn't have a safe.

Or did I?

"Tell me where."

He tilted his head. "She never showed me, but I do know it's on her property."

My heart leapt at the thought. Then sank. The person who'd broken into the criminal's safe was most likely the same person who'd set fire to the library. And if they knew about Rose's connection to this place... "I'll do my best, I promise."

I had to find it. Soon. Before the thief ended up at my house.

If he wasn't already there.

"I have to go," I said, stumbling past him, giving him a wide berth.

"I figured you might," he said, watching me skedaddle.

I was halfway to the door when I skidded to a stop. "Wait." I turned. "What's your name?" I couldn't believe I hadn't gotten it.

Where were my manners?

Then again, he'd scared the bejesus out of me.

"Augustus Crowe," he said, standing.

"Augustus," I repeated. "Thank you."

I turned to leave.

"One more thing." He strode toward me, the smuggler's swagger gone. "If you find her"—he stopped halfway—"tell her I miss her."

I nodded and slipped out the door.

Chapter Twenty-One

My headlights did little more than punch holes in the pitch black as I steered down the narrow cliff road, my knuckles white on the wheel.

"The safe is on my property." I still couldn't believe it.

"I can't imagine where." Didi braced herself as I navigated another hairpin turn. "A safe isn't exactly easy to hide."

Between us, we knew every inch of the property. Twice.

"It has to be down in the cave." It was the only place that made sense.

We hadn't exactly searched every inch of Rose's underground lair.

We would now.

I grabbed my cell phone headset and shook out the mass of wires.

"Even I know about earbuds," Frankie drawled from the backseat.

Now wasn't the time.

I plugged in my headset and made the call. "Melody," I said the second she uttered a greeting.

"Hold on," she cut in.

"I just found a key stolen from Rose's archive box. Someone used it to break into a safe at the Crowe mansion. Whoever set the fire in the library took the boxes." It was plain as day. "They cleaned out the Crowe safe—walked away with a pile of cash—but I'm hoping they left fingerprints on the key. I'm going to turn it over to Ellis as evidence."

"Let me take you off speakerphone," she said tightly. She banged around and slammed a door behind her. "I was in the middle of a staff meeting."

Oh no. "With who?"

"With everybody," she hissed. "The bank lent us their big conference room."

My heart sank.

Well, that settled it. "You can't go back into the library. Not until we know who did this."

"They need me." She clipped each word.

"And I just outed us," I said with a wince.

"You were looking out for me," she corrected. She took a deep breath. "If we do have an arsonist, a thief among us, I don't have a choice. I can't leave." Before I could insist, she added, "You wouldn't."

"But—" I hated when she was right.

"I'll call Alec," she said. "He's getting off soon. He'll stay with me."

"That will have to do." I knew better than to argue. And Alec Duranja had come in handy a time or two.

"Gotta go."

"Be careful." I'd put her in danger. We both knew it.

"Always," she said.

And then she was gone.

I looked to Didi. "I think I just made things worse."

She didn't argue. "We'll figure it out."

I wished I could be so sure. "The question is, who could have known the money was in the mansion?"

Didi gave me a sidelong look. "Could be an ancestor of Augustus Crowe."

"I nominate Mr. Hartley." I tapped the wheel. "Or any of the Hartleys." The Crowe mansion was theirs now. "If they've done any exploring, they'd know about the safe."

Didi sat back. "In that case, they could blow it. Yank it out of the wall."

"You ever tried that?" Frankie muscled his way between us, juggling a crystal decanter and what looked suspiciously like a stolen taxidermized peacock. He'd only agreed to abandon his conga line if we helped him "liberate" a few choice items from the speakeasy. "Suds and I blew a wall safe once. Scattered Boss Wiley's Federal Bank take so wide his grandkids are still finding twenties." He leaned forward, nearly catching my ear with the peacock's beak. "You need an expert to dynamite a safe, and if the Hartleys hired someone, word would get around."

This was Sugarland.

"Would it be so bad if people found out?" I took another turn, tires crunching over loose gravel. "It would be their money on their property."

"Not if the money could be linked to Rose or the suffragettes," Didi countered. "But the Hartleys don't need to be burning down libraries for old cash, they're loaded."

"Okay, true." But then who? "Lucas?" He had been up in the kids' area with Melody when the fire started. And he wasn't exactly a criminal mastermind. Neither was Mr. Watkins, the head volunteer.

Didi glanced at me. "I don't know who, but it has to be an inside job, or they wouldn't have known to take the log record of the boxes."

True.

"Which means you screwed the pooch with that phone call," Frankie said.

"Sit back. Or get control of your bird," I said as a frigid, ghostly beak grazed my cheek.

"Can't," he said, and that was when I noticed the entire back seat was loaded down with cases of Firefly Moonshine.

How had he had the time?

"This is exactly what I need to reclaim my life." Frankie hugged a case, wobbling a gilt-framed mirror with cherubs carved into the corners. "At least it's a start."

"I hesitate to ask," I said, clicking the blinker for a left at the bottom of the hill.

"She took my Tommy gun wall display." He jabbed a fistful of stolen cigars at Didi. "She made my poker table disappear and turned my barber chair into a needlepoint rocker. Well, it ends now. I'm taking my home back. I'm taking my life back, and this is my stuff now."

It would all disappear eventually.

Spirits could only keep what they'd died with. Unless they were the dominant ghost on a property, which he wasn't. That was Didi, and she'd just turn his peacock into a porcelain poodle. Not intentionally or with malice. It was simply the way she saw things.

"This time, it'll be different," the gangster vowed. He nestled his peacock between a case of moonshine and a velvet painting of dogs playing poker, his cutting gaze daring me to say a word about it.

Didi shot him an apologetic look. "I'll try my very best."

"I know you will," I said, although it hadn't made a lick of difference the last time.

She patted her hair. "It's just that home to me means quilts draped over armchairs, and tea cozies, and potpourri sachets in every drawer. Fresh-baked cookies cooling on racks, and doilies under everything. Oh, and those little crocheted covers for the spare rolls of toilet paper. A place where everything's tidy and warm and smells like lavender sachets and lemon furniture polish." She sighed dreamily. "I miss those days."

"Like a bad rash," Frankie said, lighting up a cigar.

"Not in my car," I warned him.

"You see what I put up with?" he asked his peacock. But we made it home without incident. We left him to rebuild his empire while we entered Rose's garden.

At least it would keep him busy.

Moonlight spilled across the flagstones.

The night was still except for our echoing footsteps and the rustle of leaves. A trio of stone nymphs cast shadows across the path, their marble faces watching us pass.

The secret hatch appeared exactly as we'd left it.

I pried open the lid, and silvery light poured from the caves, stronger now than before.

At least I wouldn't need my flashlight.

I swallowed hard and hurried down the ladder.

Madge stood at the bottom, her translucent form casting a pale glow against the rock. "I've been waiting for you." She smoothed her skirt. "Did you find Hope at the workhouse?"

I exchanged a look with Didi. "We did." I cleared my throat. "I'm sorry." There was no easy way to say it. "She was murdered for her key to the safe."

Madge gasped, her hand flying to her mouth. "Murdered?"

"We need to understand what Rose was protecting. We need you to show us where you keep the safe."

Madge's form flickered. "How?" She backed away, her jaw tightening. "How would you know Hope was murdered by a thief? Unless…"

"It wasn't us," Didi pressed, gliding toward her, stopping when Madge shrank back. "We're kin. We have Rose's key because she left it to us."

The ghost's gaze found my great-great-grandmother's necklace.

She wanted to believe.

"Please," I said. "We're working to preserve Rose's legacy, the suffragettes' legacy," I corrected.

"We want to help just as much as Rose did," Didi added.

But time was running out. I shuddered at the thought of meeting the man who'd broken into Augustus's office. "Where's the safe, Madge?"

She squared her shoulders. "I have no idea what you're talking about."

She was a bad liar.

I didn't want to upset her. I really didn't. "We're searching this place whether you like it or not." I brushed past her into the meeting room, where peaches littered the table.

"Viv is going to be back any minute," she said, trying—and failing—to block Didi.

Didi searched behind the posters while I checked under the table. Behind a banner.

"The peach room," Didi suggested, heading that way.

"There's nothing in there," Madge insisted, a step behind.

"Madge." Didi turned. "My grandmother is going crazy trying to protect whatever's in that safe. I let her down once. I won't do it again."

"I don't know what you're talking about," Madge cried as I joined Didi, searching behind shelves, behind baskets of peaches.

Madge wouldn't understand. She didn't know she was dead. None of these women did—not Hope, suffering eternally in jail, refusing to admit, much less examine her death, not Viv, who was still waiting with Madge for the meeting to start.

These suffragettes lived in their most crucial moments, still immersed in the battle. I wished we could give them peace, let them know it all turned out right. But I didn't see how.

Not right now, at least.

"I don't see anything," Didi said after we'd searched the storage room.

I didn't either. "Where else can we look?"

Madge's eyes went wide.

"Madge..." I began.

They widened further. "What?"

"We're not here to expose your secrets." I wished I knew how to make her believe me. "But Rose trusted us with this key for a reason. If we don't protect what's in that safe—" The bad guy would win. The suffragette legacy in Sugarland would be lost. Rose would turn full poltergeist forever. I wished I could explain it in a way she could understand.

She looked from me to Didi to me. "The suffragette cause—"

"Is safe with us," I promised.

Madge's hands twisted in her skirts as she backed toward the wall.

A metallic clang echoed through the cave, followed by a low rumble that shook dirt from the ceiling.

Didi rushed toward the sound, with me hot on her heels. She shouldered past a canvas banner glowing gray on her side, paint cracked on mine, emblazoned with *VOTES FOR WOMEN* in bold black letters. The Statue of Liberty stood beneath the words, her torch raised high against a faded white background. Didi tossed up the banner on the ghostly side, and I plowed past it in my realm. Behind it lay a chamber no bigger than Frankie's shed.

The stench hit me first—sour mash and copper.

"Verity—" Didi stopped cold.

A moonshine still dominated the space—in my world and the next. A water heater's rusted body wrapped in copper squares, each patch secured with baling wire that caught the light like a spider's web.

Flattened milk cans formed the top, their edges melted together under thick red clay. Copper pipes shot upward through holes in the rock ceiling.

Not a single joint leaked. Wooden braces and metal brackets held them in place, each support positioned perfectly.

The whole thing tilted left, feeding into a series of catch basins like a metal waterfall. At the bottom sat a washtub, its rim fitted with copper mesh to strain the clear liquid.

It was rusted on my side, uglier. The copper gone green.

The pipes overhead let out a low gurgle in the ghostly realm, followed by a harsh wheeze.

"Oh my word," Didi breathed.

Against the far wall, musty in my realm and glowing gray in the other, wooden crates bore a familiar logo—a lightning bug burned into the wood. Empty bottles nestled in their dividers, row after row waiting to be filled. In my world, a few of the cases had shipping labels partially torn away, the word *Chicago* still visible on one corner.

I stared at the still. It didn't seem real. "You're bootleggers." Under my house.

Bootleggers.

With my great-great-grandmother's full approval.

In fact, according to Frankie, Firefly Moonshine was the best, the ultimate, the one moonshine to rule them all. Every criminal wanted a piece of it, and I'd been living on top of it.

The truth of it did more than sting. It was a betrayal. A mockery. The worst kind of lie. I felt the spark, the family pride, the womanly righteousness fizzle out of me. "You're not suffragettes. You're dirty bootleggers."

"Nonsense." Madge recoiled, pressing a hand to her chest.

I flung mine at the still. "Exhibit A."

"Truly." She smoothed her already-perfect hair, every pin in place. "We are suffragettes first." She tilted her head. "And also bootleggers. The proper kind."

Was there such a thing?

No. No. I'd met plenty of dead bootleggers, and they were all criminals.

Didi circled the still, tracing the precise copper seams. "I believe her."

"You haven't met the South Town boys." Frankie's gang was a force unto itself.

Madge gasped at the mention of the mob. "Please." Her prim demeanor cracked. "You can't tell the South Town gang. You can't tell a soul."

I wouldn't—they'd have these women cleaned out faster than you could say Bob's your uncle.

Frankie alone would have a field day. Grandma had blown up his latest still, and this one was nicer than Betsy Sue the Third—I mean Fourth—nicer than any still Frankie had ever built.

So, no. I wouldn't tell.

But she didn't know that.

I met Madge's eyes. "Didi and I will keep your secret if you tell us why this still is here. Why you're brewing hooch. And what any of this has to do with votes for women."

Madge wrung her hands. "It's complicated." She rushed forward as Didi reached for a copper pipe. "Please don't touch that. The pressure has to be perfectly balanced, or the whole batch will be ruined."

Didi withdrew her hand. "Then you'd better start explaining."

"What's to explain?" Madge threw up her hands. "We're women. We don't have jobs. We can't earn money. We can't even open our own bank accounts." She paced in front of the still. "Sure, I was a secretary before I married, but now my husband would absolutely forbid me to work outside the home, and I don't blame him. Nobody would hire me. It's just not done."

Well, shoot. I blinked. "I hadn't thought of it that way."

Madge stopped and met my eyes. "Movements cost money. Organizing costs money. Bringing in speakers, making protest signs." She flung out a hand. "We didn't have the money." She dropped it. "Until we did." A flush crept up her neck. "It was Rose's idea."

Didi crossed her arms. "I can't say I'm surprised."

Truly? "I am." Rose was a proper lady with a lovely home and a rose garden and—

Didi's eyes caught mine. "You haven't met her. Well, except for the jail."

"She wasn't exactly herself then," I admitted.

She was in trouble.

Still was.

Madge ran a hand down the still's metal barrel. "It started with small batches. We'd brew just enough to raise money for a single event. Or to buy sashes. We'd call it our bake sale." Her lips twitched. "It had a nice ring to it. And believe me, brewing peach moonshine is easier than baking a hundred pies."

"You have to admire the practicality." Didi said.

Except we were supposed to be the good guys. "It's illegal."

"So are votes for women," Madge shot back. "It's illegal for me to own property. To sign a contract. To have a say in my children's schooling." She cocked her head. "And, yes, it's illegal for us to brew shine. But we're never going to get anywhere by following the rules." Her pins worked loose, and she didn't care. "You know what we'll get by staying put? More of the same, and I, for one, am not going to stand for it."

Didi burst into applause. "I'm so proud of you. All of you."

"Me too." Madge was right. They all were. I couldn't help but grin. "You ladies are revolutionaries."

She touched her hair. "We're doing it for us and for girls like you so you'll have the voice we don't."

"Oh, I think you're making your voices heard," I assured her.

She pursed her lips. "The thing is the shine has taken off like we never imagined." Madge smoothed her skirts. "Our lawyer found us a man who distributes it. He doesn't know who we are."

Oh, yes, he did. If Augustus was to be believed, he knew Rose very, very well.

"We're a premium brand now," she continued. "We're sponsoring chapters across Tennessee. Eleanor Blackwell is helping us coordinate. She's a brilliant organizer, and she knows everybody. Her coming here to speak is a great honor and a step toward change, but she's really here to receive money and distribute it across the state."

I couldn't help but wonder if that was the cash in Augustus's safe. Or if we'd find it in Rose's stash.

"Do you have any idea where Rose kept her records?" If she knew, she needed to tell me now. "We really need to find her safe."

Madge shook her head. "She never said anything to me. I'm just the moonshiner."

Didi directed a smile at her. "Well, your still is lovely."

It was. It is. "We have to go."

We had to find Rose's safe before someone else did.

/ Chapter Twenty-Two /

I climbed out of the hatch, quick as I could, numb from the shock of it all. My great-great-grandmother, my blood, had been a moonshiner—distilling illegal hooch from our ancestral land, from the orchard that had been in our family since Lucy Long grafted the first Sugar Peach.

Rose's ghostly garden stretched around me.

I mean, Rose had a reason.

Frankie also thought he had reasons. But Rose did it for her organization. And Frankie...never mind.

"Verity?" Didi asked when I clanged the hatch shut a little too loud.

I took a breath. Let it out. Looked at her. "From the time I was tiny, Mom, you, every woman in our family—we made it a point of pride that we're proper ladies who handle everything life tosses at us with charm, grace, and every bit of style we can muster." I'd always tried to live up to that legacy. "I have to admit it's knocking me sideways to think Frankie might have more in common with our matriarch than I do."

Good thing he hadn't seen what was down there. He'd take one look at that moonshine still and never leave.

"At least she was good at it," Didi said as we hurried from the garden. "The logo is gorgeous. The hooch is top notch. Grandma Rose always liked to do things up nice."

She wasn't helping.

And neither was Frankie. We found him by the pond, teetering on a stack of stolen crates, nailing his velvet painting of dogs playing poker to my favorite apple tree.

"I'm taking over," he announced. "This is all mine." He spread his arms, and for a second, I thought he'd hug the tree. "My poker parlor." The peacock watched from the shed roof, tail spread. He'd stacked cases of Firefly Moonshine into an ad hoc table and chairs. "My shed. My moonshine."

"Someone needs to remind him he doesn't need to stand on crates," Didi murmured. "He can float."

"Let him go." He was on a roll.

And he still had all his stuff. "Way to go, Frankie."

I was impressed.

"Something happened to me in that speakeasy." He hopped down. "I saw the true potential for partying. For crime." He pointed the hammer at me. "For what I can be if I put my mind to it. Oh, I've changed." He tossed the hammer. "You're looking at the new Frankie. The powerful Frankie. I'm taking my shed back. I'm taking my life back."

"Good for you." Didi began clapping for him, and to my shock, Frankie bowed. She clasped her hands under her chin. "I must say you have a lovely...eclectic touch." She tilted her head. "Although it does look quite messy—" Her eyes went wide as the velvet dogs morphed into a cross-stitch sampler that read *Bless This Mess*.

"No, no, no!" Frankie windmilled his arms, lunging for the sampler. His feet tangled in the crates, and he face-planted with a yelp. "My masterpiece!"

"Oh no." Didi waved her hands. "It's fine. I like it all. It's fine!" One of his makeshift chairs transformed into a doily-covered settee. Then another. Then another. Didi spun around, put her back to the mess, pressed her hands to her face. "I need to stop looking!"

"Too late." I stared as his prized peacock shrank into a ceramic garden gnome and toppled off the roof. The stolen mirror morphed into a hutch crammed with delicate teacups.

"Mine!" Frankie zipped around like a deranged humming-bird, trying to gather his hooch as it poofed into pots of gerani-ums, croquet balls, and way too many Franklin Mint collectible plates. "Mine. Mine—" He shrieked as the last case of moonshine morphed into a hope chest stuffed with gowns. "What am I going to do with this?" he pleaded.

"I'm sorry." I hurried to where he lay with his face in the dirt, a bridal tiara glittering beside his head. I wished I could do some-thing to make it better. To make this his home again.

He rolled onto his back and flung his hands out. "It's all gone. Done. All I've got is doilies. And china teacups. And a hope chest full of mothballs and disappointment."

"It's not all bad," I said. "Think of it this way—you can always nick more stuff." Frankie loved stealing. He thought of it as a sport.

He closed his eyes. "I didn't suffer this much when Three-Fingered Larry strapped me to a Bentley 3 Liter headed over Niagara Falls with nothing but a kazoo and my wits. At least then I got to ride in a nifty car. And I kept the kazoo. Only now it's a sterling silver pickle fork." He closed his eyes tighter. "I want my kazoo."

Wisps of smoke began curling from his ears.

Oh no. "I thought we'd put the fire out."

Didi's hands trembled as she pressed them against her chest. "I think the booze just relaxed me. It calmed my agitation. The only real way to put the fire out is to spend time in the ether."

"So go," I said.

She shook her head, eyes wide with panic. "I can't. Not yet."

Frankie rose up behind her.

"We'll fix this," I promised. "You just need to calm down. Think happy thoughts. That speakeasy was fun, right?"

"Until she killed my souvenir peacock." Pinpricks of flame glowed beneath the skin on his neck.

Didi whirled on him. "It was dead already."

Frankie reeled back. "I'll have you know Beatrice was my favorite bird."

"Beatrice would want us all to keep our cool right now," I urged.

"I don't even think the bird had a name," Didi scoffed. "You just made it up."

She'd never get him to admit it. "Let's table the Great Peacock Debate until no one's at risk of spontaneous combustion." My stomach dropped as tiny embers floated from his shoulders.

He flung a hand over his face. "This is worse than the time my racehorse ran away and I couldn't catch him because he was too fast."

"I get that." Sort of. I was proud of the home I'd helped him build here. There had to be a way for him to have that back. But he was in danger.

They both were.

"I don't know how to fix this." Didi's voice warbled.

I didn't, either, but something had to give.

A sharp crackle split the air. I spun toward Didi.

Smoke curled from her patchwork dress.

Oh no, not both of them. "Didi, you're on fire."

She recoiled. "I'm fine." She spun, swatting her dress with both hands. "No—no. I'm not fine. I'm horrible. I'm ruining everything. His things, his home, I'm yelling at my own guest—"

To be fair, the gangster made yelling easy.

Frankie leapt to his feet, sparks cascading off him. "I'm not the guest. You are." Flames licked through his hair as his voice rose. "You left. I moved in. That's my shed." The fire shot up, crowning his head like a terrible halo. "*My place.*"

"Frankie," I gasped.

"I'm not a guest. I'm *family*." Didi's voice boomed as fire raced down her shoulders. "And this is not your house. It was never your house! You don't belong here."

Frankie's outline blurred. Sparks rained from his shirt cuffs. "This place has been more my home than any place in my entire life." His tie ignited. "Or afterlife!"

"Stop it. Both of you!" *Think, think, think!* There had to be a way to stop this before—

"She did this." Frankie's finger blazed like a torch as he aimed it at Didi.

"You're doing it to yourself," she shot back.

She didn't know she was on fire, too. I stared in horror as hot embers broke through the skin on her neck. "Stop it," I commanded, desperate to douse this supernatural inferno. "Stop talking. Stop looking at each other. Just stop."

But they circled each other, trailing smoke and sparks, their eyes locked like prizefighters waiting for the bell.

"I'm doing my best to be hospitable!" Her shout sent hot embers blooming across her cheeks.

"Well, you failed, lady!" Frankie bellowed. Flames burst from his ears.

Didi's dress ignited like kindling, and my heart stopped. "Grandma!" Her earlier warning hammered through my head. This wasn't just dangerous. This could destroy her.

She met my eyes, terror washing over her face. "I need to calm down. I need to get to the ether."

"Yes." Oh, yes, please. "Go!"

"But—" The words gurgled as flames devoured her throat. "You. Need. Me."

She'd done more than enough. "Go. Save yourself. I'll handle things here."

She stared at me.

"Trust me," I urged. "Please."

She bowed her head and dissolved like mist.

"Oh, Didi." I'd never been so grateful to see my grandmother vanish. Please let her be all right. She had to be all right.

"At last." Frankie was nothing but fire now, his features melded into the flames. "Now I can get my stuff back."

He was literally burning away, and he was worried about his loot? "Look at yourself," I shouted.

"The last thing I need is a lecture from you." He reached for a pack of smokes that would no doubt ignite on contact.

"The flames are eating you. You could die." There was stubborn and there was bullet-in-the-forehead, on-fire, single-headed stupid. "You need to get to the ether, too. Away from Didi."

"Not until I get my peacock back." He whirled toward the shed. As if on cue, the peacock-gone-garden-gnome burst into flames and exploded. The ghostly shed caught fire, flames racing up the gray-glowing sides. "She did this," he shouted as ghostly smoke billowed from the roof.

"Let it go." My voice broke. "Your stuff, your pride, your need to win—none of it matters when you're burning alive." He was disappearing into the flames before my eyes.

"I stay. I win," he barked.

"Nobody wins." Not like this. And I was starting to think nobody could win. Didi and Frankie didn't mix. They'd kill each other. Or themselves. They'd both caught fire saving me, and now I had to try to save them. "Do it for Molly." His girlfriend. His love. The one he'd been ignoring to help me. "How would she feel if she saw you like this?"

He pointed a flaming finger at me. "Don't let Didi take my stuff while I'm gone."

"I'll guard your hope chest with my life," I vowed.

What was left of it.

"That's not funny," he said, and in a blink, he was gone, leaving a scorched spot on the grass.

Please let him be okay.

Please let them both be okay.

I dragged a shaky hand down my face, realizing for the first time how hot I was. Sweat rolled down my temples as if I'd been standing in front of a furnace. This was a disaster. If they survived this, if they both made it back whole, they'd never be able to share space. And how could I possibly choose? I'd trapped Frankie. I'd given him a home here. But Didi was the dominant ghost. This place had always been hers. No matter what I did, someone would burn.

I sank down onto the grass near Frankie's smoldering footprint. Smoke mixed with the sticky-sweetness of fallen apples. My home had always been the one thing I could count on, the place where everything made sense. Now it was falling apart, along with two of the people I cared about most.

They'd nearly destroyed themselves trying to help me, trying to best each other, and I had no idea how to make it right.

The plain truth of it was, I needed them both.

Didi had taught me what it meant to do good, to live with a sense of history and purpose. She'd shown me what a privilege it was to be from Sugarland, to love the people around me. To take pride in doing the right thing even when the world was falling apart. Grace under pressure, that was Didi.

And Frankie, he'd barreled into my life with guns blazing. He'd kept me on my toes, showed me how to laugh in the face of danger. He'd proven family wasn't always about blood. Sometimes it was about who showed up when you needed them most. He belonged here just as much as I did.

They both did.

The scorched grass crumbled in my hands. What kind of person was I to let it get to this point? To let them burn themselves up. They were only trying to protect me, to prove themselves worthy of a place that should have been big enough for all of us.

But I didn't see how we could ever make it work, to carve out space for both of them without anyone getting hurt. It just wasn't possible. They'd proved that time and time again. Now I might lose them both.

Didi could be damaged so bad she might never come back. Or she could come in a hundred years, after I was dead and gone.

And Frankie—he'd been burning the longest. He'd need more time to recover. Then an even more terrible thought hit. What if his tie to my property yanked him back while he was still burning up, and he had to burn for the rest of time?

The crunch of tires on gravel dragged me back to reality.

"Hey there," Ellis called from across the yard. His police car sat half-in half-out of Rose's prized garden. "You okay?" he asked, slamming the door.

I stayed seated as he made his way over to me. "Everything's falling apart, and I don't know what to do."

He helped me from the grass. "Tell me what's wrong. We'll figure it out."

That was the kicker. "It's nothing we can fix."

"You—"

"Please." Or I might break down.

Someone had to hold it together.

Ellis held me close as he scanned the yard—the apple tree, the pond, the shed. He was the most observant person I knew and a heck of an impressive police officer, but not even he could see Frankie's grandmother-chic disaster zone sprawled across my lawn. On fire.

He rested his chin on my head. "How about you tell me what you can?"

I could try. "I met the ghost of my great-great-grandma Rose in your jail cell. Ran for my life because she's going poltergeist. Then I made it over to the old Crowe mansion and met her dead fiancé, who tells me Rose has the key to her legacy hidden in a safe on my property."

"Here?" Ellis drew back to look at me.

"Here. Somewhere." No telling where. "But then I checked the hidden cave by where your car's parked, and all I found was a bootlegging operation under my rosebushes."

"Another one of Frankie's?"

"No. It turns out Rose and her friends were brewing Firefly Moonshine under my house."

To his credit, he didn't even blink. "Please tell me there's a story behind that one."

"There is, and I'd be glad to fill you in later." Once I finished processing it myself. "It's just..." Everything was an emergency at once. "We have to find the safe now."

Before the thief did.

Then we'd have our answers, and that evil man would have no reason to come anywhere near this place.

I tucked a scraggle of hair behind my ear. "Where would you hide a safe on my property? I know this house inside and out, and it's nowhere."

Ellis rubbed his jaw, eyes scanning the house. "It would have to be a secure place, easy to access but easily hidden." His gaze climbed the weathered siding to the wraparound porch, past the second-story windows. "If your great-great-grandma was anything like you, it would be a sentimental place, one with personal meaning." His hand dropped as his eyes fixed on the attic window, where a firefly winked in the gathering dusk. "You say she brewed Firefly Moonshine?"

The fireflies in my attic.

They'd always been there.

Generation after generation. It was just the way it was.

"You think?" I asked, hoping against hope.

He shot me a knowing smile. "Only one way to find out."

Chapter Twenty-Three

We rushed into the house, up to the second floor. The attic stairs creaked as Ellis pulled the trapdoor down. I went first, scrambling up the rough wooden stairs.

"I haven't been up here in years." Not since I'd ended my engagement to Ellis's brother. Not since I'd had to sell almost everything to keep my house. My footsteps echoed against bare floorboards as I stepped into the attic.

The emptiness pressed in around me, a physical reminder of everything I'd lost. Every missing piece of furniture left its ghost—faded rectangles on the walls where paintings had hung, lighter patches of wood where Grandpa's chest of drawers had protected the floor from sun damage. The space felt wrong, like walking into your bedroom to find someone's rearranged all the furniture.

Empty shelves lined the back wall. Nail holes dotted the plaster where Grandma had stored those old landscape portraits. Some of them had gone back all the way to Kitty Long's day. I'd cleaned the entire place out, piece by piece, memory by memory.

My gaze drifted to the corner by the window where I'd stashed Frankie's urn. That was years ago, when my ex had given it to me as a gift.

Some gift.

Grandma's wooden broom still leaned against the wall there, its worn handle smooth from years of use. I'd thought that broom was long gone, sold off with everything else. Seeing it now felt like finding an old friend in a crowd of strangers.

A lone firefly drifted past, its glow stark against the waning light.

"Look." Ellis had stopped, half-in, half-out. He traced the hatch frame with his finger.

"What do you see?" I bent to find an etching of a firefly, same as the one on the moonshine bottles. This one had been sketched in pencil. Underneath, in looping script, someone had added, *Hope Burns Bright*.

That was how Grandma had known the password for the speakeasy.

We had to be in the right spot.

I stood.

Then I spotted it.

On the wall directly across from us. "Ellis, look."

There was a mark on the bump-out wall between two windows. Of course, there were marks everywhere—streaks and smudges on every wall. The attic had been packed with memories before I'd had to let everything go. But this particular mark was different.

My grandfather's rolltop desk had sat there. Or maybe it had been that massive stack of steamer trunks. Years of weight pressing down had rubbed a shadow onto the wall. It looked like nothing until I knew what I was looking for. That was when the shadow took shape —curved lines forming delicate wings, a rounded body. A firefly.

My throat thickened. "How did that get there?" It appeared to be carved in the plaster, like a relief. "Wait, no." I traced the impression. It wasn't carved. "It feels like there's something under here, plastered over." Rubbed down over the years. "It's starting to show through."

Ellis was by my side in an instant. "Let me see."

I grabbed Grandma's broom. The wooden handle felt right in my hands. "Step back." I was done waiting.

Done wondering.

"Verity, there could be an easier way to—"

I swung. The handle dug deep into the plastered wall, the impact shuddering up my arms.

"Want me to do it?" Ellis offered.

"Not on your life." This was my birthright. My legacy.

I swung again. And again. Heat crept up my neck; sweat streamed down my back. A crack appeared. I hit it again, and a chunk of plaster broke free, shattering at my feet.

"You've got it."

I swung again. My broom handle struck metal like a bell. Ellis went in with his utility knife, levering out another large piece, revealing a cast-iron safe.

"We did it." My knees went weak, and my head went light. After everything—the fire, the skeleton, the prison and the very scary ghosts—here it was.

Raised on its surface was an etching of the same firefly from the moonshine bottles, with the initials DNW underneath. I dropped the broom. Didn't care. "Those are the same initials from the ring we found under the skeleton in the library. And on Rose's key." The same script. The same everything.

I dug at the edges, the plaster crumbling beneath my nails. Ellis's utility knife made quick work of the rest.

"It's here!" I could hardly believe it. "We found it!" After all this time—

Ellis locked eyes with me. "Do you have your key?"

"Yes." I trembled as I pulled Rose's heavy brass key from my pocket with the intricate scrollwork woven through the handle.

Ellis cleared away the last bits of plaster from around the keyhole cover and slid it aside with a gentle scrape.

The key slipped in like it had been waiting a hundred years for this moment. A perfect fit.

I held my breath and turned it. The mechanism ground, each tumbler falling into place with a satisfying final click.

The door creaked open, the hinges stiff. A musty, metallic smell wafted out. Ellis stood by my side while I drew out the first of its contents—a sepia photograph, its edges worn with age. A woman in a high-necked blouse stood beside a tall man in a suit. Rose and Augustus. Her chin lifted, defiant. His hand rested on her shoulder, proud and protective.

It touched me deeply. "I'm glad she had him."

I passed the photograph to Ellis.

Beneath it was an envelope embossed with the star and the motto *Deeds Not Words*. Oh, my goodness. "DNW." It was the call to action of the suffragettes.

The paper was thick, expensive. Inside, documents outlined the "grand plan" in elegant script. I lost my breath when I read it aloud. "Firefly Moonshine wasn't just a business or a way to funnel money to other suffragist chapters. It funded the entire Southern suffragette movement." My hands trembled. They were funding Eleanor Blackwell's congressional campaign in Tennessee. Women's education. Support for those seeking independence.

My throat tightened. No wonder Rose had gone crazy when her legacy was threatened. She'd fought so long and hard for something so vast I could hardly imagine it. And she'd done it here, in this house—in my house—she'd started a revolution.

The rest of the world had seen nothing more than a widow tending her garden, but she'd been working for the freedom to vote, the freedom to own property, for all the things I took for granted.

"I'm so proud," I whispered, my voice breaking. This wasn't just my great-great-grandmother's legacy anymore. This was the legacy of every woman who'd had to hide her power, who'd had to work in secret to change the world.

I traced the elegant script, feeling a connection to Rose I'd never experienced before. She was a warrior.

And so was I.

"I'm not surprised at all." Ellis beamed, taking each document I handed him as the precious treasure it was.

A bankbook showed the careful records. Mr. Hartley's signature beside Rose's on every transaction.

"Heaven forbid a widow manage her own money," Ellis growled over my shoulder.

"At least she had someone willing to sign for her." Then I glimpsed what lay farther back in the safe. "Ellis." My voice caught as I reached for it.

Paper certificates, bound in faded paper bands. Each bundle as thick as a Bible.

Strange. "I thought there would be something worth hiding in here, like money." I fanned the documents with my thumb. "I wonder what she was doing with certificates."

Ellis pulled out a bundle. "These are stock certificates." He grabbed another. "Government bonds."

"My stack says City Bank of New York."

"Citibank now." Ellis straightened. "Mine are from the US Treasury."

There was no telling how much was in there. Only it was lots and lots and—

"These could be worth millions," Ellis said. "Probably worth more than face value, being this old."

I handed him my stack. "I still don't understand what happened." I bent to draw out more. "What stopped them? Rose and the Sugarland Suffragettes had everything—a booming business, big plans, the money to make it happen." I drew out two more stacks. Three. "American Telephone and Telegraph Company."

"I'm not sure about that one."

Me neither. I put that one back in the safe. "General Electric. Coca-Cola. More City Bank of New York." Amazing. "They had it all worked out. At the same time, Eleanor disappeared. Hope died in jail. Madge and Viv were still waiting for their meeting to start. And Rose—" I swallowed hard. "She lived a normal life for years, raised her daughter, tended her garden and never said a word about this to anybody. Why?"

Ellis shook his head. "What does Didi say?"

"She didn't know about any of this." None of us had. "Why did Rose keep this so secret?"

And what could have stopped the suffragettes so suddenly that none of them except Rose even knew they were dead?

The attic hatch slammed closed.

We both jumped.

"Didi?" I hoped. She'd be back as quick as she was able.

Only she didn't have the strength to move objects.

Ellis reached the hatch first, shoving down on the handle. It didn't budge.

He shot me a panicked look. "We're not alone."

The scrape of metal on metal echoed from below—the slider bolt being drawn.

"Who's down there?" I demanded.

In my house!

But I knew deep in my twisting gut.

The arsonist had put the pieces together. We hadn't been as far ahead as we'd hoped.

Then the smell hit me. Acrid. Sharp.

Smoke.

Ellis grabbed my arm. "Stay away from the hatch."

Smoke curled from the edges.

They'd set fire to my house!

I clung to the certificates. I didn't care about the safe. Flames crackled below. Rose's legacy, her secrets, her sacrifice—someone had killed to stop her all those years ago.

And if we couldn't find a way out of this, history was about to repeat itself.

Chapter Twenty-Four

We were trapped.

Ellis slammed his boot against the attic hatch. The wood shuddered. The hinges rattled. But the thick oak stood strong.

He drew back and kicked again.

And again.

The impact echoed through the attic. Smoke leaked between the hatch and the frame. Stinging gray ribbons, curling up from the hall. My house was burning.

My house.

Then an even worse thought hit me. *Lucy.* "Lucy's down there."

Ellis slammed his foot down. "She's smart." He braced himself for another kick. "She'll get herself out."

No, she wouldn't. "Not if she's locked in too."

Had I left her in the house? I couldn't remember. How could I not remember my skunk? I was all she had. She depended on me. Lucy's tiny face flashed in my mind, her whiskers twitching as she dashed through the halls below, scared and confused, searching for me.

The smoke was getting worse, seeping through every crack in the floorboards. Ellis reeled back from the hatch, his polished badge catching the fading light from the window. He bent. "The floor's getting hot." He yanked at his collar. "We need another way out of here."

I pressed my palm against the wall. The plaster felt warm. I prayed to heaven Lucy was outside.

We had to get out of here. We had to fix this.

Ellis rushed past me, toward the window overlooking the yard. "Stay here." He squeezed my arm on his way past.

Like I had anywhere else to go.

Then it hit me.

Rose's legacy. I had to save it. The suffragettes' dream.

I hurried for the safe. Realized I was holding a stack of stock certificates. I stuffed them down the front of my dress.

They fell out.

I crammed them down again and braced them with an arm. Then I grabbed the documents from the safe. More certificates. The bonds. The papers crinkled against my skin as I wedged them between my ribs and my fitted cotton dress.

The smoke was getting worse.

It burned my eyes, tears streaming down my face. My throat felt raw. Each breath came shorter than the last. The ceiling disappeared behind a gray haze that pressed lower, forcing me to crouch.

Metal hinges screeched as Ellis wrestled with the window. Fresh air rushed in, and I staggered toward it, gulping deep. My face burned. The night air felt like heaven.

Ellis turned to me. "I'll get the fire out." His voice was steady. Sure. "I'll get you out."

My heart stopped as he ducked through the window onto the roof.

"It's steep!" I rushed forward as he clambered down the steep slope, his movements fluid. He made it look easy. Natural. Like he did this every day.

He was crazy.

He was doing it for me.

"Ellis, be careful!" The words caught in my throat as he reached the edge.

"I've got this." He flashed me that slow grin I knew too well, then gripped the gutter and swung himself over.

My breath hitched as he dangled there, two stories up, muscles bunching under his shirt. Then he dropped, landing in a crouch on the lawn.

I wanted to cheer, but instead I froze.

A shadow detached itself from the corner near the porch. A man wearing all black, his face hidden behind a ski mask. In the waning light, I could see something in his hands. A shovel.

He rushed Ellis.

"Ellis, behind you!"

Ellis dropped and rolled. The shovel whooshed past his head, catching his shoulder. He hit the ground hard. The masked man raised the shovel, metal glinting as he brought it down.

I scrambled onto the roof. The shingles burned through my sneakers.

Ellis rolled sideways and grabbed the handle mid-swing, using the man's momentum to send him stumbling. Ellis scrambled up, but the attacker charged, ramming into him. They hit the ground in a tangle.

A flash of black and white streaked from beneath the porch.

Lucy.

My brave, foolish little skunk launched herself at the attacker's leg, latching on with a ferocity I would have cheered if it hadn't scared me to death.

The man cursed and kicked, sending Lucy flying.

"Baby!" I stumbled down the roof slope.

Lucy flipped twice, rolled, and ran straight for the battling men.

My little girl was going to get herself killed.

I dangled from the gutter, feeling the metal give beneath my grip, my feet kicking at empty air. Ellis had made this look so easy.

The ground swayed beneath me, too far away. My stomach lurched.

The certificates shifted against my skin, then slipped free, raining down onto the rose garden. Rose's legacy, scattered to the wind. I had to do something.

I squeezed my eyes shut and let go.

Fell.

The impact drove the air from my lungs. I caught myself against the house, in the space where Frankie's rosebush had been, papers swirling around me. No time to hurt. No time to think.

Up close, the attacker was massive. His shoulders stretched the black fabric of his shirt, muscles rippling as he pinned Ellis down. He pulled a knife. Even with the mask, I could feel his rage. Lucy squealed and attacked his shin.

He brought the knife down on Ellis.

I grabbed the shovel and swung like a banshee, catching him on the side of the face. "Get off now!"

He rolled—right onto Lucy.

Her squeal cut through me.

He swung the knife at me.

I hit him again, harder. Lucy squirmed free and bolted. Relief flooded through me as she darted away.

He launched himself off Ellis and was on me before I could react, the knife slicing down. I stumbled into the rose garden pavers.

Ellis wrapped an arm around the attacker's neck.

Did he have him?

I had to get inside and save my house.

Lucy ran a wide arc, building speed. She'd better not try anything.

I glanced toward my porch. Smoke billowed out a shattered kitchen window.

Ellis's cry of pain brought me back as the man drove the knife deep into his thigh.

"Ellis!" I gripped the shovel and rushed forward.

Lucy was coming in from behind. My crazy, brave girl was heading straight for them. "Lucy, stop!"

She wasn't running an agility course.

Only she was.

Ellis's attacker flipped him onto the ground.

My skunk ran up the man's back like a ramp. Her claws latched onto his ski mask. He thrashed his head, trying to shake her off. The sudden movement twisted his mask sideways, blinding him—and spinning Lucy exactly where she wanted to be. Her back legs found his face through the fabric.

She dug in her claws and let loose, her back feet a furious engine raking his eyes, his nose, again and again. Lucy rode his head like a rodeo champion. She was fierce. Vicious. This was pure street fighting, and my little girl was magnificent.

He screamed, knife falling as both hands flew up to protect his face.

But Lucy was having none of it.

Her tail whipped like a battle standard as she dodged his scrabbling grip.

He tried to shake her off, and she dug in harder, her tail lashing in a blur of black and white. She let out a throaty war cry that would have done a mountain lion proud.

Ellis didn't waste the opening. He swept the man's legs, taking him down. My skunk leapt free, tail swishing.

In one fluid motion, Ellis had the attacker facedown, cuffs clicking shut.

"You picked the wrong house." Ellis hauled him up. "And the wrong girl."

The man stumbled, still protecting his face as Ellis hustled him to his cruiser. A quick duck of the head, one firm push, and the attacker folded into the back. The door slammed with a heavy thunk.

Lucy bounded into my arms, trembling but triumphant. I

pressed a quick kiss to her head. "My brave, crazy girl." But the victory was short-lived. Thick black smoke poured from my kitchen window. "I have to save our house."

Chapter Twenty-Five

I yanked the phone from my pocket and called 911. A familiar voice answered. "Nine-one-one, what's your emergency?"

"Tina Louise." She'd run dispatch since I was in diapers. "My house is on fire."

"Sugar, I know. Hailey Mae down the road called it in as soon as she saw smoke. I got three trucks headed your way right now." She lowered her voice. "You stay clear of that house, you hear?"

I wished I could. Instead, I pressed a quick kiss to Lucy's head, deposited her on the grass, and made a beeline for the house.

"Verity!" Ellis demanded. "Where are you going?"

"It's Frankie," I shouted over my shoulder. Ellis was bleeding bad from the gash on his leg. "I have to get his dirt." After I'd dumped his ashes over my rosebush, I'd taken the bush and the dirt and placed it in a trash can for safekeeping. It currently resided in a place of honor in my parlor, and I'd be damned if I'd let it—him—burn.

We might never free him without that dirt.

Ellis, to his credit, didn't argue.

He just covered his hand with the bottom of his police shirt and reached for the door handle.

Smoke poured out.

"Let me go first." He pulled his shirt up over his nose, but I was already blazing past him into the house, through the kitchen, into the parlor. There it was. Frankie's ashes and the dirt, sitting in a trash can under a big, fat rosebush.

The crackle of flames echoed from upstairs. Thick waves of smoke billowed across the ceiling, stinging my eyes.

I wiped them with my sleeve and gripped the handle of the trash can, yanking with all my might. It slid an inch. The weight of soil and roots made the plastic sides bow. The rosebush swayed, branches catching my hair, scratching my face.

Ellis grabbed the trash can from the other side, his face pale. Blood soaked his pants leg, spreading down past his knee. "On three."

"Your leg—"

"One." His jaw set. "Two."

Together we heaved. The can scraped across the hardwood.

"Again," I urged.

The bush wavered between us, thorns snagging our clothes. Smoke burned my eyes, my throat. My muscles screamed in protest.

Inch by grinding inch, we made it across the parlor, into the kitchen, trailing blood onto the linoleum. My face felt hot. The smoke was everywhere. I tried to hold my breath. Ellis's grip was white knuckled on the other side of the can.

"Almost there." My voice came out rough. We were going to make it.

We had to make it.

Another heave. The can caught on the door frame. We twisted it sideways, the plastic catching and groaning as the weight shifted. The bush tilted dangerously, threatening to spill. "Ellis, watch out."

"I got it!" He righted his side, his leg buckling. He caught himself on the wall, leaving a bloody handprint.

One final push and we were through, out onto the back

porch. The night air hit my face, and I gulped it in, sweet and clean. We dragged it to the edge of the porch by the stairs.

Headlights swept across us as trucks and cars skidded into my yard—Royce Davidson's ancient Ford pickup, Tommy Ray's gleaming Silverado, Marcus Johnson's mud-splattered Bronco. I'd known them since forever. The cavalcade of vehicles barely stopped before doors flew open.

"How did you—?"

How did they know?

Bobby Thorne, Walt Peterson, and Mark Sawyer charged past us, fire extinguishers clutched to their chests. Right behind them came Big Ken McClary, volunteer fire chief for twenty years, leading three more neighbors with extinguishers. They lived in the bungalows near the end of my drive. Two more trucks blazed across my backyard from the farm behind my property. "Second floor first!" Big Ken bellowed over the chaos. "Mind that smoke!"

A fire truck wailed in the distance.

My throat burned, and my eyes felt like straw. But my heart swelled as I helped Ellis down the steps. I wasn't alone. Not in Sugarland.

Second-grade teacher Sarah Beth McClary stood in my back-yard, organizing a bucket brigade from my pond—a human chain stretching across my yard. The Hendersons' teenagers passed buckets alongside Peggy Wilson from the post office. Eight-year-old Dwane Wilson Junior darted between adults, distributing empties. Even Mr. Patterson, leaning on his cane, directed traffic.

"I got you." Kip Williams, EMT, rushed up and met us halfway down. "Easy, now," he said, taking Ellis's other arm. His sure grip steadied us both. "I'm parked over there," he said and nodded at a nearby ambulance.

He must have just pulled up.

The fire truck cleared the side of the house, lights and sirens blazing. It parked by the pond. Firefighters leaped out before it fully stopped, unrolling hoses with practiced speed. They moved in sync with the bucket brigade, my neighbors seamlessly adjusting their line to make way for the professionals.

"I've got it from here." Kip guided Ellis toward the ambulance, its lights painting everyone's faces in alternating red and white. "Let's get that bleeding stopped."

I let them go. Ellis was in good hands.

More people poured into my yard, running toward the house with fire extinguishers from their garages and cars. The Martins. The Hopsons. The Garcia family from the blue two-story.

They'd come for me. To save my house.

Lucy leapt and danced from person to person, cheering them on.

They'd come to help because I needed them. I needed my neighbors and my friends, and the people I only knew by name or in passing. I needed my town and their bravery and their love like I needed my home and my legacy.

My legacy.

The papers.

Ohmygoodness. Grandma Rose's papers. The carefully preserved documents she'd protected—proof of every penny she'd earned and invested in the movement. Stock certificates worth thousands, maybe millions now. The bonds she'd bought to fund women's education. All her work for justice, scattered in the dark.

I ran to the back of the house. Three rosebushes stood sentinel against the wall. The empty space where Frankie's bush had been gaped like a missing tooth. But the lawn was empty. No scattered papers, no precious documents.

It couldn't be. There'd been so many.

Panic crept up my spine. Had they blown away? Had the arsonist escaped the patrol car and made off with them?

I couldn't see him in the dark.

A flash of orange caught my eye. A burning paper sailed past on the wind, edges glowing. I sprinted after it, sneakers pounding across the grass. Not this too. Please not this too. The paper dipped, and I lunged, catching it right before it hit the ground. I smothered the flames with my dress.

In the flashing emergency lights, I made out the ornate border of a stock certificate, mostly burned away. But there might be more.

There had to be.

And there was only one person who'd had a bird's-eye view of the entire debacle. I prayed he was still there. Captive. I clutched the charred paper and ran for Ellis's cruiser. If any of Grandma Rose's legacy survived, I had to find it.

I yanked open the driver's door and threw myself inside. The interior was dark, quiet.

But not empty.

Good.

I hit a switch on the dashboard.

Light flooded the back seat like a single bulb over an interrogation.

"You're going to start talking," I said. "Now."

The arsonist sat handcuffed in the back, dressed in black. His ski mask twisted sideways, exposing one eye and part of his mouth. Blood caked the skin at the corner of his eye. That eye widened when I clamped my hand on the metal grate separating us.

"The papers." I gripped the metal until it hurt. "The ones I dropped in the yard. What happened to them?"

He drew back. "I-I don't know what you're talking about." His exposed eye darted left.

He was lying.

"I don't have time for games." My house was burning, Ellis was bleeding, and Grandma Rose would go poltergeist forever if I didn't get those papers back.

I kicked the driver's door open. "Lucy!"

My little skunk had been weaving through the bucket patrol. She turned, saw me, and made a mad dash for the cruiser. I turned to the arsonist. "Talk, and it's just you and me. Don't talk, and you'll be sharing that back seat with an attack skunk."

The arsonist let out a startled cry. "You—you can't do that!"

"Can and will." I leaned closer to the grate and stared him in the eye. "There's no one stopping me."

I didn't relish opening the back door. I didn't relish what Lucy might have to do. But we were the same, Lucy and me. We'd do what needed doing to protect our own.

"I—" He scrambled sideways across the seat, cuffs rattling as he pressed himself into the corner. "That's a wild animal."

Was he even from Sugarland?

"Oh, she's worse than wild," I said, grateful she wasn't wearing fairy wings and a bow. "That timeshare guy who wouldn't take no for an answer? His presentation folder is still stuck in my oak tree. Shredded like it came out of a confetti cannon." I leaned closer. "Makes me wonder what she'll do to someone who tried to burn down her home."

Lucy leapt up into my lap, her nose twitching with interest.

"And between you and me?" I let my voice go low. "I'm not entirely sure her shots are up to date. Rabies is a bitch. So maybe you tell us what happened to those papers in the yard."

He stared at me with his one good eye.

He'd already tried to burn down my home. No way he'd just sat here watching those papers blow past without making note of where they went.

"I know you were after Rose Landry Long's papers." There was no other reason to attack my house. No other reason he'd tracked Grandma Rose's legacy from the library to the Crowe mansion to here. "I dropped them in the yard. What happened to them?"

His whole body went rigid, shoulders hunching. "I have no idea." He shrank back as my eyes narrowed, words tumbling out faster. "I swear. It's true. I can't see anything."

"Take your mask off."

He hesitated. Lucy chose that moment to bare her tiny teeth and let out a menacing hiss.

"Whoa, okay, okay!" He twisted awkwardly, maneuvering with his hands cuffed behind his back. "You do it."

"Don't try anything," I warned as he leaned forward toward the grate.

I reached through and grabbed his mask. It caught on his ear, then slid free.

The dashboard light illuminated a face I knew. Lucas Greene, with his tousled blond hair and sharp jawline. Dark circles under his eyes spoke of sleepless nights. Blood matted his hair where Ellis had taken him down. The eager grad student who'd spent countless hours in the archives with Melody now looked more feral than academic.

I could hardly believe it. Him. "You were supposed to be preserving history, not destroying it."

His lip curled. "Who says I did?"

Oh, that was it. The absolute gall—to take a job at our library while plotting its destruction. To preach about historic preservation while pocketing the matches. To try to erase the Sugarland Suffragettes' life's work brutally and permanently.

"Showtime, Lucy." Her claws clicked against the metal console as I reached for the door handle. "I hope you like your skunks angry." I slid out of the front seat, the weight of Grandma Rose's charred certificate heavy in my pocket. "Because we both really hate liars."

Chapter Twenty-Six

The interior light cast harsh shadows across my attacker's face. "Not the skunk!" He wedged himself into the corner of the cruiser's back seat, pressing against the window. "Stop. Okay. Fine. I admit it. I burned the library. But I wasn't trying to burn it down, and I have no idea about your papers."

I eased back into the seat, cradling my skunk. "Then why are you here?"

He hesitated.

Lucy's tail twitched against my arm. "You are on our last nerve," I warned. "One word from me and your night will go from sweet tea to vinegar real quick."

"I was trying to get my key," he said, voice cracking. "The one you took from the safe in the Crowe mansion."

Heat crept up my neck. "That's not your key."

"It was. It is." His shoulders bunched as he tried to make himself smaller. "I found it in an old box nobody cared about but me."

The nerve. "You mean you found it in my grandmother's donated items."

His chin jutted out. "That sat in a basement longer than

you've been alive. And how many times did you bother to check it out of the library? Hmm...I know. None."

I hadn't known it existed.

But I certainly wasn't going to explain myself to *him*.

I shifted Lucy higher. She was ready for thunderdome, and I didn't blame her. She scrabbled for the grate, claws clicking against metal. "Tell us the whole story. Start from the beginning."

He pressed his lips together, gaze darting between Lucy and the door handle.

"Last chance." I reached for my door. "Full confession or full skunk. Your choice."

"Fine. Stop." Sweat beaded on his forehead. "I got the job at the Sugarland Library to make the money to go to grad school. My history undergraduate put me in debt up to my eyeballs." He paused, but at my sharp look, rushed on.

"I was working on the suffragist exhibit, going through boxes." His eyes lit up despite his predicament. "That's when I discovered their underground moonshine operation. Do you know how remarkable that was? These women built an empire right under everyone's noses. And they did it for a cause. Firefly wasn't just moonshine. It was legendary hooch. I decided right then this had to be my dissertation topic."

"Good for you." And for them. I drummed my nails against the grate. "But that doesn't explain what you did next."

"I researched," he said. As if that said it all. "History is juicy if you know where to look. And I'm good. I am." He scooted forward. "From the meeting minutes, I knew Rose was having trouble with her lawyer, Clayton Rutledge. So I dug through his papers." A trickle of sweat ran down the side of his face. "He had a safe-deposit box in the suffragettes' name. I looked up those records." His voice dropped, his eyes fever bright. "Rose was making the deposits, but Rutledge was making all the with-drawals. He bought a nice house on Second Street, a few blocks north of downtown. You and I both know it was the swankiest part of Sugarland back in the day. I can't *prove* he was stealing from them, but he was stealing from them."

My grip on my attack skunk loosened. "I think you're right."

He plopped back onto the cushions. "I know I am." He shook his head. "Thieving bastard."

That was rich. "Are you talking about the crooked lawyer or yourself?"

He made a face. "Rose needed to do something. About Rutledge."

"She did. She ordered a safe built in the Crowe mansion."

"Of course!" He was on the edge of his seat in a flash. "I found the receipt in the box."

"The receipt you stole," I pointed out. "Did you take the money, too?"

"I needed that key. Don't you get it?" His cuffs rattled as he surged toward the grate. "You don't understand what it's like. I've spent years working dead-end jobs, scraping by, watching people less qualified than me get those spots in grad school because they had the money. The connections. I didn't have a way in—not really—until I found this." His breath hitched. "This was my chance. A real discovery. Something big enough to make me stand out. Something that could fund everything."

"Something that wasn't yours."

"Do you know how it feels to work so hard and still come up short?" His head jerked up, a flicker of defiance in his eyes. "You know what it's like not to have money."

I did. I'd suffered. But... "I never stole."

He hesitated. "The key was right there in the box. I figured, why not check it out?"

I shot him a stern look.

"Only I get there, and it takes two keys." His words tumbled faster. "But you know with the suffragettes' plans to fund chapters, to bankroll Eleanor, they have cash." He tilted his head forward, eyes bright. "You can see it on their books. Big deposits. Conservative withdrawals." The corner of his mouth lifted. "I figure there's a fortune—abandoned—if I can find that second key."

"A fortune that doesn't belong to you."

He cocked his chin. "I was the only one looking."

My jaw clenched so tight my teeth hurt. These women had fought and bled and sacrificed, and this jerk thought he could just walk in and help himself to their legacy.

"But that's not even the good part." He shifted forward, metal cuffs scraping against the seat. "I figured I'd try the simplest solution first. I took the key to Nashville. Better to stay anonymous, you know? I found a locksmith who'd copy anything, no questions asked."

"Because all of this was so aboveboard."

He could hardly pretend to be in the right.

"I had the original purchase order for the safe and the keys," he said quickly.

"That you rifled out of a dead woman's belongings," I snapped.

Lucy's tail twitched against my arm.

"Don't freak out on me," he warned as if Lucy and I were the unreasonable ones here.

He'd obviously hit a roadblock, because having a second copy of the key from the box wouldn't get him anywhere. If it was the crow key I'd discovered at the scene, he'd found Augustus's key. Rose no doubt kept it after his death. Lucas would then need a suffragette key as well to unlock the safe at the Crowe mansion.

"Keep talking," I ordered.

"Fine." He eyed Lucy. "I found the answer to the key in the meeting minutes." His knee bounced rapidly. "They gave out three keys to the suffragettes."

"Two," I said. "Well, according to Madge."

"You didn't read Rose's private records. One key went to Rose. The other, to Hope."

I knew that much.

"Then Rose had one made for Eleanor Blackwell." He licked

his lips. "Rose's and Hope's keys could be anywhere by now, but Eleanor? She had to have her key on her when she vanished. All I had to do was find Eleanor."

It made sense. I shifted Lucy's weight. "She was in from out of town. It wasn't as if she'd leave the key to the suffragette fortune in her hotel."

"Exactly! So I went back through Rutledge's papers. His date book showed a meeting with Eleanor at the library the night she disappeared." He flashed me a sly look. "I looked up the old newspaper accounts. According to my timeline, he was the last person to see her alive."

Lucy looked at me, and I knew what she was thinking.

Here was a man who'd found precious history and decided to melt it down for pocket change.

"What else did you learn?" I pressed.

He lowered his chin. "Rutledge was holding onto the Sugarland Suffragettes' account at the First Bank of Sugarland—because he was a man, he had control. But he'd been flashing lots of cash. He was in the newspaper buying a new Cadillac, going on fancy jewelry-buying trips to St. Louis. Selling off stock certificates to fund his fancy lifestyle. Only he's just a small-town lawyer. Where's he getting that kind of cash? Then Rose cuts him off."

I gripped the wire mesh between us. So that was what the suffragettes had been up against—not just fighting for their rights but fighting to keep their own money safe from the lawyer they'd thought they could trust with it. No wonder Rose had moved everything to the safe in the Crowe mansion. She'd found a way to protect her people and her cause.

He smiled at my surprise. "From what I've seen, Rose was no shrinking violet."

"You don't know the half of it."

"Rose would have told Eleanor why she moved the club's finances, or at least Eleanor would have suspected. Now Rutledge wants to meet Eleanor alone. She agrees but makes it somewhere public and out of the way. The second-floor library renovation was perfect."

Rose had been trying to protect their legacy, their cause. "Rutledge went after Eleanor for her key."

"No, he didn't." Lucas shook his head hard. "It was one of his biggest regrets that he didn't know about it when he killed her. I read all about it in his private journal. He said he buried Eleanor with the key, and there was nothing he could do about it."

Lucas's breath hitched. "From the way Rutledge operated, my guess is he wanted to threaten Eleanor into giving him cash payments out of the Crowe safe. He knew all about their moonshining. I can't prove any of that last part, and believe me, I've been looking. Either way, it got ugly. Rutledge killed Eleanor and stuffed her behind the fireplace."

Rutledge murdered Eleanor to keep his crimes hidden.

He hadn't planned it, so he'd need to find something quick. "He bricked her into the wall," I said, trying it on. It was possible.

So very possible.

All this time, the truth had been sealed in the nook behind the fireplace, while Rutledge lived out his days respected and wealthy.

"The brick was weak and sloppy where I tore it out," he said thickly. "I knew she had to be there." He licked his lips. "I mean, why was the wall thicker at the back of the fireplace? It's not like that downstairs. And there was nothing like that on the original renovation plans. I checked."

Of course he did. "But why did you set the fire?"

"Who says I did?" he shot back. "That would be illegal."

"Do I have to show you the skunk?" I warned.

He breathed heavily through his nose.

"I wanted to see if I was right." His eyes gleamed.

"And steal the key," I corrected.

He ignored me. "I volunteered to prep for the festival after hours," he said, lost in his own story. "I started digging into the wall and—" His breath caught. "There she was. Just like I thought. But I wasn't ready. Nobody could be ready." He swallowed hard. "She was curled up. The bones were so delicate. Dark hair still clinging to the skull."

I'd seen.

A shiver ran down my spine at the memory of Eleanor's fragile skeleton. Her last moments had been spent terrified and trapped, betrayed. My grip tightened on the grate. "She deserved better than to be your treasure map."

"That blue dress—it was beautiful once. You could still see the beading on the collar. But the fabric was like tissue paper. I touched it, and it crumbled. I feel terrible about that."

"That's what you feel terrible about?" I managed.

"But the key." His eyes lit up. "It was there, hanging from this thin silver chain around her—around what was left of her neck. The metal was tarnished black, but when I lifted it—" His cuffed hands jerked behind his back. "Do you know what it feels like? To research something, to follow the trail, and to be right? To touch history?"

"To tear up a library and desecrate a woman's grave? To steal what isn't yours?"

"I had the key, but I made too big a hole." He slumped back. "I got carried away." He shook his head. "I tried covering it with festival posters, but I knew that wouldn't last. I needed a reason for the damage."

Lucy's whiskers twitched.

"I didn't mean to set the fire," he said quickly.

Who was he kidding? "You purposely set the fire."

"A small, contained fire." His words picked up speed. "Just underneath the damaged spot. The old flue would keep it controlled. I researched exactly how to do it."

"And in this case, your research was terrible."

"It should have worked." His voice rose. "Fire follows the chimney. That's physics. Then I set it during the festival so if anything went wrong, people would be there to help."

"Only you didn't count on the fire trucks getting backed up by the crowd."

"It wasn't supposed to get that bad!" he snapped, his face flushing. "It wasn't supposed to spread to the basement. The archives. I'd planned for everything, every detail. It's not my fault they couldn't get out fast enough."

He actually believed he wasn't to blame, after everything he'd done. "How can you possibly think that's okay?"

"Oh, please. This was the older section of the library. There were no research books. No rare books."

"Just people," I said dryly.

"The Children's Section," he said, as if it meant nothing at all. "All those books are still in print. Everyone made it out okay."

"My sister almost didn't. A little girl almost didn't." The memory of smoke-filled hallways and Olivia's desperate coughing hit me like a punch to the gut. "They were trapped in there while you sat safe outside, congratulating yourself on your clever plan."

"I'm sorry!" He pressed back against the seat. "I watched them bring everyone out. I made sure—"

"You don't get it." Lucy's claws dug into my arm as my voice dropped. "While you were playing treasure hunter, that little girl was crying for her mother. My sister was risking her life. They could barely breathe. And you're sitting here talking about your research and your dissertation and your treasure hunt."

"That's not—"

"You're not sorry at all. You're only sorry you got caught."

His mouth opened and closed. "It's my word against yours."

We'd see about that.

Lucy's tail flicked against the grate, making her opinion known.

"You took Eleanor's key to the Crowe mansion." That explained the two sets of matching footprints—both his. "You opened the safe and stole the money."

He hung his head.

"But you left Augustus's key."

"The one from the box." He glanced up. "I got the safe open, but then—" His face went stark. "The room went ice cold. I swear someone was standing right behind me. I ran. Just... ran. Didn't even think about the key still in the lock."

Lucy's whiskers twitched. We both knew he wasn't trustworthy, but I believed he'd felt a ghost.

Augustus had watched him steal.

Then Augustus had done something about it.

"I figured the key didn't matter." His voice steadied. "The only proof it was missing was the fact it wasn't in the box anymore."

"The box you stole."

"I'd never displace history."

"But you did."

He shifted. "I didn't have a choice. Melody wanted to go poking around. I figured she'd quit if the box was gone."

"But she didn't give up."

"Neither did you. I heard you on the phone, telling her about finding the key, seeing my footprints, preserving fingerprints, and I knew I had to get that key back."

"And robbing one safe wasn't enough." He feigned surprise, but he wasn't fooling me. "Once you learned about Rose's second safe, you attacked me at my house."

"Whoa, no." He jerked upright, cuffs rattling. "I never attacked you."

"You hit Ellis with a shovel! You stabbed him with a knife!"

"I was just trying to get him out of the way," he insisted as if that made it okay.

"Do you hear yourself?"

His mother had taught Sunday school. Volunteered at the food bank. And here was her son talking about assault like it was a trip to the Piggly Wiggly.

"I only wanted the key back," he pleaded. "I'd never get it with you and Ellis holed up in there, and it was only a matter of time before you handed it over and I was screwed."

"So you set fire to my house?"

He shrugged. "It's just a house."

The cruiser suddenly felt too small to contain what I wanted to do to him.

"You have insurance."

"That's not the point!"

"Well, I had to get you out, and that did it."

Lucy's tail bristled. She and I were in complete agreement about turning her loose.

He looked askance. "Ellis should have gone down easy. I had the jump on him—"

"And me."

"I wasn't going to hurt you. I needed my key."

"Augustus's key."

"Only your skunk attacked me, and Ellis cuffed me, and look, you got your way." His voice rose, then fell as he caught my eye. "But I was only trying to learn about Sugarland history, pay for grad school, make something of my life." His shoulders slumped. "It got out of hand, okay?"

It sure did.

"And my great-great-grandmother's papers got scattered across the yard."

He was sweating again. "I didn't see them. I swear."

"I believe you. If only because you didn't try to swipe them." That and the fact his mask had been turned around, blinding him.

His eyes darted to the door. "That skunk would rip my eyes out."

"Count on it." I held Lucy close. She was a softie until someone threatened her home and family.

"You still can't prove anything," he said like he had one up on me.

As if he dared.

"Don't you worry about that," I said sweetly.

I could prove it, and I would. I had all I needed.

Chapter Twenty-Seven

I shifted Lucy to one arm and slid my phone from my pocket. His eyes widened at the screen, where the recording timer ticked away. "You know what they say about pride going before a fall?"

He threw himself forward. "You can't—"

Lucy's tail shot straight up.

He shrank back so fast he cracked his head on the window. "That's not admissible."

"Single-party-consent state." I tapped the screen. "And boy, did you consent to running your mouth." My thumb hovered over play. "Want to hear yourself explain how you torched the library? Or maybe the part about attacking Ellis with a shovel? Or how you stabbed him with a knife."

A bead of sweat traced his cheek. "Delete it."

"Now why would I do that?" I tucked my phone away. "Your dissertation's about to take an interesting turn. Instead of writing about the suffragettes, you'll be joining Rutledge in the history books. You both tried to rob these women of their legacy."

His face crumpled. "Please. My mother—"

"Taught you better." I knew that for a fact. I reached for the door handle. "Some crimes stay buried. But not yours. Not Rutledge's. Not anymore."

~

Back on my porch, the air still reeked of smoke, but the fire was out. I'd checked on Ellis, who was doing well. My neighbors had set to work righting fallen flowerpots and gathering scattered hose lengths. No sign of the papers. Just mud and boot prints tracking across the lawn, up my steps.

Well, wait. Not for long on the porch. Mary Ann Galvin and Valeen Nielson were already headed that way with buckets and brushes.

Three ladies from church rushed over, two embracing me at once. "Don't you worry about dinner," Miss Patricia said.

"Or lunches or breakfast," Janey Mae added. "We're off to make you some this instant."

Ah, casseroles. The love language of Sugarland, served up in nine-by-thirteen pans.

Bobby Ray Tompkins stepped out my back door, his firefighter's jacket slung over one shoulder. I'd known him since second grade when he'd eaten an entire box of crayons on a dare. These days he ran the station and coached Little League.

He closed the door gently when he saw me. "How are you holding up?"

"I'm scared." I glanced past him at my smoke-stained windows. "Grateful." I nodded toward the yard full of helpers. "Really grateful."

"Your neighbors did good work until we got here." He looked back at the house. "If the fire had spread—" He whistled low.

I might not have a house.

He shifted his jacket. "It started in the upstairs hall, right under the attic access."

My stomach squinched. "That was no accident."

"It wasn't," he said, not bothering to sugarcoat it. "An arson investigation team will be here in the morning."

And Lucas would be charged with the crime.

"How bad is the damage?" I squared my shoulders. "Tell me." I could take it.

I could face it.

Bobby Ray's expression softened. "You'll need new planks in that hallway, smoke remediation throughout." He squeezed my shoulder. "But she's solid. Built to last."

Just like my family, who'd loved this home for generations.

My throat tightened. "Thank you, Bobby Ray. For everything."

He smiled that crooked smile that won him Best Coach three years running. "It's my job to look after you and everybody in this town."

It was my job, too. Just in a different way.

Same for everyone here. For Bobbie Jean Clift, who taught needlework at Sew What Creations and now cleared debris from my flower beds while her granddaughter entertained Lucy with a sock toy.

For Mick Roan from the hardware store, who'd arrived with a truck full of cleaning supplies and box fans. I went down to thank him and Bobbie Jean and everyone else.

Duranja pulled up with Melody. Ellis hobbled over to intercept him while Melody ran to me.

"Verity!" She enveloped me in a hug. "I can't believe—I just can't—" She drew back, pressing her hands to her cheeks. "Lucas?"

"Let's sit." I gestured to the porch swing. "Before we both fall down."

She sank onto the freshly scrubbed white wood. "I mentored Lucas. I helped him research grad programs. For two years, I watched him pour his heart into everything Sugarland. He was brilliant, passionate." Her voice cracked. "What happened? How did I miss it?"

"You see the best in people." Plain as that. "And I, for one, would never want to see you change that. Not for Lucas or for anybody."

"Oh, honey." She gripped my hand tight. "That's exactly what I needed to hear, even if I don't quite believe it yet."

Out in the yard, Duranja transferred Lucas to his patrol car while Ellis held the door.

And took great pleasure in slamming it shut.

"At least it's over," Melody said, twisting her engagement ring. "Alec will take care of him."

"I have no doubt." Alec Duranja was the last person to let anybody get away with anything.

Duranja pulled out with Lucas a prisoner in the back.

We'd caught the arsonist. We'd protected the town and my house. I was the luckiest girl in Sugarland to have these people at my side.

I felt almost selfish wishing for more.

Ellis winced as he struggled up the porch stairs, his bandaged leg barely taking weight. I rushed to help, slipping under his arm. "Here, let me." He didn't have to do it alone.

I looked out at the yard where I'd dropped Rose's papers. I'd searched again but found nothing. Everything the suffragettes had worked for, all that Rose had preserved—precious history—had vanished.

The legacy of the suffragettes, Rose's legacy, was gone.

"You'll stay at my apartment until this is sorted," Melody said as Ellis thwumped down on the porch swing.

"Actually," he cleared his throat, "I was thinking my place. Lauralee taught me her famous chicken and dumplings. I was going to surprise you next week, but I think you've earned some serious pampering."

Melody mock scoffed. "Are you bribing her with comfort food?"

"Is it working?" He grinned, then sobered as he caught me staring at the yard again. "The papers." He explained to Melody what we'd discovered, what we'd lost, and with every word, my regret deepened.

If I hadn't jumped off the roof...

I'd have succumbed to the smoke.

If I'd somehow dropped down while holding the papers...

I'd have broken something. Or landed on my head.

If I'd set the fire patrol on a paper chase...

My house could have burned down.

"Let me give it a second look." Melody leapt off the porch swing and headed down the stairs.

More like a fourth look, but I appreciated the effort.

Only it wasn't just that. I turned to Ellis. "Didi and Frankie were terribly hurt when they disappeared into the ether. I haven't seen them since." My voice caught. "What if..."

What if they weren't coming back?

I scanned my darkened backyard. I saw no dogs-playing-poker painting strung up on my tree. No cross-stitch either. No ghostly garden gnomes, flags, or gun collections. No silvery gray light radiating from under the door to Frankie's shed.

No sign of the ghosts at all.

I wouldn't put it past Frankie to pout, but Didi?

She'd have been here if she could.

"I'm sorry," Ellis said, pulling me close.

"Me too," I murmured, leaning in.

We'd caught the arsonist. Stopped him from destroying more history. Saved my house. But at what price?

Rose's legacy was gone forever.

Didi had given it away. I'd scattered the rest to the wind. Or let it burn.

The result was the same. It was gone. We'd failed her.

Poor Rose would go poltergeist for good. Didi and Frankie could be in trouble, and I couldn't help them.

We'd uncovered the truth about Rutledge, about Lucas. But looking at my smoke-stained house, my empty yard, and the spaces where my ghosts should be, I wondered if the price had been too high.

Melody tromped back up onto the porch empty-handed. Bless her for trying. She was trailed by Adelaide Taliafero Brown, her short, silver hair curled in tight ringlets, her pink slacks spattered with mud.

"Verity," Melody began.

"It's all right." They'd tried. That was all they could do.

Adelaide rubbed at her eyes. "I'm sorry, dear. I wanted to help, but I'm not as fast as the others, and I can't heft a bucket anymore." She stepped forward, cradling a thick manila envelope and a messy stack of papers against her cardigan. "All I could do was clean up your yard. There were papers blowing everywhere. I've been trying to organize them. I thought they might be yours."

She held out the stack.

Stock certificates.

Bonds.

The envelope from the attic.

I stared, hardly daring to breathe. "I—"

"I think I got them all." She smoothed a wrinkled corner. "Most were easy, but I had to fish some out of Mrs. Henderson's azaleas, and a few nearly went into the pond."

The neat typescript peeked out from beneath her hands. Meeting minutes. Membership rolls. Letters to the scattered Tennessee chapters. Rose's legacy, saved by the granddaughter of one of her own suffragettes.

Hope would be proud.

I leapt up so fast the porch swing nearly toppled Ellis. Adelaide let out a surprised "Oh!" as I wrapped her in a careful hug, mindful of the precious cargo between us.

"Thank you," I said against her sweater. She smelled like magnolias.

"It was the least I could do," she said, patting my back.

And more than I ever expected.

Rose's papers were safe. Her story would be preserved. And somehow, that felt like more of a victory than I could have deserved.

Chapter Twenty-Eight

The thing about victory is, it doesn't always feel like winning. Standing in my smoke-stained parlor the next morning, I couldn't shake the feeling that somewhere between catching Lucas and saving Rose's legacy, I'd lost something precious. The empty spaces where Didi and Frankie should have been echoed louder than any fire alarm.

Lucy curled around my ankle as if she'd been thinking the same.

"They'll come back," I told her, scratching her head.

They had to.

In the meantime, I popped a batch of Lauralee's famous cinnamon rolls into the oven. She'd stopped by Ellis's last night, loading me down with hugs and homemade treats. Every time the doorbell rang—and it rang plenty—another good citizen of Sugarland arrived with their signature dish. Miss Patricia's chicken pot pie. Sarah Beth's pulled pork. Three different mac and cheeses, each claiming to be the best in town.

By midnight, Ellis's freezer couldn't hold another casserole. We'd filled Melody's too, and this morning I'd hauled the overflow home. Enough food to feed half of Sugarland, all wrapped in tinfoil and love, with detailed reheating instructions written in familiar handwriting.

Sweet cinnamon overtook the bitter tang of smoke drifting through my wide-open windows while fans whirred in every doorway. The fire had left its mark—streaks of soot tracing walls and ceilings, telling a story I'd rather forget. But sunshine poured through those open windows, and there was nothing downstairs that a good scrubbing and fresh paint couldn't fix.

Kat Richards of Sugarland Citizens Insurance stopped by first thing to fill out her report. She photographed the charred floorboards, the burned walls leading to the attic, and the blackened hatch. Kat assured me it wasn't nearly as bad as it could have been, promising she'd take care of me and my house—and not just because I'd babysat her oldest, but because we took care of each other in Sugarland. It was the right thing to do.

My house had withstood the storm.

I'd be fine.

I'd fix things up just the way they were.

The first order of business was to rescue Frankie's dirt and the surprisingly resilient rosebush that had survived both the fire and the rescue. Somehow, that didn't surprise me a bit.

We Long girls grew them strong.

I pushed and pulled and dragged the entire arrangement back to the hearth where it belonged. Then I straightened Frankie's urn so it sat nice under the thorny bush. "You'd better be okay," I said, rubbing a smudge off the brass, right above the dent near the bottom.

I didn't know what I'd do if Frankie didn't make it back.

Then the air cooled, and the energy behind me shifted.

I turned as silvery light filled the parlor. My breath caught as ghostly outlines of Didi's floral couch and doily-draped coffee table shimmered into view, glowing bright against the soot-stained walls.

"Grandma?" My pulse skipped, then raced, then skipped again.

I didn't see her at first. But then the air shimmered, and there she was, smiling from the arched doorway between the parlor and the kitchen.

"Didi!" I raced for her, wishing I could hug her. "What happened to you? Are you okay?"

"I'm fine." She reached out, halted when she realized it. "I recovered. I healed."

She'd come back to herself.

"So fast?" My voice caught. The last time I'd seen her, she'd been so hurt, so undone.

Her expression grew tender. "I had you to look forward to."

Warmth bloomed in my chest. Even when her world had shattered, she'd kept faith in our connection—in me.

I hoped what had happened in the meantime wouldn't send her spiraling again.

"While you were gone—I'm sorry." I could hardly say it. "We caught the thief, who was also an arsonist, but not before..." I gestured at the smoke damage marring her beautiful walls.

Grandma nodded. "I saw when I arrived."

"You did?" But she didn't seem upset.

She ran a hand over the wall. "I know everything that happens to this house. I love this place almost as much as I love you."

"I'll fix it," I vowed. "I'll make it all right, I promise." Yes, it looked bad and smelled worse, but I'd restore it if it was the last thing I did. "I'll make it the way it was when you left it to me. Down to the last detail." She'd see. "I'll track down your cherrywood dining set, and that inlaid secretary desk from the entryway." I'd restore the house and her legacy, just like we'd done for Rose. "I'll make it my full-time job." Ghost hunting could wait.

"Verity." Her tone stopped me cold.

She wore the same expression she'd used when I was seven, hiding vegetables under my napkin and feeding them to the dog.

Then came the indulgent smile that always followed. "I know you want to fix this, sweetie."

"I will." I'd given my word. "You can count on me."

She strolled to the hearth, pearl-gray against the blackened walls. "You have to understand." Her hand traced the marble mantel. "This isn't my house anymore. It's yours."

"That you left me to take care of." To protect. "I understand."

She dropped her hands. "I left it to you so you could live in it and love it as much as I have." She tilted her head. "Not so you could turn it into a shrine to me."

I stared at her. "I don't understand."

She drifted closer, reaching as if to caress my cheek. The air cooled where her hand would have touched. "This house is yours now, sweetie. Not mine."

"But—"

She straightened her shoulders, the way she always had when laying down the law. "You don't need to go chasing down my old furniture. You don't need to keep everything exactly as it was." She gestured at the soot-stained walls. "You need to make this place yours. The way I made it mine. The way my mama made it hers before me. That's how this house stays alive." Her smile encompassed the walls, the mantel, the graceful archway that had welcomed generations of Longs to rest and gather. "That's how you really live."

I stood startled. Gobsmacked.

Dare I say inspired?

In all my years here, I'd never once thought about what I wanted for this house. Not really. Every decision had been filtered through what Grandma would have wanted, would have done. I'd needed that—her approval, her pride, the comfort of keeping things exactly as they'd always been.

For her.

For my family.

But now, standing in my smoke-stained parlor, it felt shockingly good to imagine leaving my own mark on my family's history.

Did I dare?

I could create cozy corners where formal furniture used to be. And the dining room? I never used it. Not when meals at the kitchen felt so right, with Melody, Ellis and Duranja around my weathered oak table, elbows bumping and stories flowing. The dining room could become something lived in and loved. Built-in bookshelves, maybe, with a deep window seat where Lucy and I could curl up on rainy afternoons. I could paint the walls a buttery yellow or sage green. Hang gauzy curtains.

My bedroom upstairs was already spacious, even when Grandma's carved mahogany bed had commanded the center of the room. Now, despite my futon and garage-sale dresser—not to mention Didi's massive wardrobe still standing near the door—it felt...empty. Colorless. I could layer thick, plush rugs over the hardwood floors, where Lucy could sprawl in sunbeams. Add oversized armchairs by the big picture window overlooking the pond. Maybe a cute side table for my morning coffee.

And plants—I'd always wanted a bedroom full of plants. Trailing pothos vines winding along the top of the wardrobe. Delicate ferns spilling from macramé hangers in the windows. Potted herbs on the windowsill—lavender and rosemary, their scents carried on the breeze.

This house deserved to be lived in, not just preserved. And maybe, just maybe, that was what Didi had been trying to tell me all along.

I couldn't help but smile. "I have some ideas." Exciting ones. And like with all things, "I'll do my best," I promised.

"Then you'll succeed," she assured me. And for the first time since the fire, I truly believed it.

A flicker of movement caught my eye through the kitchen window. A ghostly butterfly. Then another.

I hurried to the kitchen door and opened it.

A ghostly form sat on the back patio swing, her booted feet barely brushing the weathered boards as she swayed. Her hair coiled in an elaborate hairdo above a stiff, lace collar, and her bearing spoke of generations of grace and pride.

Rose.

Even in death, she commanded attention.

I slipped out the screen door, letting it whisper shut behind me. The morning air was thick with the sweetness of roses in bloom.

Soon I saw why.

The ghostly rose garden had transformed. The bushes towered twice as tall as Didi had remembered, their stems as thick as my thumb and as thorny as barbed wire. Blooms bigger than my fist nodded in the breeze, and butter roses climbed a lattice clear to the second story, creating a living frame around my bedroom window. The silvery blooms caught the morning light, their petals unfurling in graceful layers against the weathered white siding.

Round, tight mini blossoms tumbled over each other, spilling across the brick path and reaching for the porch rails.

"Your garden is magnificent." It truly was. It was an honor to see it as she had, the way it had looked in its glory days when she'd spent countless hours loving it, caring for it, making it hers.

Rose didn't turn. She merely patted the empty spot next to her.

I dutifully slid onto the bench.

She turned, and I caught my breath. Her face held none of the rage that had twisted it before. Instead, her features were refined and striking, with high cheekbones and eyes that held quiet determination—the kind that came from years of proving herself in a world where women weren't supposed to have opinions, let alone property.

"Did you know legacy roses can live for more than a hundred years?" She glanced at me, her dark lips curving into a gentle smile. "The one in your parlor came from a cutting Alice Paul gave me when I first began organizing the ladies of Sugarland. Just a small thing, passed between friends. But like us, it grew strong and endured." She pursed her lips. "It was always my favorite."

"I know it's unusual to bring it inside—" I began.

And in a trash can, no less.

"Do you love it?" She faced me fully, her posture speaking of the careful dignity she'd cultivated like her roses.

"I do love it. With all my heart." I thought of Lucy playing beneath those thorny branches, batting at falling petals. Of all the bouquets I'd cut that had filled the house with their scent. Of the day I'd first met Frankie, when I'd tried to baby the roots and accidentally trapped my gangster. How it had become his as much as mine. His dirt. His land. His home.

"Then I'm happy." She settled back and gave me a side-eye. "Delia was right to trust you with our legacy."

I stared at her. "You know about that?"

"I've struggled. At times, I've let the cause consume me. Let my emotions control me." She pressed her lips together. "I couldn't always afford to be soft. I regret that now." She turned to me in earnest now. "But I've watched you. The way you love not just this house, but all of Sugarland's history. Every family's story matters to you, not just ours." She clasped her hands. "I've seen how you care for this house, my roses." She caught herself with a rueful smile. "Your roses now. I can't imagine who I'd trust more."

It was all too much. And everything I'd wanted, all at the same time. "Thank you." I wished I could take her hands in mine. "I'll do everything I can to earn that trust."

"You already have." She beamed. "Because of you, our legacy lives. The truth of what we fought for, what we sacrificed—the secret meetings, the marches, the arrests, the hunger strikes, even our Firefly Moonshine." She clucked. "Quite the scandal."

"You love that." I could tell.

"I kind of do," she admitted. "Thanks to you, the truth is out. What we did matters again. And now we can keep making a difference."

"The money?"

"When you read the documents, you'll see. It belongs to you

and the descendants of the Sugarland Suffragette League. Use it in our spirit to help the women and families of Sugarland."

"I will," I promised.

I'd honor their legacy. I wasn't sure how yet, but they'd fought so hard. How could I do any less?

I gazed toward the pond, past it to the scattered farms in the distance. Sugarland had always been special, a place where people truly cared for each other. Just as they'd proved last night.

When I looked back, Rose watched me with deep affection. "I saw it clearly when your neighbors came together to save our house. This legacy isn't just mine or yours. This house, this town —we all belong to each other. We always have."

As if her words had conjured them, silvery figures began materializing in the yard. Hope Taliafero stood beneath the oak tree. I recognized her from the jail, unnaturally thin from her final hunger strike, her high-necked blouse and dark skirt unchanged from the night she died. She spoke quietly with a tall, commanding woman.

Near the pond's edge, Madge and Viv appeared delighted to at last welcome a gathering crowd of women in long skirts and shirtwaists, some still clutching their weathered *Votes for Women* signs.

The garden filled with women in Gibson Girl hairdos and high-necked blouses, their expressions bright with purpose. Some wore the prison badges I'd seen in photographs. Others wore sashes across their chests. They glided over the lawn in small groups, greeting each other like old friends.

Then I spotted Didi at the edge of the yard, half-hidden by the apple tree.

Rose saw her at the same time. She hesitated.

"It wasn't just me making things right," I said. She had to know. Had to see. "I couldn't have done any of this without Didi."

"I—" Rose went still beside me.

Didi closed the distance with measured steps, shoulders

straight, head high. I caught the faint tremor in her hands before she folded them behind her back.

Rose came to her feet as Didi mounted the steps and stood before her.

"I'm sorry I gave away your legacy." Didi cleared her throat. "Our legacy. I didn't understand what I had, what it meant." She met Rose's gaze. "I should have protected it, like you protected us all those years."

For a long moment, Rose said nothing. Then her face crumpled. "I'm sorry, too. For letting my emotions get the better of me. For losing myself."

"You were upset—" Didi began.

"Scared," Rose corrected. "But it's not an excuse. You didn't know." She pressed a hand to her cheek, then let it drop. "It's not what we do when we don't know that matters. It's what we do after, when we understand. And you?" A smile touched her lips. "You helped make it right. You and Verity both."

Didi stepped forward. Rose met her halfway, and they embraced. Grandmother and granddaughter, coming together, understanding each other, forgiving each other.

I remembered the darkness that had nearly claimed Rose, the anger that had almost destroyed her and everything she cared about. But love had brought her back. Didi's love for her, and her love for us.

And now, watching them, I understood once more what Rose had meant about belonging to each other.

I left them to it, walking down to the apple tree where Hope lingered. Her friend had left to help Viv and Madge gather the troops, but Hope was content to just be. Her shoulders were lighter. She carried herself taller. And for the first time, I saw her smile.

"You look well," I told her.

"Rose came back for me. She explained everything." She tilted her face to catch the sunlight filtering through the leaves. "I'm free." Her voice held quiet joy. "Finally, truly free."

I followed her glance to where Didi and Rose gathered on the porch, deep in earnest conversation. "Your granddaughter was the one who saved your legacy in the end."

It was Adelaide Taliafero Brown who had gathered the documents, Adelaide who had helped in the best way she knew how.

"I know." Hope's face glowed with fierce pride. "I'm so proud of her. And of you."

I thought of all the small acts that had brought us here. Ellis asking for my opinion on the skeleton. Adelaide saving those papers. And the big ones. Frankie saving me from the library fire. Grandma returning to set things right.

I was proud of everyone who'd tried to make a difference. "We were glad to help."

Rose came down the steps to join us under the apple tree. "We'd like to thank your gangster too," she said. "Where is he?"

My throat tightened. "He's gone." I hadn't seen him since he fled for the ether... on fire.

Frankie wasn't one to miss a celebration. Not to mention a pat on the back. And it should have been easier for him to return than it had been for Didi. I truly hoped he was all right.

Rose's face fell. "That's a shame. I have a reward for him."

The gangster materialized right next to her, wearing his pin-striped suit and wide tie, betraying no sign of the fire that had almost consumed him.

"Frankie!" I gushed, thrilled, ten kinds of relieved and not even mad he'd scared me half to death.

His hair was tame. His ears were no longer smoking. He lowered his white Panama hat over the bullet hole in his forehead. "So, what's this about a reward?"

Chapter Twenty-Nine

Rose stepped forward. "Welcome home." She gestured for her ladies to gather round. "We want to thank you for helping to preserve our legacy."

The suffragettes' much-lauded moonshine still shimmered into existence next to Frankie, glowing gray. The ad hoc contraption looked like someone had beaten a water heater with an ugly stick and then mummified it in copper and baling wire.

Frankie gazed at it like he'd just seen the *Mona Lisa*. "It's...it's beautiful!"

That was one word for it.

Hope's eyes sparkled like she'd handed him the keys to the kingdom. "Consider it a gift."

An ugly, ugly gift.

It picked that moment to let off a loud, smelly burp.

"We'd like you to keep the recipe." Madge drew an envelope from her sleeve, its edges softened by decades of careful handling.

Frankie grabbed it and clutched it to his chest. "This is even better than the time I got lost looking for the bathroom in Chicago and stumbled on Al Capone's diamond-smuggling operation. Who stores rocks like that in a bowling alley back room? Made more off that than my first three bank jobs combined."

Didi gasped. "Didn't he hunt you down?"

"I told him Ice Pick Charlie did it." Frankie bent to hug the washtub at the bottom, its rim fitted with copper mesh that strained the clear liquid dripping through. "I shall call you Betsy Sue the Fifth." He pressed his cheek against the rusty metal. "Queen Betsy for short."

Didi leaned my way. "Is he crying?"

I didn't want to know.

But it was clear Betsy Sue the Fifth was coming to live in my backyard.

"You know, some families pass down antiques or china," Didi said.

"You tried," I told her.

Yes, every family needed its traditions, and it seemed ours included illegal moonshine stills.

This one was a small price to pay for Frankie's happiness.

And to be fair, Didi had made the last one explode.

Rose turned to the women in the yard. "And now, ladies, I think we've earned our peace."

The light started as a pinprick, a glimpse of gold breaking through the clear blue sky. Then it spread until it bathed my yard in a glow that felt like summer sunshine, fresh-baked bread, and being wrapped up in my favorite quilt all at once.

I'd seen my share of the other side, but this was different.

This was perfect.

Liberty stepped forward, her suffragist sash gleaming white against her practical Gibson Girl suit. The women behind her—dozens in shirtwaists and long skirts, some still bearing protest signs—moved as one.

"Thank you. You've given us back our voice," Liberty said, her stern features softening. "Our sisters can rest now, knowing you'll carry on." She rose like a dandelion seed on the breeze, her suffragist sisters trailing in her wake, their forms dissolving into points of light.

Hope was next, her back straight and her head held high, no

longer cowering. No longer living in fear. "Thank you for finding me," she said simply. "For helping me realize it's time to rest. To live." She drifted upward, finding her peace at long last.

I watched her go, grateful I could be a part of her story. Humbled to have met her.

Madge and Viv stepped up together, Madge with her sweet round face and Viv as stark and practical as ever. "Take good care of my girl," Madge said to Frankie, patting the newly crowned Betsy Sue the Fifth. "Feed her all the peaches she wants."

Frankie brought a hand to the recipe he'd stashed in his suit coat pocket, the one right over his heart. "I'll treat my girl like the queen she is."

Madge shot him a wink as the two rose together.

Rose stood apart, her hands clasped in front of her, gazing at her friends rising. Moving on to the next adventure.

Then a tall ghost in a dark suit emerged from the rose garden behind her.

Augustus.

He hesitated, like a man who'd rehearsed this moment a thousand times but found himself speechless now that it was here.

But when she saw him, her face lit up like she'd spotted the North Star. She ran to him, her skirts flying, and he caught her in his arms, spinning her in a circle. When their lips met, the years between them vanished.

"I'm sorry," she said against his chest. "I'm so sorry. It's been so long."

He tucked a strand of hair behind her ear. "My radical girl," he murmured. "You were worth every minute of waiting. And now it's done." He smiled. "Now we have forever."

Rose turned back to us, her joy making her radiant. "Thank you for everything, Verity. You are fierce. You are brave. And you see the truth in people's hearts. The Long legacy couldn't be in better hands."

Her gaze shifted to her granddaughter, and something deeper flickered in her eyes. She wrapped Didi in a fierce hug. "And you, my dear girl. You didn't just fix what was broken, you made it shine brighter than ever. That's what real strength is. That's what changes the world."

Didi squeezed her back, standing tall. "I learned from the best." She drew back. "I love you, Gran."

Rose cupped her cheek, her face luminous with affection, joy, pride. "I love you too."

Then Rose took Augustus's hand, and they rose together into the light. The bad boy and the suffragette. The rabble-rouser and his radical girl. The two who'd started it all.

Two souls who'd found each other across time and death and everything in between, finally getting their happily ever after. At last.

And as Rose and Augustus vanished into the light, the towering rosebushes in her garden shimmered and grew less grand, their wild, sprawling blooms settling into the more modest garden Didi remembered. And as a massive bush at the entrance to the garden disappeared entirely, there stood Frankie, leaning against the wooden trellis arch, taking a drag off a cigarette.

Frankie pushed away from the trellis and sauntered toward Didi. As he drew near, he pointed at her with two fingers, the cigarette dangling between them. "You'd better not put me in a sweater."

"I think I can control myself this time." Didi let her gaze drift over the garden, up to the weathered siding of the house. "The truth is this place isn't mine anymore. It hasn't been in a long time."

Frankie halted in front of her, taking a long drag that made the cigarette's ember flare. Smoke curled from his lips as he spoke. "I'm glad you finally listened to me." He flicked a bit of ash, a small smile playing at the corner of his mouth. "Now that you're leaving, you're not half bad." He rocked back on his heels. "I mean, you did get us into the Crow's Nest."

She matched his smirk with one of her own. "Now that you know the password, you can visit anytime."

Frankie ground out his cigarette beneath his heel. "You can come back anytime, too."

Didi barked out a laugh. "Do you mean that?"

He shoved his hands in his pockets. "No."

"But you will anyway." I smiled at Didi.

We'd give the gangster time.

Didi's smile never faltered. "I'll try my best, Verity."

Frankie looked past her, his expression shifting from sardonic to shocked. "My peacock is back!" He ran for his shed. "Oh, Beatrice. I thought you were gone forever."

The bird stood regally on the lawn next to his shed, its tail feathers spread like a beacon.

"I have an even bigger gift for you," Didi said when we'd reached the pond. From behind the apple tree, she retrieved a gleaming silver frame. Inside, preserved behind ghostly glass, was the yellowed newspaper page Frankie had stolen from the work-house, the one he'd thought he'd lost.

SUGARLAND'S MOST WANTED — MARCH 1919 blazed across the top.

Frankie pressed his hand to his chest and staggered back. "Sweet mother of crime, it's my greatest achievement!"

"You've earned it," she said.

Frankie hefted the frame and cradled it like it was his firstborn as he carried it to the shed. "I'm hanging this right above my barber chair."

How wonderful. "You mean it's back?"

Frankie threw open the door. "It's all back. My poker table! My bar!" He let out a small shriek. "My crystal ashtray shaped like a Tommy gun!" He leaned his head out the door. "I stole that one from Babyface Nelson." He disappeared inside again. "My home is mine again. Mine!" He emerged clutching his prized silver cocktail shaker engraved with *Property of Public Enemy #1*.

I turned to Didi. "You're really leaving, aren't you?"

She dipped her chin. "This is only goodbye for now, Verity."

She made that familiar gesture, the one that used to end with her tucking my hair behind my ear when I was little.

"You come back anytime, you hear?" I did my best to put on a brave face, even as my voice warbled. "You're always welcome to live with me." She needed to know that. To always remember.

We'd had so little time, barely enough. There was so much I still wanted to say to her, to do with her.

I just wanted to be with her.

Didi stood beside me, her ghostly light warm and soft. "There's never enough time, is there?" She looked to the shed, the house, the garden that had changed so much. "Still, I don't belong here anymore. You know that."

I did. I just knew I'd miss her more than I could say.

Didi looked to the sky. "I'm happy in the light." She drifted upward slightly, as if drawn to something I couldn't see. "It's my favorite place." When she turned back, she glowed with a peace I'd never seen before. "I need to go home now."

I nodded. I understood.

"Grandpa Jack will be missing me. And now that Rose has found her way too..." She pressed a hand to her heart. "It's like everything is finally as it should be."

I found myself smiling. "Do come back and visit."

"I will. And I'll do you one better. Remember this, Verity. Even if you can't see me. Or even if I'm not right there. Even if you change the furniture or, for goodness' sake, liven up that dining room."

I already had ideas.

"I'm always with you." She smiled.

"Good. Because I love you." More than that... "I am who I am because of you."

Didi's eyes shone. "Then I have truly lived a good life."

A bright light opened above us, bringing with it a warmth like sunshine. "It's time," she said simply.

I nodded and let her go. I watched her rise until I could no longer see her.

But I felt her. Deep in my heart and in this place. And for that, I'd be forever grateful.

~

The police searched Lucas's house and found artifacts from several Sugarland families, stolen from the archives. Including ours. They also found the suffragette money from Augustus's safe. Each bill had been stamped with the Firefly logo, settling all dispute. It seemed the suffragettes had gotten the last word after all.

Lucas pleaded guilty to arson, theft, vandalism, and a host of other crimes that would keep him in jail for a long time.

It was sad, really. To see his potential go to waste. He'd had such a mind for history, such a curiosity about the past. If he'd only sought to understand our history rather than possess it.

But all was not lost. The Hartley family made a ridiculously large donation to help restore the library. Between that and the insurance money, Mr. Hartley vowed to help the town of Sugarland rebuild the library even stronger. According to Melody, they had plans for a new children's area and the money to move the town archives out of the basement and into a light-filled former sugar warehouse that had once been a thriving centerpiece in the heart of downtown. Now it would be again.

Melody would see to that.

There, they could catalog and store the artifacts properly. And I hoped it was a sign of great things to come.

Dare I hope for a Sugarland History Museum in the making?

Eleanor Blackwell's signet ring would go on display in the lobby, along with a display of Firefly Moonshine bottles and crates, and even the original still. Melody was sure her experts could bring it up from the cave and reassemble it.

I told her she was welcome to do so, that we'd wear our family's history with pride.

Some families passed down silverware and china.

We Longs, it seemed, had a penchant for 'shine.

And speaking of moonshining, Ellis was right. The stock certificates I'd found in Rose's safe were worth millions. Not to mention the government bonds.

We referred the matter to lawyers, who determined the money belonged to the Sugarland Suffragettes and, therefore, to their heirs.

That included me and Melody, of course. Along with Adelaide, who'd saved them from the fire. It included my friend Bree, who worked at the animal shelter. And Madge's great-great-great-great-grandniece Emmy, who worked as head barista at the coffee shop downtown.

Together, we founded the Sugarland Suffragette Memorial Fund, dedicated to bettering the lives of women and families in Sugarland. Our logo was the firefly over a single star, and our first order of business was to open a Family Center in the heart of town, offering free childcare and after-school programs for working parents, parenting classes and support groups, literacy programs, and free legal services for anyone who needed them.

The casserole warriors volunteered to serve up hot meals every day of the week. And Adelaide organized the greeting committee. We would make everyone welcome.

This would be a place like Sugarland where everyone belonged. Dedicated to helping our friends and neighbors reach their full potential.

Just like Rose had always dreamed, and just as Didi had always taught me.

We also searched for Eleanor Blackwell's kin, and when we found she had none, we laid her to rest in a place of honor in Holy Oak Cemetery, in the same section as Colonel Larimore, the town founders, and others who'd made a real difference in the world.

There, Eleanor would be visited and remembered, as she deserved to be.

Lucy and I stayed with Ellis at his house while Bill Roan and his crew made repairs to mine. It sent the grapevine to growing and more than a few tongues wagging, but that was all right. I was a rebel, just like my great-great-grandma Rose.

That's not to say we didn't return to my home often. Heck, we did every day.

If only so Lucy could nap under her favorite apple tree.

And on this particular day, after the workmen had left, I found myself sitting on my porch swing, overlooking the yard.

My rose garden was back to the way it was—small, but loved, with one bush missing from the row and sitting in a place of honor in my parlor.

I rocked gently next to Lucy, who wore her championship sash. She wasn't the kind of girl to save her fine china for special occasions, and neither was I.

I sipped lemonade I'd squeezed myself out of a crystal glass I'd bought from the resale shop downtown. It was etched with ribbons and bows, and I loved it.

It was my taste, and I'd bought a full matching set as part of my new renovation.

Frankie was out by the pond, fussing over Betsy Sue the Fifth. He gave a proud whistle as she belched a perfect smoke ring that drifted lazily across the pond. "That's my girl."

He'd set to brewing his very first batch of Firefly Moonshine.

Heaven help us.

Lucy tilted her head as the gangster left Betsy Sue to her devices and began rigging a trip wire from the still to the apple tree to the roof of his shed. This one connected to his prized barber chair, positioned precariously on the shed roof.

Of course, that wasn't the half of it.

He'd rigged his entire brewing area with his lethal contraptions. His stuffed peacock was now mounted on some kind of spring-loaded catapult. He'd appropriated Suds's pickaxes and bank-tunneling gear and arranged it into something resembling a trebuchet. And he'd made a skull and crossbones warning sign out of my favorite sheet.

At least on the ghostly side.

"I'm trying to score some Civil War cannonballs," he explained, adjusting the tension on a rope that would send the barber chair careening down onto any dead thief or lawman who dared get close to his still.

Lucy shot me a look that clearly said, 'You're going to let him get away with that?'

I would. For now.

I smiled and sipped my lemonade. I'd come to realize it was his house now, just as much as it was mine.

"So, what do you think?" he prodded, standing directly under the barber chair, turning slow circles under a fraying rope.

"I like it, Frankie. It's very *you*."

His dream still.

His home.

We were both where we belonged.

Note from Angie Fox

Thanks so much for dropping in on Sugarland for Secrets, Lies and Fireflies! *I had so much fun exploring the hidden history of Verity's family and watching Grandma Didi shake things up a little. Okay, a lot.*

Speaking of shake-ups, the next book is called Garters, Ghosts and Wedding Toasts. *In it, Melody's big day turns into a murder mystery at one of the most haunted hotels in the South.*

I'm talking cursed brides, restless ghosts, and a real-life killer. Frankie's stirring up trouble as well (this time with a rogue ghost hunter), and Lucy the skunk might just sniff out the biggest clue of all.

Until next time...
Happy reading!
Angie

**Check out the next
Southern Ghost Hunter mystery
Garters, Ghosts and Wedding Toasts**

When Verity Long agrees to be her sister's maid of honor, she expects wedding cake and champagne—not a dead hostess, a cursed honeymoon suite, and a ghostly bride reliving her tragic final moments.

With a killer on the loose, a ballroom full of restless spirits, and Frankie teaming up with a rogue ghost hunter, Verity must race to uncover the truth before Melody's dream wedding becomes her worst nightmare.

About the Author

New York Times and *USA Today* best-selling author Angie Fox writes sweet, fun, action-packed mysteries. Her characters are clever and fearless, but in real life, Angie is afraid of basements, bees, and going up stairs when it's dark behind her. Let's face it: Angie wouldn't last five minutes in one of her books.

Angie earned a journalism degree from the University of Missouri. During that time, she also skipped class for an entire week so she could read Anne Rice's vampire series straight through. Angie has always loved books and is shocked, honored and tickled pink that she now gets to write books for a living. Although, she did skip writing for a week this past fall so she could read Victoria Laurie's Abby Cooper psychic eye mysteries straight through.

Angie makes her home in St. Louis, Missouri with a football-addicted husband, two kids, and Moxie the dog.

Connect with Angie Fox online:
www.angiefox.com

www.ingramcontent.com/pod-product-compliance
Lightning Source LLC
Chambersburg PA
CBHW061754190726
48289CB00007B/1942